OF SONG AND WAR

Yolanda Prieto Grimaldi

TO SALVADOR, THE LOVE OF MY LIFE

AND

IN MEMORY OF ALL THE ALPINE SOLDIERS
WHO DIED IN WORLD WAR I

CHAPTER ONE

A town in the north of Mexico at the dawn of the Revolution of 1910

The hooves trampling on the cobbled stones came to a stop.

"Evaristo Gomez, open the door in the name of the revolution!"

The winter morning stillness was pierced by the young but forceful voice that echoed through the town, followed by three knocks on a massive wooden door. Roberto Madariaga, a man in his early twenties now stood beneath the carved sandstone portico. He was dressed in khaki pants and shirt, both creased and worn. Two bandoliers of ammunition crossed his chest. A small brigade of horsemen followed him to the main square of Santa Rosalia.

As it had done for the last hundred and fifty years the six o'clock mine whistle would soon call and men, young and old, would step out of their humble homes wrapped in their woollen ponchos ready to face another day in the hazardous darkness of the underground tunnels.

Almost a year had passed since Roberto had heard about the work plan of presidential candidate Francisco I. Madero. His proposals to change the future of Mexico had stirred Roberto's mind and fuelled his desire for social justice. He had returned to Santa Rosalia determined to demand better and safer working conditions for the miners.

And as he stood waiting, he recognized how strange this situation was. He was standing in front of Don Evaristo's house, demanding his presence, the mine owner who had employed him for several months.

About a dozen men accompanied Roberto, all carrying carbines and wearing ammunition belts across their chests. Roberto could discern other shadows entering the plaza cautiously curious to find out what the turmoil was about. In the last few weeks the plaza had witnessed several confrontations instead of the usual religious pageantry, and the inhabitants had grown fearful.

The door was not opening. The exasperation of the horsemen was increasing. Finally, hurried footsteps were heard behind the massive door.

"Gomez, we're waiting!" shouted Quijano. In his early forties, Quijano was the only man who had not dismounted. He kept his horse moving in circles as he shook his carbine in the air.

"You're coming with us to the mine, señor," another shouted.

"Yeah, to the mine, to the tunnels," shouted others.

"Silence everyone!" commanded Roberto, hoping the door would open soon.

Just as his voice fell, the door was opened just a crack by a manservant and Don Evaristo Gomez, the owner of Santa Rosalia's mine, stood heavily behind the wrought iron gate. With his right hand at his waist resting on a gun he gazed at the men. Roberto felt his contempt.

"What's the problem Roberto? Are you ready to work for me again?" Don Evaristo stared at the dust covered boots and the khaki outfit; very different from the polished boots and jacket he wore every day in the mine office.

"No, sir. Not until you do the reinforcement work that we proposed."

"That you proposed. And who are you? You're an accountant, Roberto, and a stupid one to boot!" he hurled. "The mine engineer doesn't think that work is necessary."

"The engineer doesn't want to lose his job, Don Evaristo."

"And you, rich son that you are, can afford to stop working. Isn't that so?"

Roberto fought to keep calm and remain silent.

"Eh, Roberto, you don't want to get into trouble, do you?" Gomez's attitude was changing. "You know who my friends are."

"Señor, your friends are powerless now. They are gone. We are here to go to the mine and examine the conditions of the tunnels and you are coming with us. You shall see them for yourself."

"It's not a good time," replied Don Evaristo.

"This is the time, the only time. You must come with us. You have four deaths on your shoulders. How many more will it take for you to do something about it?"

"There's no money, Roberto!"

"No money? I was your accountant, Don Evaristo…"

"What would your father say about this?"

"Leave my father out of this! He has nothing to do with it. My best friend and three other workers died in your mine because of the collapsed tunnels. Almost a year has gone by and you haven't fixed them. You have done nothing." Roberto's voice escalated with impatience.

"I cannot go with you now," Don Evaristo replied as he handled the grip of his gun.

"Cannot go with us?" shouted Quijano, still astride his horse. "The hell you can't!" He edged closer to the gate.

"This is my house and you can't come in!" Don Evaristo tried to push the heavy door shut.

"We'll see if we can or we can't," retorted Quijano. And saying so he fired his rifle twice. Don Evaristo fell to the ground behind the gate. The manservant stood there frozen. The blast of the gunshots echoed on the walls of the church and the buildings surrounding the square.

"Damn it, Quijano! What the hell do you think you're doing?" Roberto barely controlled his impulse to yank the man from his horse and hit him.

Shutters were now pried open and faces were peering from behind lace curtains. A small group had gathered some distance away, watching in silence. The mine whistle blew its six o'clock call to work. Suddenly, another shot fired from the same carbine, stopped all movement.

"You cowards!" shouted Quijano laughing. "Don't you see? He had it coming… He asked for it, the big mining king!" He spat to one side.

The powerful Don Evaristo Gomez lay against the iron gate.

Suddenly, the clangour of the church bell filled the air. Agustin, the bell ringer, at the top of the tower was thrusting his arms with all his strength and rolling the enormous bell. The bell only rang for emergencies in the mine. Roberto was well aware things were out of control.

"Stop it, Quijano! Run to the church and tell the bell ringer to stop," ordered Roberto.

But Quijano, instead, waved the carbine and shouted: "Stop the bell!" and the bell continued to ring.

An older woman pulled at Quijano's boot and screamed at him: "He's simple! He cannot hear! Don't you understand?"

And before anyone could react, Quijano kicked his boot loose and pointing his rifle he fired towards the church tower. A sepulchral silence followed the detonation.

"Perfect shot!" he exclaimed triumphantly as everyone watched in horror.

The body of Agustin, the bell ringer, fell from the tower to the ground. His head was splattered over the stones in front of the old church doors and blood was slowly seeping from under his body. Roberto was seized by a desire to use his gun against Quijano.

The same woman screamed: "My son! You bloody murderer! You miserable killer!" And she ran to the lifeless body.

At the foot of the church was Agustin, twenty years old, feeble-minded and poor. At the entrance of his mansion lay Don Evaristo Gomez, fifty-five, powerful and rich. An eerie silence enveloped the town. The mine whistle was mute. Only the faint murmur of prayers floated in the air.

On the day the tunnels had collapsed, the mine whistle had blown its message of tragedy and the church bell had rung death as the miners lifted the bodies of Roberto's friend, Felipe, and three others. Don Evaristo dismissed the demands of the workers claiming that a minor earthquake had caused the accident. He had cleared his conscience by paying for the burials and buying flowers for the graves. *Would anyone bring flowers to Don Evaristo's grave? Would anybody accompany his funeral procession?*

The silence of death was broken by Quijano's voice: "Captain, we can enter the house now."

"Silence! We do no such thing! We're leaving!" shouted Roberto.

"But Roberto, there will be money and probably gold..." said Quijano.

"We're getting out of here. Now!" shouted Roberto as he mounted his horse and spurred it to a gallop.

A current of hatred followed the horsemen as they raced from the plaza.

Captain Roberto Madariaga was sick from all that had happened. He had gone to the home of Don Evaristo Gomez to show him that the conditions of the mine tunnels were intolerable and unsafe.

Now he was leaving Santa Rosalia with the death of this very man in his wake.

While he had worked at the mine, Roberto had studied the cavernous interior and had presented Don Evaristo with clear plans for carrying out the necessary improvements. But the profit-hungry mine owner delayed the reconstruction work and one day the tunnels finally collapsed. After that day, everything had changed for Roberto, for the miners and for the town.

The miners had gone on strike, but strikes were forbidden in Mexico. In any case, Don Evaristo had hired people from the next town and the men had been left without work. Roberto had resigned from his job at the mine, vowing not to return until the working conditions of the miners were improved. But his plan had backfired and now he felt only guilt and despair. The death of the mine owner would bring persecution from the federal troops and the death of the bell ringer would bring hostility from the locals. Nothing had been accomplished. But two people had died.

The group galloped for several hours towards the outline of the Sierra de la Gloria. When they finally arrived, the sun was already casting shadows in the canyon. They dismounted and pulled their horses to the entrance of a cave. A few weeks back they had found an underground creek inside and had adopted the place as their campsite. There they filled up their metal canteens and their gourds and carried water for the horses. Everyone was silent –exhausted.

Finally, Roberto spoke: "Since we must stay away from the towns for a while, we need to trap some hares. Traps. Understood?"

"It's easier to shoot them," interjected Quijano.

"No guns. We must save our bullets. Is that clear?"

"Yes, Captain. Whatever you say," Quijano replied with a grin. Roberto felt the scorn and glared directly at him but Quijano turned away whistling.

Roberto could guess what Quijano's thoughts had been when he had killed Don Evaristo, but could not help but wonder what had been swirling inside his mind when he had fired at the poor bell ringer.

Most of the men were miners and they had asked Roberto to guide them in their quest for justice. Their families depended on their work for survival. Now, they would have to stay away from home and from Santa Rosalia and fight in the hope of winning something in the end.

After setting up the traps for the hares, the men sat down around the fire. Quijano had walked far from the camp to drink the *pulque* that he always carried in a leather bag. Somehow, he made certain to secure the strong drink in every town but never shared it with the men and they resented him for that.

Roberto remained pensive. He knew now that eventually they would be forced to fight the federal troops, who protected the dictatorship of President Porfirio Diaz.

"Now they'll be after us," said one man. "Those *federales* won't give up."

"Let them get Quijano," another mumbled. "Why us? We did nothing! And he's not in this for work, like us. He's in it for the looting."

"I hated Don Evaristo, but that wasn't the way. We won nothing," said another.

"What a life! One day bloody rich, the next bloody dead!"

"And the bell ringer? What about him? He got dealt a rotten card, poor devil!"

"He didn't deserve that," said Roberto sadly. The fire was glowing, the smell of roasting meat diffusing and one of the men started to play his harmonica.

Every night they had sang together but tonight Roberto couldn't sing.

The yowl of the coyotes merged with the night sounds as the other men sang softly.

Adios, adios lucero de mis noches
Dijo un soldado al pie de una ventana..."
(Good-bye star of my nights, said a soldier to his beloved as he
stood below her balcony...)

Sitting by the fire, Roberto's thoughts were carried to those countless evenings when his family hosted friends for an evening of dinner and song. There would be about twenty people and everyone would sing accompanied at the piano by his mother, Maria Eugenia Pugibet. Roberto himself loved to sing, and while studying accounting in Chihuahua to please his father, he had taken singing lessons with Maestro Baldini, an aging Italian musician and retired opera singer. The maestro had dedicated his last years to teaching singing to a few well-chosen pupils and had not been happy when Roberto had told him he was joining the miners' cause.

"That's not for you," he had told him. "I'm leaving Chihuahua and, like your family, I'm moving to Mexico City."

Roberto had disregarded his advice and almost without wanting to, he had become part of a revolutionary movement. It was like a whirlwind, a force that could not be stopped. Now he realized how little he knew of the world and of himself.

His thoughts were interrupted by Molina's words: "How long do you think this struggle will last, Captain?" Bernardo Molina had been the mine's foreman and was anxious to return to work.

"I don't know, Bernardo. The mine owners are holding tight. No improvements, nothing has changed except that now... Don Evaristo... and the boy... What a disaster!" Roberto said, anger once again rising to his throat.

The fire was dying and the men were sleeping now. Roberto replayed in his mind the events of the last months. This was not what he had hoped to achieve. Everything was lost. His elbows were resting on his knees, his locked hands pressed against his forehead. He was choking from disgust. Never had he felt so hopeless and guilty at the same time. What had prompted him to even join the revolutionary movement? Maybe it had all started after hearing the idealist message of the liberals. He had embraced their principles but like him, they were not practical. They were far removed from the reality of daily life and from the people they most wanted to help. Some middle class enthusiasts were impressed by the presidential candidate's message but the oppressed classes had too much anger kept under restraint through oppression or hunger to wait for the changes to happen. Roberto realized now that nothing would change by talking with the mine owners. Only the prospect of violence or severe economic loss would force change.

Roberto moved slowly towards the horses. Suddenly, by his side was Molina. "Captain where are you going?" he whispered. Roberto just shook his head.

"I'm not a captain, Bernardo. I can see that now. I'm not even a soldier. I would be proud to die for the cause but I cannot handle the killing. You need a real war horse and I'm not it. I can't stay with you anymore. I will only be a hindrance. Please explain this to the other men. I have left the carbine and the bandoliers and bullets in the cave."

"But Captain, we need you!"

"No, you don't. You'll be better off without me. You know what you want and you will get it," he said. "I now know that talking with the mine owners is useless."

"*Adios Capitan!*" said Molina extending his hand. Roberto shook it and in silence saluted him.

Man and horse walked away, down the ridge towards the plateau, sheltered by the darkness of the Chihuahua autumn sky.

CHAPTER TWO

Just before daybreak, Roberto found himself standing on top of the ancient stone bridge that joined the two sides of town. He wanted to see Santa Rosalia one more time before leaving for good. He remembered that not all that long ago the river flowed under the bridge and the peasant women sang while they did their washing. They carried their tunes rhythmically, accompanied by the beating of the soapy clothes on the stones.

But the mine owners had changed the river's course. It was not even a creek now. There was no more singing and no more washing. The music had been replaced by the sound of dry stones kicked by the children when they walked from one side to the other. The willows that bordered the riverbed were dried out, their musky smell gone. The fields that became green with the rains where Roberto had played ball with his friends had disappeared under the rubble of the surrounding adobe walls that had slowly fallen to the ground.

The landscape had changed but the church tower could still be seen in the distance, its pink sandstone façade carved by stone masons centuries before, could not be distinguished, clouded as it was by the smoke coming out of the mine stacks.

It wasn't that long ago that he'd been crossing the river on horseback together with his friends, Juan and Felipe, when a huge wave of muddy water carrying trees and branches swelled against them. They had screamed in fear, their horses had panicked, but they had been able to reach firm ground before the flood had covered the fields. The dyke that contained the river further up had burst.

Now, eight years later, Felipe was dead because of the collapsed gallery in the mine and Juan had gone away. There had been too many deaths, too many changes. His town was not the same. Standing on the bridge he knew that he was seeing his birthplace for the last time –the place that gave him a sense of belonging.

No use pretending he was a captain or a revolutionary. He couldn't even control the men. He wouldn't use a gun on anyone. In fact, he promised himself never to carry one again.

For six days he rode his horse through small towns, avoiding the bigger places and eating whatever he could in exchange for a few coins. He left the arid northern plains and rugged mountains behind him and reached the fertile fields and pine forests of the center of the country. The people he encountered in the small towns shared with him their meagre pots of beans and tortillas around a coal brazier where they sat and ate in silence. They worked and tended the land of the big *hacienda* owners day after day, from sunrise to sunset, returning to their shacks in the evening to sleep on a mat made of palm leaves on top of a dirt floor. They worked hard. They deserved a better life.

The older people were resigned to this misery. "It's our fate," they said. The younger ones were not as accepting and underneath a veneer of complacency and even joviality, there simmered deep anger for the hardships they had to endure. They were at the mercy of the farm foremen whose abuses and infamies they suffered. They did not get paid when they couldn't work due to illness. It was up to the owners to provide the basic medical care, but more times than not the peasants had to ask for help from the *shamans* to cure them. Also, their wives and daughters often endured in silence the sexual advances of these bosses. The law failed to protect them.

Roberto listened to the few peasants who dared to talk about the situation. He had little to offer except his insistence that they should all learn to read and write, despite of age and sex. That was the first step. "Education is the only way," he said.

These people were not permitted to have any more than a religious education that encouraged their acceptance of poverty with the hope of a better life after death. Roberto now understood the magnitude of the problem and had begun to feel helpless against it. At the end of this short journey he had stronger feelings about what he considered to be the right of every man but also realized that the change would take a long time.

He stopped at a former classmate's house in the outskirts of Mexico City. It was a big property, surrounded by gardens and paddocks. Further away stood the stables where the family kept pure bred horses.

He had been here once before. But, now Roberto felt uncomfortable seeing so much wealth not far from the humble dwellings and the living conditions that he had witnessed in the last few days. There was such an enormous gap between the people who worked the land and the families like his school friend's –a gap that could not be easily bridged.

"Roberto, thank God you're alive! We've heard alarming reports about happenings in the north and wondered where you were," Manuel Dominguez said, embracing him.

"Well, here I am, bruised but alive."

"I hope you're not going back. Are you hurt?"

"No, just discomfited, Manuel. Listen, can I leave my horse here, for you?"

"For me? What do you mean?"

"I'm not going to need it any more. I'm going away –far away."

"Where?"

"I still don't know. You always liked this horse. Right?"

"Well, yes, but…"

"No buts, Manuel. Please take care of it for me and… could you lend me some clothes?"

"Yes, of course!"

"I want to go to the opera tonight in Mexico City."

"To the opera? Why on earth?" asked Manuel.

"Because, I love it. It's the one thing that gives me real delight."

"Yes, I remember. So do you still sing?"

"I did, until a few months ago."

"Right! Until you started your crusade for the miners, am I wrong? Your brother mentioned something about that."

"I'd rather not talk about that…"

"As you wish," said Manuel shaking his head as they entered the house. "Let's have something to eat."

For the first time in months Roberto enjoyed a sitting down meal. They had rice and mole with chicken and fresh quesadillas with pumpkin flowers and hot peppers.

They talked about the new presidential candidate and the rising hopes of the middle class.

In the afternoon Manuel drove Roberto to the train station in his father's new car. Roberto had managed to avoid the subject of Don Evaristo's and the bell ringer's death.

A few hours later, he entered the opera house in Mexico City. He climbed the three floors of marble stairs as fast as possible, not looking around and not wanting to be recognized by anybody. He sat in the top balcony of the theatre waiting for the opera to start. Roberto had always loved the minutes before the conductor's

entrance, when the orchestra tuned up and each musician practiced specific passages that required more effort. They played
oblivious to one another. That reverberating moment when every
instrument executed its own tune was the prelude to grand opera
performance.

The lights went dim, the conductor climbed the podium and
the first notes of the overture to Verdi's *La Forza del Destino* filled
the theatre with their powerful drama.

Roberto closed his eyes as he entered the world that he loved.

He remembered clearly the first time he had been deeply touched
by the world of opera. He had been ten years old then and was living in Santa Rosalia with his family. There was great excitement at
home because two opera singers –a married couple- were visiting
the town and were going to stay at Roberto's parents' house for two
nights. The singers were on their way to Guanajuato and Mexico City
where they were going to sing in several opera performances. The
household was energized and everybody worked feverishly preparing
for the guests. The piano was tuned and flowers adorned every room.
Roberto expected to meet a fairy tale couple –a prince and a princess,
but when Monsieur and Madame Carre shook his hand and smiled
at him warmly, he was disappointed that they didn't look as he had
imagined they would. M. Carre was short and balding, not quite the
image of the Egyptian General Radames of "Aida" that he was to interpret. Madame Carre had a beautiful face with eyes that lit up as
she talked. She was quite portly, a disadvantage when standing beside
her husband, but she had a contagious laugh which seemed to inject
liveliness and joy into the most serious of gatherings.

After the main meal was finished, the adults spent the rest of
the evening in animated conversation and the children were sent
to bed. During the night, Roberto woke up to the sound of two
voices that were singing the final duet of Verdi's *Aida*, saying farewell to the earth and the valley of plants *O terra addio, addio valle di
piante…* He was familiar with the duet from his parents' Victrola

but this was a true performance. He did not get up. He listened from his bed, holding his breath, electrified by the sound of the voices that were expressing eternal love. He waited for the final notes that he had heard many times before, never fully appreciating the sublime music. That night, he decided that he would be an opera singer. The next morning when he greeted the opera singers, they both looked magnificent to him. Now, twelve years later, Roberto listened with a sense of foreboding to the music and words of one of Verdi's most tragic operas with its eloquent undercurrent of misfortune and unavoidable destiny.

What is my fate? Roberto thought. He felt like an outsider in his own country, maybe because he could not accept its present situation. He was opposed to the government and angry with the people who profited from contracts that exploited the workers. Those magnates lived in splendour right beside the poorest of folk, completely blind to their misery, never looking into their eyes. The outcries of discontent did not seem to upset them and Roberto couldn't understand that.

When his parents had left the town of Santa Rosalia, he thought that the miners' situation in town was the worst in the country and that he could do something for them. Now, through his short riding trip across the center of the country, he had seen true poverty. He felt a tremendous urge to vanish, to disappear without a trace.

The lights went on for intermission. "Hello Roberto!" said a sweet voice behind him. It was his sisters' friend, Marianela, whom he knew from his hometown and had not seen for quite a while. Roberto turned around and stood up to greet her.

"Hello Marianela!"

"When did you arrive? Your sisters told me you were still in the north. We have moved to Mexico City too," she added.

"Oh! I just got back," he answered, becoming terribly nervous. He shook her hand politely and added: "I should be on my way to see my family before it gets to be too late tonight."

"Are you not staying till the end?" she asked.

"I don't think I should," he replied. "Good-bye, Marianela. Enjoy the performance!" And with this he made his way out of the aisle in a desperate effort to stay away from conversation. By tomorrow, his family would know that he was in town and had been seen at the opera.

He went down to the next floor wishing to hear the rest of the opera and stood at the back behind the separating wall, together with the theatre ushers who attended all performances on their feet. *Pace, pace Mio Dio,* the voice of the soprano soared in the theatre echoing Roberto's need for peace of mind.

The opera ended and he walked as fast as possible, following the people who were making their way out of the theatre in the midst of talk and the sound of heels on the marble stairs.

"Roberto!" The low-pitched voice of his old singing teacher shook him.

"Maestro Baldini! How good to see you!" He turned to face him with relief.

"What are you doing here? I thought you were in the north."

"I got in this afternoon, Maestro. And you?"

"I've been here for some months already. It was not good in Chihuahua; too much disorder these days. Now I have a place not far from here and I always have good coffee. Come! Let's talk, Roberto." And in saying so, Maestro Baldini took Roberto by the arm and led him towards the exit.

Outside the theatre there were presidential guards protecting the entrance and keeping distance between theatre patrons and the poor people who stood or sat along a cordoned area. Not a word was uttered by the surrounding group, made up mostly of indigenous women carrying sleeping children in their *rebozo* shawls, they only stole recriminatory glances at the women coming out of the theatre dressed in their best gowns of muslin and damask, their shoulders covered with mink capes. These women

and their escorts did their best to ignore the poverty that surrounded them.

The Maestro still holding Roberto's arm squeezed through the
guards and after some apologies got the two of them walking on
an empty street away from the crowd.

"That was bad!" said Roberto.

"And it will get worse," replied Maestro Baldini as he took a key
out of his pocket and stood in front of a heavy door. "This is my
new place. Just one flight of stairs." He climbed it with difficulty.
He opened the apartment door and turned the lights on. "Not a
palace, but there's room for the piano and the music, and it's close
to the theatre."

"This is nice, Maestro," said Roberto taking in the room. The
beautiful baby grand piano occupied a good part of the room and
a few bookcases lined the walls.

"Much better than facing the disturbances taking place up
north, although after what we saw tonight, I don't know how much
longer will the government be able to control the situation. The
movement is growing in the south too. But enough of that! Sit
down Roberto and I'll make some coffee." He went to one corner
of the room to turn on a kerosene double burner and set a coffee
pot on it.

"What did you think of the opera tonight?" Baldini asked.

"It was inspiring but I had to leave my seat halfway through it. I
ended up standing on the second floor, at the back."

"Why?"

"Oh Maestro, I didn't want to talk to anybody and one of my
sisters' friends was sitting right behind me. After we exchanged
greetings I gave some excuse and left. I'm in no mood to talk to
people at the moment."

"I hope that doesn't include me, Roberto."

"Of course not, Maestro! You are one person I'm always happy
to see. You bring me close to my greatest joy, music."

"Well, then, would you like to play and sing something?"

"Maestro, I haven't played for almost a year."

"*Bene, bene.* Fine, I'll play and you sing." Roberto tried to vocalize to warm up, but he couldn't relax.

"Let's have the coffee first," said Baldini. He got the coffee pot and poured two cups. "*Allora?* So what's wrong?"

"Maestro, my joining the movement was a total disaster." And, as he drank the coffee, he explained the death of Don Evaristo Gomez and of Agustin, the bell ringer. "Everything happened so fast and I couldn't do anything. I felt impotent and frustrated at my inability to prevent all that from happening. I didn't accomplish anything with the mine owners. I was so wrong to even try."

"No, it's never wrong to look for solutions. But I wish this day had never come for you, Roberto. Idealism has little to do with day-to-day reality. The rich only learn when their pockets suffer.

"I thought I could help, Maestro. I had good plans for reconstruction and they were not that expensive. But the owner just wouldn't listen."

"Well, that's greed. The dispossessed lose their patience and killing becomes part of the bargain. History teaches us so."

"I don't know what do. I have nothing but shame and a feeling of complete despondency. I couldn't even stay with the miners. I became an obstacle to their plans and they knew it. I believed that was my calling. Now, I have nothing. No plan. No dream!"

"Roberto, you have a life in front of you."

"For what? I don't want to be an administrator for a rich owner, or a lawyer, which is what my father would like me to be."

"I know, but what about your first dream? What you wanted to be only three years ago? You are young. You can become an opera singer. Music was your passion until you became involved in that disastrous endeavour. You were given the gifts of a good voice and a good ear. Develop them. Go to the heart of opera. Go to Milan and study."

"Oh Maestro! That was a dream. I don't know if I can afford it now."

"Nonsense! Listen, I have a good friend in Milan, Federico Stracciari. He's an excellent singing teacher and will be glad to help you. We both studied at the Accademia Santa Cecilia years ago and he became a renowned opera singer. He may introduce you to people who can give you a job."

"You make it sound so easy."

"It's not so difficult if you resolve to do it, Roberto. Youth is on your side."

"Come with me, Maestro! You're always thinking about Italy."

"No, Roberto. I'm too old and my heart is failing. I don't mind staying here. My daughter and her family live here and I have some new students."

They talked until the early hours of the morning. By then, Roberto's mind was clear and filled with determination.

"Thank you for everything, Maestro," he said embracing him warmly. Maestro Baldini kissed Roberto on both cheeks.

"Don't let them dissuade you, Roberto. Be strong and *Avanti! Buona fortuna!*" As Roberto stepped out into the cool morning mist, he turned around to wave. He probably would never see the Maestro again.

It was early when he arrived at his parents' home. It was a two-story house with an imposing entrance framed by two stone planters and four marble steps with a balustrade on either side. It was a combination of French provincial and Spanish colonial styles, quite different from the unobtrusive elegance of their house in Santa Rosalia.

The caretaker, who had followed the family to Mexico City, opened the door.

"Master Roberto, it's good to see you!" he said.

"Hello, Panchito! How are you?" said Roberto smiling.

"Everything is well! And now, even better! Your parents will be happy to see you."

"Thank you, Panchito! I want to see them too. But I would like to wash and shave first."

Panchito showed him to the guest room and the washroom. "Oh, they are going to be delighted," he added. "I'm going to tell my wife so she can prepare your favourite dish." Roberto couldn't remember which one it was. It seemed like an age since he had savoured Marta's delicious cooking.

When Roberto entered the dining room, a while later, his father and mother were already sitting at the table.

"Mother! Good morning, Father!" he said politely as he rushed to embrace his mother. "It's so good to see you."

"My dear son, how are you?" his mother cooed.

His father, Don Gustavo Madariaga, stood up and shook Roberto's hand gravely.

"So you're here. Are you ready to start your law studies?" asked Don Gustavo.

"Please, Gustavo. I would like to hear how he has been, what he has done, before we talk about studies," pleaded Roberto's mother.

"The time has come for him to make a decision about his life and not the life of the miners. Did you get any satisfaction from the owners?" Roberto shook his head. "No? I knew it! You could have avoided all that aggravation if you had only listened, Roberto."

"I'm sorry father!" was all he could muster. He had no intention of giving Don Gustavo the details of his failure.

"It's time to be practical. The entrance exams for law school are in a couple of months and you have just enough time to prepare yourself."

"Father, with all due respect, I am not going to study law. It's not for me."

"Not for you? You think that university has to fit your wishes?"

"Of course not, Father. But I want to go to Italy and study music, opera to be precise."

"Opera? Are you out of your mind? An opera singer in our family?"

"Why not, Father. I remember when Monsieur and Madame Carré visited us in Santa Rosalia and we went all out to receive them in our house. For days afterwards, you and mother talked about their talent and their artistry," said Roberto.

"Do you know how difficult it is to earn a living from music or art, for that matter?" How would you support a family?"

How could Roberto answer? He didn't even have a girlfriend.

"Oh, my son! You have a beautiful voice, but Italy is so far..." interjected Roberto's mother.

"And how do you intend to travel, pay for your studies and live?" asked his father.

"Professor Baldini has given me a letter of introduction for a friend of his in Milan. He is a voice teacher and he may be able to help me find a job to support myself."

"And the trip? Do you know how expensive is to travel to Europe?"

"I saved most of my earnings from the work at the mine, Father. I think I have enough to travel to Italy and get started there. And... I would like to have your blessing to do that, Father."

"My blessing! You didn't need it to go on your mining adventure. You could have saved your mother all the anxiety that she has gone through. Why on earth can't you study law like your brother? Right here at the university!" exclaimed Don Gustavo.

"Please Father, try to understand that Francisco and I are different, even if we are brothers."

Doña Maria Eugenia had listened to this exchange and knew that Roberto would not convince his father. Don Gustavo was attached to a family tradition that firmly believed that their contribution to their country was to provide an uninterrupted line of lawmakers and barristers. For three generations the sons of the family had graduated in law and now, one of his sons was rejecting the idea.

"I'm sorry Roberto. I have to go to court now. You know what my feelings are about this matter. I have nothing more to say. Good-bye, my dear!" he said addressing his wife.

"But Father…" Roberto stood up to say good-bye but his father was out of the room.

"Oh my dear!" said his mother, "I wish I could convince him."

Roberto embraced his mother tenderly. "You understand, Mother, don't you?"

"Yes, I do, and you have my blessing. But please be careful. Write often and let us know how you are. The truth is that your father worries about you and cares a lot about your future, but I understand your love of music and you have to follow your heart, my son."

"Thank you Mother! Thank you for everything! I hope Father will come to terms with my decision."

"When are you leaving, Roberto?"

"Tomorrow evening. I'll take the train to Veracruz and then the ship to New York. From there, probably to Genoa."

Roberto embraced his mother and left the room.

CHAPTER THREE

Saying good-bye to his family was hard. Roberto had hoped that his father would change his mind or at least wish him well, but he remained stern. His mother instead was supportive and serene as the gentlewoman she was, but suddenly, as he embraced her, she looked frail and Roberto was filled with apprehension. His brother was encouraging and his sisters were enthusiastic about his travelling to Europe.

He had mixed feelings as he closed the door to his home.

"To the train station, please," said Roberto as he climbed on a barouche and rode along the Reforma Boulevard. Once again he admired the majestic *ahuehuete* trees and the gardens that adorned the avenue. Large quantities of roses and shrubs were planted at the time of Emperor Maximilian's rule, almost forty five years before and the avenue became a favourite promenade for all residents whether on horseback, riding in carriages or simply walking.

The boulevard had been designed to emulate the Champs Elysees in Paris and it connected Chapultepec Castle, the official residence, at the time of Emperor Maximilian and Empress

Carlota, with the government palace and the Cathedral located in the centre of town. Halfway between the castle and the Cathedral now stood a towering marble and sandstone column with a golden angel at the top. All this mounted on a huge marble platform decorated with sculptures of the fathers of the Mexican independence movement.

"It's a magnificent monument!" said Roberto to the driver as they came to a stop. The splendid monument had been commissioned by the president, General Porfirio Diaz to celebrate the first centenary of Mexican Independence. A few weeks back, on the 15th of September 1910 the monument had been the stage for a huge parade depicting the history of the Mexican people. Allegorical floats had moved along the boulevard carrying Aztec emperors, surrounded by their eagle and tiger warriors who walked in great numbers brandishing their shields and weapons. Behind them followed Hernan Cortez, the conqueror, mounted on a splendid white horse and his army of Spanish soldiers and Franciscan friars, the viceroy and his court. The people, rich and poor, had lined the streets watching in awe the splendour and the excesses of the celebrations.

Different countries presented gifts to the Mexican government to honour one hundred years of Mexican independence. A civic procession, made up of various associations of bank, industry and commerce and of the military, was organized to attend a ceremony in memory of the heroes of independence at the Cathedral. This was followed by a sumptuous reception.

That night President Diaz, the governor of the city, the cabinet ministers, the diplomats and the representatives of many countries and their wives, dressed in formal outfits, gala uniforms and exquisite gowns, gathered in the government palace. The Cathedral and the government buildings in the heart of the city glittered with millions of newly installed lights, while they listened to the call of "Viva Mexico!" and the clangor of the bells. The populace at the central plaza, below the main balcony of the national palace, admired the lights and joined in the joy of a free Mexico.

The next day a military parade took place to inaugurate the Independence Monument. All the members of the Mexican army, navy, cavalry, artillery and the Military College marched along the Reforma Avenue and were joined by contingents of marines from France, Argentina, Brazil and Germany.

Today, however, instead of the rejoicing crowds, the cheers and the sound of the bands, a large group of people had gathered around a speaker. His forum was the highest platform of the Independence Monument, beside the statue of Miguel Hidalgo. He had a powerful voice and from the carriage Roberto could hear: "No more oppression!" "No more starving wages!" "We want the right to strike!" "We want freedom!" "Yes, freedom!" "We are slaves in our own country!"

Roberto could still hear him as the carriage gained distance from the monument. More and more people were walking towards the speaker making it impossible for the carriage to move in the other direction.

"Sorry Señor," said the driver. "It's impossible to continue."

Roberto stepped down and pulled his trunk. A man with a small pushcart offered to help. They walked against the crowd that kept moving and calling out: "The candidate, the candidate! Madero is here!" Roberto didn't think that Madero, the charismatic candidate to the presidency, would come. President Diaz would not allow that. He was determined to add still more time to his thirty-year presidency. His power was now sustained through oppression and through total control of the newspapers.

"To think I was in the parade dressed as a tiger warrior," said the carrier.

"Were you really?" said Roberto.

"Oh yes, Señor. I was proud to be there. All my family was cheering."

"I read in the newspaper that it was a grandiose show."

"It was. But just look now. Everyone is upset. They say too much money was wasted."

So, thought Roberto, *the people who were silent at first are now raising their voices.*

Finally they entered the esplanade in front of the train station. While he was paying the carrier Roberto saw in the distance a group of presidential cavalry guards galloping towards the Reforma Avenue, swords drawn. A horrible vision crossed his mind. But his thoughts were interrupted by the noisy arrival of a group of carriages that lined up outside the station. Ladies dressed in long travelling suits and ample hats scrambled out of them looking around with anxiety and lifting their skirts not to dirty them. They rushed towards the entrance accompanied by children, nannies and husbands and by porters wheeling trunks and boxes along the platforms.

Outside the walls of the station there were groups of indigenous women and children sitting stoically waiting for the men to come back. Not too far away the men were listening to yet another speaker whose face was not visible from the station but whose arms and hands spoke exaltation. The winds of revolution were blowing their way to the south. Fearing the worst, people who had families outside of Mexico City were leaving for places they thought safer.

Roberto hurried towards the tracks. A supervisor checked the railway ticket and directed him to the second-class sleepers. Porters were giving information in loud voices. "Pullman 32, further ahead." The conductor was shouting instructions to teamsters and brakemen. People were saying good-bye, crying and embracing each other. Every so often the rush of steam let out by the locomotive dampened the din. It was a long train with first, second and third-class coaches, dining cars, freight cars and an observation car at the end. From this moving balcony many heads of state had saluted the people upon arriving in the city and had praised the work of President Diaz, for it was he who had brought Mexico into the twentieth century.

Above the confusion, the distinct sounds of gunshots were heard in the distance. Some people forced themselves to believe that the blasting noises were caused by firecrackers and not by gunfire. Roberto had a sudden impulse to stay and remain by his parents' side.

Train windows were lowered and people were looking out. Some were waving and some were crying. *How very different from the only other time he had taken a train.* Years before the experience had been exhilarating. But things had changed and something was terribly wrong in the country. *Was he doing the right thing? Leaving his parents, leaving his country?* "You must go, Roberto," his mother had said. "This may be the only opportunity."

He feared for her because he sensed she was hiding some illness. He feared for his father because he was part of a dwindling social class –a class made up of the children or grandchildren of Europeans who had arrived in Mexico to work in the mines, or the railways, as teachers or businessmen seeking opportunities in the New World. His father was a lawyer who believed in justice. But these days, justice was not being served and Don Gustavo was upset.

"All aboard!"

Roberto felt a lump in his throat. Nobody had come to say good-bye to him. He imagined his father standing very straight and looking at him with his light blue eyes reproaching his decision to leave.

He went out of his compartment as the last passengers were coming in. The train started to move. Roberto was submerged in his own thoughts. How things had changed. The peaceful towns where he had grown up in the north had become battlegrounds. Hatred and discontent had spread among groups that had worked together for ages. A major conflict seemed to be brewing.

Roberto believed in negotiation, in finding solutions. He believed in peace and rejected the use of arms. He loved music and loved to sing. That was what he hoped to do –to learn enough to sing the operas he loved, to interpret the drama that they conveyed and relive, every time, the desperation of a Cavaradossi waiting for the firing squad or the desolation of a Rodolfo when his Mimi dies.

He was considering all this while standing on the platform between the train cars –the marvelous place that allowed travellers to look at the countryside, feel the wind and hear the whistle of the locomotive as the train moved leaving a cloud of smoke along its trail. Leaning on the half-door of the platform area, which was left open for the people who wanted to smoke, he saw fields and mountains pass before his eyes. There were problems in the country, but here, along the tracks, away from the towns, everything seemed peaceful. He could see the farm hands pushing primitive ploughs pulled by oxen. The fields were cultivated and looked prosperous. The land here was noble and rendered citrus fruit, coffee, sugar cane and cereals. There was a great difference between this area and the north of the country, where mining and cattle were the sole products.

Childhood memories kept coming to mind filling him with nostalgia. He could recall the sheep races and the mock rodeos during the yearly feast of Santa Rosalia. In the evenings the band played in the kiosk of the central garden. While the older people sat on the wrought iron benches to listen to the music, they watch the young groups walk around the square, chatting and laughing –the girls clockwise and the boys counter-clockwise. They ate ices and sometimes threw confetti at one another –the only way to tell a girl that she looked pretty. All of that was now just a memory.

Eventually, Roberto entered his train compartment.

"Good evening," he said to the fellow passengers as he sat down.

A mature lady with inquisitive eyes and a nose that seemed to inhale higher air replied: "Good evening, young man. Where are you travelling?"

"I'm going to Veracruz to take the ship to New York and then to Genoa."

"How lovely!" she replied. "I'm Mrs. Harding. This is my husband, Mr. Spencer Harding and my niece, Miss Clara Gillespie. We are also travelling to New York." The young woman smiled with little enthusiasm.

"Great place Mexico, but getting a bit dangerous," said Mr. Harding.

"Oh! My dear, please don't talk about it!"

"Clara is going to study in New York. She is an artist. Painter, I should say."

"That's exciting! I've heard that there are marvelous art schools and galleries in New York. People say it's a wonderful city," said Roberto.

"It is," replied Mrs. Harding. "We lived there before we came to Mexico. Are you going to stay in Genoa?"

"I'm going to Milan and I hope to be able to study singing, opera and everything related to it." Roberto looked at the girl, trying to guess the effect of his words.

Two splendid blue eyes looked at him. "That's wonderful!" Her voice was sweet and clear. "Do you know any music teachers in Milan?"

"No, I don't. But I have a letter of introduction for a music teacher, a friend of my singing teacher in Chihuahua. I'm hoping he'll accept me as a student. My name is Roberto Madariaga," he said, standing up and extending his hand to Mr. Harding. "Mrs. Harding, Miss Gillespie," he added bending his head politely.

"Call me Clara, please," she interrupted under the surprised expression of her aunt, who immediately interjected.

"We had to travel second class because all the sleepers in first class were taken," she explained. "Most inconvenient, I may say!"

"Don't worry Aunt Margaret, we'll be fine."

The porter, playing his marimba-like chime announced: "First call for supper," as he walked through the second-class Pullman cars.

"Would you like to join us for supper, young man?" Asked Mr. Harding.

"Well, thank you! If it is all right with you," Roberto said, looking at Clara and Mrs. Harding.

They stood up and walked through some sleeping cars to get to the dining room. The tables were elegantly set with white tablecloths, fine china and gleaming silver cutlery.

During dinner the Hardings carried most of the conversation, and the two young people barely spoke. Roberto felt the young woman's eyes studying him and wondered.

Clara was pleased to have a young man sitting at dinner with them. She often felt like an outsider with her aunt and uncle. They talked about things that held no interest for her like business, the stock market and money. She was grateful that they had offered to pay for her studies and had opened their house to her in New York. But she was leaving Mexico and felt sad. She missed her parents very much. When they had died, two years before, she felt there was no point in living anymore, yet over time, she had learned to face her new reality. For nearly two years she had lived with her Aunt Margaret and Uncle Spencer. They were her guardians and had taken her away from Tepoztlan to their house in Mexico City and were trying their best to help her carry on. She had enrolled for art classes at the Academia San Carlos and during that period, she had become obsessed with her parents' faces. When they were brought to the funeral home, after the car accident, she was not allowed to see them. And once she had recovered enough from the shock of the tragedy, she was stricken by the realization that their faces were disappearing from her memory. So she had dedicated herself to drawing and painting countless portraits of her father and mother in a desperate attempt to recapture their features and their essence.

She would like to have a friend like the young man across the table. She liked his looks and his manner. But she was going to live in New York and he was going across the ocean to Milan.

The sudden voice shook her a bit.

"Could I invite you all for coffee in the parlor car? Roberto asked.

"I'm terribly tired and would like to rest. But, thank you very much!" was Aunt Margaret's reply. "But, if you would like…" she added, looking at Clara.

"Yes, I would. Is it all right?"

"Fine, but don't take too long. Remember it's not easy to sleep on the train."

"I understand, Aunt Margaret."

"Well, good night and thank you again!" said Roberto extending his hand to Mr. Harding.

"Not at all, young man. It's been a pleasure to meet you!"

Clara and Roberto walked to the back of the train to the smoking car. It was a friendly room. People were reading newspapers and others were talking and smoking pipes and cigars.

"I know of a better place where we can talk without smoke," said Roberto as they made their way through the car.

They got to the very end of the train. It was an open place with a handrail and a wonderful view of the countryside. It was getting dark and a bit cool.

"Are you cold?" he asked.

"No, I'm fine." Clara leaned on the railing and looked dreamily at the countryside.

"Oh, I love this country! I'm going to miss it so much. This is where I have lived most of my life, you know. It's my home. I wonder if I will ever come back."

"You will, I'm sure. Just as I know that I will come back one day," Roberto replied with an air of confidence that he didn't really feel.

"I have spent the best and the worst days of my life here," she said, reminiscing. "My aunt keeps telling me that I'm going to lead a different life in New York. I'm going to have to attend receptions, go to benefit concerts and participate in church activities and also meet the children of her friends. I'd love to go to concerts, but I would loathe the rest. And I can't go to church now."

"I haven't gone to church in a while," said Roberto. "I often ask myself just when and how this change took place. I know part of the answer lies with the social ills of our country. The rest I can't explain."

"I don't know either. I want to believe, like I did a few years ago. I used to go to church and find solace in communion and prayer. But something happened after my parents died. It was horrible! There was no warning. The impermanence of life has haunted me ever since."

Roberto was shocked to hear what she had just said and added softly: "Would you like to talk about it? I don't want to upset you."

Clara shook her head and paused for a few seconds. She breathed deeply.

"I have not talked about this in a long time, but I'll try. We came to Mexico when I was about two years old. My father was an artist and he became well known in his last years. He was considered quite talented. He was also fun and sometimes impulsive. My mother told me that he had wanted to live in a houseboat, originally, but the lack of rivers in Mexico made him change his mind. Instead they decided to live in Tepoztlán, by the shadow of the powerful *Cerro del Tepozteco*, close to Cuernavaca. They rented a house with some land where my mother grew flowers that she sold to flower shops and vendors. She also loved to sing and dance and she could play the guitar. We had a lot of fun.

"Your parents must have been very interesting and special people."

"Yes, they were. Both were inspired and hard working. And although once in a while they would go away for a few days when my father had exhibitions, most of the time we were together. When they went away Eufemia stayed with me. She was my nanny from the time I was a baby. She is such a loving and kind person. I know I will miss her terribly. She gave me strength when it all happened."

They were silent. Then she continued.

"It was a horrible car accident in my father's new car. I never saw them again. They would not allow me to see anything. I only imagined them. Their beautiful faces! Their bodies, destroyed!" Clara's eyes were fixed on the distant mountains as she continued. "Aunt Margaret, who is my mother's older sister, took me away with her to Mexico City, while Uncle Spencer took care of everything. He's a wonderful person. But, I never saw my parents again..." Clara's chin was shaking and her eyes filling up. "I miss them so much...!

Suddenly a painful sound, like the snapping of a cello chord, came out of her throat. She started sobbing uncontrollably. All the sorrow and loneliness of the last two years came out like an avalanche.

Gently, Roberto put his arm around her shoulder, attempting to calm her. A feeling of loss united them as they leaned side by side on the railing, looking at the distant mountains and the darkening sky.

Clara finally calmed down. "I'm sorry for that!"

"Please, don't apologize, Clara. I thank you for your trust and sincerity. It must be such an inexpressible loss. I wish I could give you some comfort."

"Thank you, Roberto. You know, I would like to believe in another world after this, where I could meet my parents again, but I don't."

"I know. I don't believe in it either. But, on the other hand, faith gives hope. And that's the one belief that poor people have for a better life. Without that... well, they have nothing."

"But, you see? That's what makes me angry, Roberto. How can they be told to hope for something that isn't true?"

"We don't know, Clara. Do we, for sure?"

"You're right. Maybe it is good to believe in something."

"I believe in love. Do you, Clara?"

"Yes, I do, I do. My parents had great love and they loved me too. I believe in beauty, too."

"You see? One has to believe in something, if not..."

"What do you love Roberto, apart from family?"

"I love opera! The music, the words, the tragedy... it fills my senses!"

"I have only been to two operas, but I liked them very much. You said you're going to study singing, what voice are you?"

"I'm a tenor."

"Are you good?"

"I hope to be with study and discipline, just like you as a painter."

"Thank you, Roberto! I hope you will be my friend forever!" she said kissing him on the cheek.

"I hope so too," he smiled, surprised at her unexpected enthusiasm. "It's getting cold. We must go in."

"Yes, my aunt will be worried," said Clara.

"I hope to see you tomorrow, Clara," he said as he took her hand between his.

"Good night, Roberto and thank you. It's been lovely to meet you."

After accompanying her to the Pullman car, Roberto returned to the open section. He went outside and thought. He had never felt so close to a woman before. Clara was beautiful and sensitive. He liked her blond hair and light eyes. He realized he hadn't talked to a young woman for a long time.

The countryside was now in total darkness and only the outline of the mountains was visible in the distance.

CHAPTER FOUR

When the train arrived in Veracruz the next day, the newspaper boys were shaking the printed pages and shouting:
"Armed forces repress political meeting in the capital city!"

"More disturbances in Morelos and Michoacan!" "Angry miners take action in the north!"

Roberto's heart skipped a beat. He gave the boy a coin and right
there, with his luggage at his side, he read an inaccurate account of
what had happened in the town of Santa Rosalia a few days before.
No names were mentioned. The bell ringer was not mentioned. He
was standing in a state of shock when Clara Gillespie and her aunt
and uncle came out of the station.

"Roberto, is something wrong?" asked Clara.

"Bad things are happening all over the country," he replied.

"Is it serious?"

"I think so."

"We must hurry to our hotel and get ready for tomorrow," said
Clara's uncle.

"Can we give you a ride to your hotel?" asked Clara.

"No, no thank you! I have still to find a place for tonight." Roberto could hardly talk.

"Well, do rest up young man. Tomorrow we have to be at the ship's dock very early. We sail at ten o'clock," said Mr. Harding. "Hotel des Diligences," he continued, as he signaled the baggage porter to load their luggage into one carriage, while they climbed into another.

"Good-bye Roberto. We'll see you on the ship tomorrow," Clara said, already sitting in the carriage.

"Good-bye," he answered, taking off his hat.

He knew that he could have been more attentive but, at that moment, his thoughts were in turmoil. He called a young boy with a pushcart and asked him if he could direct him to an inexpensive and clean hotel. The boy immediately said yes and putting Roberto's trunk in his cart started to walk.

"How are things in Mexico City?" he asked, glancing at the newspaper.

"Not too good," Roberto replied.

Everyone had told him that Veracruz, Mexico's busiest port, was a cheerful town. A carnival took place there every year. It was a feast of colorful costumes and constant dancing. Celebrations ended with lent when the images in the churches were covered in purple cloth to remind people to observe forty days of abstinence.

There was a lot of activity today and many ships were docked. Young men in different navy uniforms were parading down the boardwalk, laughing and talking in loud voices. There was nothing to indicate that there were problems in the country. Stevedores were unloading ships and deckhands were cleaning and working, getting ready for the voyages.

After registering and washing, Roberto returned to the streets to enjoy the warm atmosphere and the gaiety. The centre of town was vibrant with people and the movement of carts, carriages and one or two automobiles. There was a group playing marimbas in the main plaza kiosk and farther away three musicians played a small harp and two guitars as they sang. The cafes were bursting with people drinking large cups of coffee and fresh fruit juices. Others walked around just listening to the music. With all this activity, Roberto's optimism slowly returned. He needed very little to look at life in a positive light. He sat at a café and wrote a long letter to his parents and postcards for his brother and his two sisters.

That night Roberto kept thinking about his town and the incidents in Mexico City. He was up very early the next morning with the first call of the ship's siren.

The ship cut a handsome image against the clear morning sky. The deckhands could be seen running from one side to the other on the various decks of the liner. The rest of the crew, dressed in white uniforms, were taking their posts and getting ready to board the passengers.

The air was clear and a soft breeze made the palms that adorned the promenade by the sea, move like slow undulating waves. The Gulf of Mexico looked calm and inviting. It was already warm, and elegantly dressed gentlemen, brandishing walking canes, were buying newspaper and walking towards their favourite outdoor café where they would read accompanied by freshly roasted cups of coffee and freshly baked bread. Roberto did the same, unable to believe that the news he had read the day before had not altered the cheerful atmosphere of this town. He looked for more news but could find nothing else in the newspapers. It was as if nothing had happened at all.

He was already crossing the platform when the ship's siren whistled for the second time. The porter escorted him to his second-class cabin. It was tiny but it was only for him. He lay down on his bed and closed his eyes. Outside he could hear the passengers walking along the corridors and the cabin-aides opening and closing doors. He was dozing off when the sound of the third siren enveloped the ship. He got up and walked to the deck.

Standing on the quay were women in long gowns and men dressed in beige linen suits, wearing Panama hats and holding canes. They waved hands and handkerchiefs, looking like the scene of a stage play that at any moment would break into a song. Around them, the local people, dressed in white, had stopped their activities to watch the departure of the liner.

The ship moved out of the harbor. The white town with its lines of palm trees became smaller and Roberto was overcome with emotion as the last view of the coastline disappeared. His country! Just a few years back he had had an argument with his friend Juan who had told him that Mexico was not really his country. Roberto had always considered Juan his soul mate. They both cared deeply about the country.

"What do you mean, Juan?"

"That you are really European," Juan replied.

"But I was born here, I live here and my family has lived here for two generations."

"Still. You will always be a foreigner."

They were seventeen year old and full of idealism, proposing what they would do to change the many things that they thought were wrong. They had read about democracy, about Rousseau's Social Contract and were ready to adopt the ideology and apply it in their country. Inequality would disappear. Roberto thought that education was the only way to affect change. Juan believed instead that the owners of enormous tracks of land should be forced to give most of it to the peasants –the people who really worked the land.

"When does one become a citizen of a country?" Roberto asked himself. He had brown hair and brown eyes, but people called him *"güero"* which meant blond. He had light skin but he did not see himself as different from others, yet something in his demeanor made people think that he was a foreigner. It was at this moment that he understood that maybe he would always be a foreigner no matter where he might be.

He was musing about all this as he walked around the ship and realized that he would not be able to see Clara during the voyage. She was in first class.

The sound of an accordion reached the deck. He followed the music until he entered the second-class dining room. The tables were set up for six or eight people and passengers were walking in and sitting down. The accordionist was playing a popular Spanish tune and some people were following the rhythm with their heads but without the enthusiasm that is usually roused by happy music. The smell of freshly baked bread engulfed the room and pretty soon the conversations became alive. Some groups spoke Spanish and others spoke French.

"May we sit here?" someone asked.

Roberto turned around and was greeted by a smiling redhead man wearing a tweed jacket accompanied by a tall black-haired woman dressed in a dark-green stylish suit. The pair offered a pleasant and cheerful contrast.

"Of course!" replied Roberto standing up and pulling the chair out for the lady to sit down. "Madam, please!"

Two young men who looked very much alike also asked permission to sit with them. Soon a young woman and a distinguished looking lady, both dressed in black, joined in and everyone sat down.

"My name is William Stevens," said the redhead man, "and this is my wife, Francisca de Leon," he added with a sweeping motion. Everyone followed suit and pretty soon the table was engaged in animated conversation. William Stevens was an impresario who was leaving the country because, in his vaudeville act, a comedian had managed to offend President Diaz and the show had been closed down by the authorities.

It was easy to ridicule the eighty-year-old president, now turned dictator. He had been a hero during the government of Benito Juarez and had fought against the French during the invasion of

Mexico. But all that was forgotten. The dashing general had become corrupt and was now the laughing stock of comedians and caricaturists. In his thirty years of government he had transformed himself from a fighter for a free and independent country into a plutocrat who, in trying to push Mexico ahead, had let the wealthy become a controlling force. The needs of the lower classes and the indigenous people were forgotten. He wanted the country to become part of the cluster of industrialized nations and had impressed those nations with the rapid development of transport and communications and industrial progress. He had adopted French customs, and his government officials and their families followed the French fashions. A good portion of the population felt betrayed and although he was building dams, highways, bridges, hospitals and railways, the benefits did not filter down to the poor.

As dinner was served, the conversation veered around the political situation.

Mr. Stevens explained that fearing the possibility of being jailed, he had decided to leave the country. His wife was secretly joyful to be returning to her country, Spain.

She was an accomplished singer of *zarzuela,* the Spanish operetta, and *couplet,* the cheerful and frivolous songs, popular in light theatre revues.

"In Madrid we will open a show, and we are going to be successful, Billy, you'll see," she said with an encouraging smile.

"I'm sure we will, my dear! But I was happy in Mexico," he added. Although he had lived in Spain and Mexico and spoke perfect Spanish, his English accent still surfaced when he was tense.

"You know," she said, addressing the rest of the table, "nobody can joke about the old fogy and get away with it these days."

"That's why we're leaving," said one of the two young men. "We are students at the Faculty of Economics and members of the Liberal Party. Lately, we were arriving to our lectures at the National University of Mexico only to find out that our professors were suspended or fired for expressing negative opinions about the Mexican economy. And those were the lucky ones, others were sent to jail as political prisoners."

"Incredible!" said Mr. Stevens. "Just a few years ago President Diaz was considered an extraordinary statesman. He was acclaimed by the Secretary of State of the United States as an example to humanity, and as someone devoted to justice and liberty."

"Well, as Plato said, 'Democracy passes into despotism," said the other young man. "And I believe that is what has happened to our former hero. He forgot what he had fought for. He forgot the workers and the poor. Wages are miserable. Strikes are forbidden and people who demand a salary increase or a reduction of working hours are severely punished with fines or incarceration. Those in government who support all this are compensated with land, contracts, favors or political power in their own towns."

"Now, you tell me if we should continue living in Mexico," the other young man added.

"He may drop dead at any moment," said Stevens, "He's nearly eighty!"

"Please, do not talk like that," intervened the distinguished lady who had been quiet up to this moment. "My husband came to advise on the construction of the tracks and the operation of the streetcars in the cities. He thought President Diaz was a good man"

"I'm sorry Madam!" said one of the young men. "I apologize."

"My father had a heart attack a couple of months ago," said the young woman. "He was having difficulties," her lips tightening to control the tears.

"Dear Maria, please stop!" said the mother.

"I'm sorry, Mother!"

"If you would excuse us," said the mother, standing up and followed quickly by her daughter.

"Won't you stay for coffee or tea?" asked Roberto standing up.

"Thank you, but we must go now," the lady replied curtly.

Roberto had been quiet through the whole exchange. He didn't want to enter into any political debates. But regretted that he had failed to observe that the conversation was upsetting the lady and her daughter.

The meal was finished and the accordionist started to play again. The atmosphere relaxed and the music flowed.

"Come, Paquita, sing us a song!" said Mr. Stevens to his wife, eager to forget the conversation that had taken place.

"Francisca de Leon! My 'nom d'art,' my dear!" she said smiling.

She stood up and walked gracefully towards the accordionist who immediately stood up as he continued playing. He leaned forward to hear what she was saying. Then stopped playing as Francisca de Leon said in her clear voice: "Ladies and gentlemen, for you, La Violetera.'"

The dining room became silent and the warm voice of Francisca de Leon filled every corner of the room. Her singing captivated Roberto. She looked stunning and was totally immersed in her song. Her voice rose easily to the highest note and then flowed down like a soft petal falling from a fairy's hand.

When the song finished there was a second of silence and then "Bravo! Bravo!" Enthusiastic clapping filled the room. Roberto wished Clara were here to enjoy the music.

"Would anyone like to join me in a song?" Francisca asked the audience.

Roberto wanted very much to say, "I would!" but he remained quiet. However, the light in his eyes gave him away and William Stevens picked up on it.

"You can sing, yes?" he said, addressing Roberto.

"A bit, but I'm not professional," replied Roberto

"Come on, this is for the joy of it. Believe me! Nobody is going to pay money here," "Paquita! He added, "this young man here is going to sing with you."

Roberto walked toward Francisca. "Would you like to sing a duet?" she asked.

"I'd love to, if I know it," he answered.

"The duet of the *Africana?*" she said.

"Yes, that's good," he replied.

"Maestro, do you know it?" she asked the accordionist.

"Of course, Señora!" and he started to play.

Francisca and Roberto were now singing. She was an experienced performer and was able to draw the young man out. Pretty soon, Roberto stood beside her in complete control of the character he was performing and although he was much younger than Francisca the two were able to convince the audience that they really were the couple in love, depicted in that piece of music.

No cantes mas La Africana, vente conmigo a Aragon.

William Stevens was delighted to hear them sing. He was smiling blissfully, already imagining a great show in Madrid.

"Bravo! Bravo!" The audience was thrilled. Nobody had left the room. "More, more!" And the musical evening continued until both singers and the accordionist were exhausted. By this time, the ship captain had been called to hear the music. He was impressed and decided to ask both singers to perform during the last evening in the first class dining room.

"But, what about the second class dining room?" said Francisca.

"We will arrange different hours so that both groups may enjoy your singing. The second class earlier and first class a bit later. Would that be acceptable?" Asked the captain.

"Perfect, señor Capitan!" replied Francisca for both of them.

"Thank you Captain!" said Roberto.

The thought of singing in the first class dining room in front of Clara excited him but also made him nervous. What a fantastic beginning of a trip it had been. The political and social concerns were momentarily forgotten.

"Señora Francisca, Mr. Stevens, thank you very much!" said Roberto as he wished them good night.

"Well done, young man!" replied Stevens extending his hand.

"Roberto, if we are going to sing together, you must call me Francisca, please."

"Yes, Francisca," he said softly "and thank you!"

The two young men got up and made a sign of approval with their hands. "Good night everyone! We'll see you tomorrow!" They bowed and put on their hats.

"Wonderful evening!" people were saying as they walked out of the dining room.

Roberto stayed out for a while, leaning on the railing and smiling at the night and the sea. The ship travelled swiftly through the waters of the Atlantic Ocean, not too far from the American coastline.

CHAPTER FIVE

Two days later, Francisca de Leon and Roberto Madariaga were rehearsing for the captain's closing dinner event. The small orchestra that played for the first class passengers went over the music with the singers.

"Roberto, you look a bit nervous," said Francisca.

"I admit that I am."

"No reason. You have a wonderful voice and your interpretation is flawless."

"Yes, but first class… I will be singing in front of someone I met during the train ride to Veracruz and…"

"Aha! Perhaps you are in love?" said Francisca jokingly.

"I don't know."

"Even better, you will be addressing your arias to her. Just follow your heart!"

On the last evening the first class dining room sparkled with the lights of the chandeliers that hung every four meters and reflected on the crystal and the silverware. Napkins folded in the shape of Japanese fans completed the set tables. Two hundred people dressed in evening clothes walked in to enjoy their last dinner on the ship. The trip had been an extremely pleasant one regardless of the reasons that had prompted each passenger to make it. As they were getting to the end of the meal, the Captain announced the musical program they'd all been looking forward to.

"It is my pleasure, ladies and gentlemen, to present to you the famous zarzuela and couplet singer Francisca de Leon and the tenor Roberto Madariaga, who will delight us tonight with their beautiful singing on this, our very last evening together."

Francisca and Roberto walked across the room to the small stage accompanied by the reserved applause of the first class passengers. Francisca was splendidly dressed in a black evening gown of the latest style that accentuated her gleaming eyes. She smiled with the confidence of an experienced performer and giving a nod to the orchestra started addressing Roberto with her coquettish song. They sang parts of *La Verbena de la Paloma* and *Marina*. Their voices filled the dining room, making everything even more special. At the end of the pieces the audience was applauding enthusiastically.

Then Roberto entered to sing alone the aria "Che gelida manina" from *La Boheme* by Puccini. He searched for Clara in the audience and looked at her briefly. Then he concentrated in the singing. By the end of the aria everyone was standing up, shouting: "Bravo! Bravo!" He couldn't make out Clara's expression from the distance. His own emotions only permitted him to bend his head and his lips read, "Thank you, thank you!" He walked out of the room where he encountered Francisca's open arms and a big kiss.

"I told you," she said. "You were great!" and kissed him again. No feeling of jealousy clouded her sincerity. Now it was her turn again and she went out and sang "Connais-tu le pays" from Thomas' opera *Mignon*. Her heart poured into the beautiful aria and many people in the audience instantly related to it as they were on their way to their old country. Others were despairing because they were leaving the place where they had lived all their lives.

For the conclusion of the program, Francisca and Roberto sang the "Duet of La Africana." The listeners were captivated by their style and expression and amused by the light ending they gave to the duet. The last evening was an enormous success both in the second-class dining room and later in the first class dining room. People stayed drinking champagne while the orchestra played for another hour.

Clara went to the back of the small stage, where the singers were talking.

"My aunt and uncle would like to invite you all for a glass of champagne," she said to Roberto and the others standing beside him.

"Francisca, Mr. Stevens, this is Miss Clara Gillespie," said Roberto.

"I imagined so," said Francisca with a smile. "It's very kind of you. Thank you! We will join you in a few minutes. You go right ahead, Roberto. Our young star," she added jokingly.

Roberto offered his arm to Clara and she held it close to her. "That was beautiful, Roberto! I didn't expect you to sing so... so brilliantly," she said as they crossed the dining room.

"Thank you, Clara! You inspired me," he replied as his heart was racing from her closeness. "If I could, Clara, I would ask you to marry me. But I have nothing to offer you."

She looked at him but had no words to reply when she realized that he was serious. She became quiet as they were approaching the table where her aunt and uncle were waiting.

"My boy, that was outstanding!" said Mr. Harding standing up and shaking Roberto's hand.

"Very beautiful!" added Aunt Margaret. "Please sit down. Are the others coming?"

"Yes, they will be here shortly. Thank you!" said Roberto sitting down.

Was he mad? What was he thinking —saying that to Clara? It was probably the singing. He couldn't look at Clara. She, instead, was composed as the waiter poured the champagne.

"To your health and to a successful singing career!" said Uncle Spencer lifting his goblet.

Presently Francisca and her husband arrived and were introduced by Roberto.

The conversation became animated between the two older couples, while Clara and Roberto were very quiet. Francisca was telling them an anecdote about her stage experiences when she was younger, "And then in the middle of the couplet this man jumped onto his table and started to clap his hands and dance flamenco. I had no other choice but to follow suit on the stage and very soon he was dancing beside me."

"I could have sent him out," said Mr. Stevens, "but Francisca was impressed and she has an eye for artistic talent."

Roberto could hardly swallow the champagne and follow the conversation.

"In fact, he stayed with our company as a flamenco dancer until recently, when we decided to go back to Spain," said Francisca.

"That's what I call a well-timed opportunity. Critical decisions in one's life can change its course forever," said Mr. Harding.

Roberto closed his eyes and breathed deeply as if Mr. Harding's statement were intended just for him. His words to Clara had been untimely and totally out of place. She was probably thinking about what her uncle had just said.

"Why don't you invite Clara to dance, Roberto?" said Francisca making him even more uncomfortable.

"Come on, you young people, you should be on the dance floor," added her husband.

Roberto stood up and went to Clara's side to ask her to dance.

They walked to the dance floor closely observed by the four people at the table.

"They make a splendid couple!" said Mr. Stevens.

"Better to let God decide," said Aunt Margaret. "My niece is very young and we barely know this man. Furthermore, he is going to study in Italy and he may meet a beautiful Italian girl and forget about Clara in no time. Clara must be introduced to our group of friends in New York. She may find someone well established who would want to marry her. She is an orphan, you know. And my sister didn't leave her much. Still, we are happy to take care of her."

"It's great to have a caring family," said Francisca. "My mother is waiting for us in Madrid. That's where Billy and I met," she added –her eyes shining. "It was like magic!"

"Yes, it was," said Mr. Stevens standing up. "Would you like to continue the magic and dance, Paquita?"

"Always!" And they went whirling around with other couples to the melody of the waltzes of Juventino Rosas and Johann Strauss.

Roberto glanced at them as they danced, thinking that although they had told him that they had been married for over fifteen years, they seemed to have still the spark of love.

Clara looked intently into Roberto's eyes. "I think the music prompted you to tell me what you said before," she started, "but I know that you have to study and you have a long road ahead of you."

"Clara, I think I'm in love with you. I would not have told you anything otherwise."

"Maybe," she said, "I like you too, very much. But we have to follow our roads until we are ready."

Roberto knew she was right and she was more mature. He felt like an inexperienced fool. He had been so lonely in the last while that her friendship seemed like the greatest love he'd ever know and perhaps it was. "I will write to you and one day I will go to New York and I'll look for you."

"That will be grand! In the meantime, let's enjoy ourselves and dance the rest of the night away." She was smiling and feeling animated for the first time in the two years since her parents' death.

He pressed her hand softly and continued to dance. They floated in a cloud of tender feelings.

"I may not see you tomorrow when you leave the ship," said Roberto. "You will be gone by the time the second class passengers disembark."

"I thought about that and have written down our address in New York. Put it in your pocket," and handed him a folded piece of paper. "Write to me."

"Maybe we can meet sometime tomorrow," said Roberto, "go for a walk and see some of the sights."

"I think my aunt and uncle have other plans."

"Clara, please don't forget me!" he said.

"You'll be in my heart, always!" she replied, as the music ended.

They walked back to the table. Mr. and Mrs. Harding were already saying good-bye to Francisca and Mr. Stevens.

"It has been a pleasure meeting you, Roberto!" said Mr. Harding. "If you ever come to New York, do call on us," he added sincerely.

"Thank you, sir. It has been a pleasure meeting you all. Mrs. Harding. Good-bye Clara!" he added holding her hand for a moment.

"Good-bye Roberto!" She said composedly.

As the others left the table, Francisca said: "What? No kiss?"

"Well, they are strict people," answered Roberto.

Suddenly, they saw Clara almost running between the tables towards them. "I forgot my night purse," she said picking it up from the table. "And this!" and she kissed Roberto hurriedly on the lips. He was so shocked that he couldn't even stand up. By the time he reacted, she was already out of the room.

It took a few minutes for him to talk again and Francisca and Mr. Stevens just smiled. As they stood up to leave, Stevens exclaimed:

"Oh youth! Is just wonderful!" He shook Roberto's hand. "Good night Roberto!"

"Sweet dreams, my friend!" said Francisca.

"Good night!" he answered as politely as he could. He could hardly talk. He walked through the corridors to the second-class deck and stayed there quietly, looking at the sea. He wanted to retain forever the glorious feeling of Clara's kiss.

CHAPTER SIX

In the morning the ship approached New York harbor. The passengers came out of their cabins and contemplated the imposing view. Rising above the fog stood the Statue of Liberty proclaiming its message of freedom. A respectful silence extended among the passengers and the crew. Roberto thought about the similarity between the Statue of Liberty and the Angel of Independence in Mexico City, both proclaiming freedom and self-determination. Perhaps the answer was here, in this country.

The ship moved toward Ellis Island, the port of entry for all travellers arriving in the United States. The first class passengers were cleared by the immigration authorities on the ship before all others and were not required to line up or wait around.

It was a cold December morning when the rest of the passengers set foot on American soil. They joined many other men, women and children who were waiting to enter the huge buildings, where they would go through the immigration process and be cleared by the health officials. Many children wrapped in blankets sat beside their parents, or hugged them with great anxiety.

As they entered the huge building the confusion of tongues echoed on the tall ceilings and the walls. A large American flag hung from a balcony at the very front and through the high windows on the sides of the building, the sun shone in, spreading a feeling of hope.

"Have your documents ready!" shouted a uniformed officer, waving a passport in his hand. He walked back and forth between the rows of people who waited patiently for their turn. The lineups were slow moving but the people, many of them tired and hungry, were not upset. Instead, there was eagerness in their expressions. They were arriving in great numbers from Russia, Albania, Italy and Ireland and from other countries that Roberto could not readily identify. Most little children slept peacefully, lulled by the constant murmur, while the older ones looked scared in such surroundings and stayed close to their family.

People wore their best clothes to enter the United States. Some carried suitcases and some carried their belongings inside large canvas bags or baskets. Roberto noted that some of the children looked hungrier and more frightened than the Mexican children he had encountered back home in the mountains.

In the next lineup Mr. Stevens and his wife were talking: "Look at them. They could really do with a Spanish *tortilla*," said Francisca. "Did you know that eggs, onions and potatoes saved Spain from starvation a century ago?"

"No, I didn't. I guess potatoes are a treasured root all over the world," replied Stevens.

"God knows what these people have gone through," said Roberto from the next line.

"You can imagine just from looking at their faces. Those children need to play and laugh," said Francisca.

"I hope they find what they are looking for," said Roberto.

"Isn't that what we all want? Peace, acceptance and a place to work and live." Francisca's voice faded as she imagined the pain and indignities these people had endured through pogroms and massacres in their own countries. Their eyes gave testimony of great suffering, but when their names were called a sudden spark of hope brightened up their faces. They were identified and questioned by the authorities. Many names were difficult to pronounce so the immigration officers readily simplified them and registered men, women and children with their new names in large books. Most people didn't understand much but some did and were not happy with the sound of their new names. However, when they were informed that their entry into the United States was approved, their uncertainty disappeared. Their exhausted bodies straightened in pride and determination. With signs and bits of English words they proclaimed to the authorities their intentions to work hard and honor their new country.

Roberto was deeply moved by this human drama.

As they got closer to the front of the lines, a faint smell of food filtered into the huge area. In the next room, long tables were arranged and women in uniforms served hot soup and bread. People were thankful and ate avidly while they waited for the nurses and doctors to listen to their lungs and inspect their skin and ears and throats. Most were given the health clearance, while a few were separated out for further medical investigation.

Several hours went by before Roberto and his friends, Francisca and William Stevens, cleared the entrance gates to the United States. Together with many other visitors and immigrants they boarded the ferry that would take them to Manhattan. The atmosphere had changed. Many new immigrants were talking animatedly in their own language and were seconded by the noise of the tugboats and other vessels crisscrossing the Hudson and the East Rivers.

"What a view!" exclaimed Roberto as the ferry approached the quay. He had never seen anything like this. The tall buildings stood at the southern point of Manhattan Island like guards protecting the assemblage of wealth and culture.

"Stunning," said Francisca, who was leaning on the railing.

"This entrance to the country never ceases to surprise me and every time it is a bit different," added Stevens.

Francisca turned to Roberto. "Please keep in touch with us, Roberto. We would like to know how you get along in Italy. Here is my mother's address in Madrid," she said as she handed him a small card. "Do write to us!"

"Maybe you can come and visit us in Madrid," added Mr. Stevens. "Remember distances seem shorter in Europe."

"Thank you!" Roberto shook William Stevens' hand, "I will write."

"Don't forget!" said Francisca as she kissed him on both cheeks.

Amazing people! Thought Roberto. Their friendship had helped him overcome the feelings of sadness and despair that had accompanied him for days. He could now envisage a bright future.

In minutes the multitude disappeared between the buildings, hauling their precious possessions and the memories of their countries, to venture into "the land of promise."

They dispersed in small groups looking for the relatives, church groups and agents who had helped them travel to this country. Many carriages and several automobiles rolled along the avenues and people wearing heavy coats and hats crossed the streets talking animatedly, contributing to the exuberant atmosphere of the city. *This is a younger country and how much faster it has grown,* Roberto had once believed that there was no place quite as big as Mexico City, but now he could see that New York was probably bigger and livelier.

He stopped a carriage and asked to be taken to Mott Street. Professor Baldini had told him there were many Italian families who rented rooms in that part of the city. The houses and buildings were different from the ones in Mexico. They had metal staircases at the front, zigzagging all the way up to the top floor.

Roberto later discovered that these were used in case of fire, while inside there were staircases which rose to the top floor, made out of wood, marble or granite and usually bordered by bronze railings.

When he stepped out of the carriage he was surprised by the sound of the language. It was not English that he heard; it was Italian. He looked around and chose a small building that had a sign "Rooms". He climbed the few steps and knocked on the door. The smell of fresh tomato sauce filled his nostrils as a middle-aged woman opened the door.

"*Buon giorno!* She said.

"Good morning, signora, I would like to rent a room for two nights. Is that possible?" Roberto asked.

The lady replied: "*Si, si, venga, venga.* Come in!

They climbed a set of stairs and the lady opened the door to a spotless room with a bed, a small table and a chair and a wooden valet hanger like his father had in Mexico.

Roberto thought it was perfect with the washroom at the end of the corridor. He carried his trunk, paid for the room and went out.

What a city! He could breathe the energy at every corner. He stopped dead in front of a barbershop at the sight of a poster that announced Enrico Caruso singing at the Opera House. Compelled to find out more, he entered the shop, where everyone seemed to be talking about the famous tenor.

"Where is the opera house?" asked Roberto.

"At Broadway and 48th street," replied one of the customers. "But all performances are sold out."

"I'll try anyway. Thank you!" he rushed out of the shop. *Caruso! I can't miss that!*

He walked fast towards the theatre. New York was a city to be enjoyed with every step, but as predicted, the performances were sold out.

"Sometimes," said the ticket vendor, "people sell tickets at the entrance, just before the performance, but usually for quite a pretty price."

"I'll try my luck," said Roberto.

He entered a cafeteria. The place was totally different from any *merendero* or café in Mexico. He saw what other people were doing and followed suit. It was good to take a tray and choose whatever you wanted from a kind of *smorgasbord*. As he paid, he noticed a few empty tables at the back and moved towards them. An attendant approached him and said:

"I'm sorry, sir, but you cannot sit in here."

"Are they reserved?" asked Roberto.

"No, sir, but this area is for colored customers only."

"What do you mean?"

"Look at the sign, sir. You cannot sit here."

Roberto was aghast. Was this possible in the country of Abraham Lincoln? He felt his anger rising and disgusted, he left the cafeteria without touching the food he had just paid for.

A couple of blocks later he bought a roasted sausage from a street vendor and a coffee. He admired the buildings surrounding Central Park but with a sense of disillusionment. Where was the equality guaranteed by the constitution of the country?

Evening started to fall and the lights shone inside stores and buildings, all decked out for Christmas. Light snow was falling but not enough to make walking difficult. Roberto went to the theatre and waited. He was standing at the front well in advance of the performance when a black man approached him. "Looking for a ticket, sir"? The man was polite and well dressed.

"Yes, I am."

"Sir, my employer went on a trip this morning and as he went out the door he gave me the ticket. He knows I like opera very much but, I guess he forgot that I cannot use this ticket."

"Why not?" Asked Roberto.

"This seat is on the main floor and colored people aren't allowed to sit there."

The man added, "I cannot use it but you could."

"No, under the circumstances I don't feel I want it," replied Roberto feeling upset for the second time in the day.

"But, Sir, you'll do me a favor if you buy it from me. I seldom have extra money. I could go somewhere with my wife and children."

"I don't think it's right."

"Sir, you will enjoy yourself and I will enjoy myself too."

Roberto was deliberating. "Please," he told the man, "let's go and have a coffee together and talk."

"We cannot sit together in any coffee shop around here, Sir."

"Well, then, let's sit on a street bench," said Roberto.

They talked for a while as the snow kept falling. Ted Anderson was a butler at an industrialist's home. His wife did the cooking. They had two children, still very young but he intended to send them to school, he told Roberto. They had good living quarters and were well treated by the family. He felt lucky. He loved to listen to opera. He had once attended a performance with his mother on the top floor of a theatre and he had never forgotten.

Roberto listened and decided he would do something for this good man. Without thinking of the consequences, he pulled a generous bill out of his wallet and gave it to Anderson.

"No, Sir, this is too much," argued Anderson.

"I have to do what I think is right," refuted Roberto. "If not, I cannot live with myself. Do you understand?"

"I do, sir. But it's too much."

"One must pay for good things. And please call me Roberto. Roberto Madariaga is my name."

They stood up and shook hands.

A while later Roberto was at the entrance to the theatre Anderson's ticket now in his hand. The excitement was overwhelming. Women dressed in long gowns and wearing fur coats stepped out of carriages and new automobiles and crossed the vestibule, which was covered with a red carpet. Every person sitting in the orchestra section had to enter this way. Roberto had never been in an orchestra seat before and this was a luxury. How many opportunities would there be in his life to hear Enrico Caruso in person? He took his seat conscious of the fact that he was one of the few men who were not wearing a tuxedo or dinner jacket. But, had he thought of it, he could not have bought one and, once the lights went off, the stage, the music and the voices were all that mattered.

Puccini's newest opera *La Fanciulla del West,* sung by Enrico Caruso as Dick Johnson and Emi Destin as Minnie, was a tragic love story with a hopeful ending; taking place in the Wild West during the Gold Rush. The composer's dramatic notes and dissonances intensified the atmosphere of greed and disappointment that permeated the work. As Caruso sang "Ch'ella Mi Creda Libero" Roberto thought of the dreadful things that had happened in Santa Rosalia and how in an instant a whole town is transformed into a place of death and revenge.

He was impressed by the singing and by the inspired manner in which Arturo Toscanini, the famous Italian conductor, had brought the orchestra to incredible heights during this most difficult piece of musical orchestration. He wasn't sure that the opera had been as fulfilling as Puccini's *Madame Butterfly* or *Tosca,* but he still came out of the theatre fully convinced that opera was the right road for him. His whole being was immersed in music and emotion.

The next morning he went to the French steamship offices. There were people lining up all the way to the street while an employee announced in a loud voice:

"No more space in third class."

"But we need to get to Paris. What can we do?" someone said.

"Try the Italian Lines," was the response.

"But we want to go to Le Havre."

"Sorry! First class only, please!"

When Roberto got to the front of the line he asked about other alternatives.

"There are some merchant ships that have a few cabins for passengers. You may try them. There's an Italian ship sailing tomorrow morning from Pier 42. Good luck!"

Roberto thanked him and rushed to the pier. There was no passenger ticket office or waiting area. It was a cargo ship but he was able to arrange and to pay for a cabin on a merchant ship travelling to The Azores, Lisbon, Barcelona and Genoa. He knew he couldn't spend any more time in New York. He would run out of money.

He enjoyed his last afternoon in the city walking and breathing in the prosperity that was evident all around. He walked by the Park Avenue building where Clara now lived. He did not go in. He would write to her.

Later he picked up his trunk and went to the pier to board the ship. He was assigned a small cabin with a water closet. There were only four other men travelling as passengers –a different experience from the trip from Veracruz to New York. The sailors were loading the last of the cargo amidst jokes and swearing while they lifted and pushed the heavy loads into place. Nobody was dressed in white jackets with golden buttons.

There were no women waving good-bye with flowing handkerchiefs or gloved hands as the ship was pulled out of the port. Like Roberto, the other four passengers were leaning on the railing and looking silently towards the shore. The shapes of the buildings were hardly visible through the heavy fog and Roberto experienced a vague sense of loss. Only the crew was moving around.

Once the shore had disappeared from sight, the day was slow and heavy. It seemed as though the ship was barely moving. The horizon was the same for hours and the sea looked like an indomitable force in its never-ending immensity.

CHAPTER SEVEN

Clara

As Roberto embarked on his trip across the Atlantic, Clara started her new life in New York. When she entered the apartment building on Park Avenue she realized her life would be different now. The view of the mountains and the feeling of openness that she had enjoyed in Tepoztlan were gone. Her aunt and uncle's apartment was spacious and she was given a bedroom with a small sitting area for her own personal use.

"I hope you'll like living here, Clara," said Mr. Harding.

"Of course she will, Spencer!" Aunt Margaret added.

"Oh Aunt Margaret, Uncle Spencer, I'm very grateful and I'm sure I will be very happy here." Clara said as she went inside the room trying to hide her tears. She was thankful and yet sad. In no other place had her mother's memory stung as in here. Like her mother, Clara did not like the few big cities she had ever seen with their tall buildings that blocked the view of the countryside. Clara hoped that one day she would live in the country again.

Aunt Margaret knocked on her bedroom door early next morning. "My dear, I have written the schedule for the coming week for you," she said as she handed her a sheet of paper with the Harding name embossed. Clara started to read as Aunt Margaret added: "Make sure that you are ready fifteen minutes before the time I indicate for every engagement. We must never be late."

"I understand, Aunt Margaret. Thank you!" Clara closed the door and sat at her desk. She needed to talk. She could write to her nanny Eufemia in Mexico. But what could she tell her? She had not ventured out of the building as yet. Maybe she could tell her about the ship, about Roberto. After her parents died, Eufemia had encouraged her to paint. "You have talent, just like your father, Clara. Don't waste it. I'm sure that he would like you to follow on his footsteps." Although Eufemia was a woman from the Puebla Mountains who could barely read and write and had no formal schooling, she possessed an artistic sensibility that showed in her embroidery. She was wise and accepted hardship with aplomb. She had helped Clara to sort out her life. She was a real friend and Clara missed her deeply.

She looked out. Across the street there were more buildings just as tall as the one she was now living in, built in the same style. The avenue was wide with a middle lane planted with trees and shrubs that would bloom in the spring. Although her room was comfortable and spacious, Clara felt cramped. She had hoped to have a balcony but the only one in the apartment was located in the living room, where her aunt entertained. *It will be strange for them to have me around.* Clara thought. It would take time for all to feel at ease.

The following days were full of social activities. Clara met the Sloan's, who had two sons, Alfred and Curtis, and a daughter, Christine. She also attended a social event at the Johnsons, who were in the drugstore business. Both families were wealthy and enjoyed a life of continuous parties, suppers and theatre. All of this was foreign to Clara and every night she was exhausted to the point that the next day she could do very little and although she had promised herself to start drawing again, she did not.

Soon she felt trapped in a merry-go round of social activity. In trying to please her aunt she was putting aside her aspirations. However, she was meeting people her own age and she was having a good time. She was learning to dance to modern music and all these gatherings made her forget her loneliness for a few hours. She seldom talked about her parents.

"Are your parents away?" asked Christine one evening.

"No," Clara swallowed. "They died in a car accident two years ago in Mexico."

"In Mexico? Oh, you poor thing! I'm so sorry!" she kissed Clara on the cheek and there was an awkward moment quickly interrupted by one of Christine's brothers.

"Come, let's dance!" said Curtis pulling Clara to the dance floor. Nobody really wanted to know more. Nobody talked about losses, let alone death. Late that night, Clara cried herself to sleep but woke up with new determination.

What's wrong with me? What's keeping me? She went out and spent most of the day at the Metropolitan Museum of Art looking at different art forms. On her way back she stopped and entered smaller galleries exhibiting painting, sculpture and some photography. At the end of the day she felt strong and purposeful. She would talk to her aunt and uncle. Her natural inclination was to be accommodating but she had to be strong.

"Aunt Margaret, Uncle Spencer, I would like to have a frank and honest discussion with you," Clara started at the dinner table.

"Is this a good moment, Clara?" asked Aunt Margaret.

"As good as any, Margaret. Let's hear what Clara has to say," said Uncle Spencer.

Clara took heart and continued. "I know that you are trying to integrate me into your group of friends and I really appreciate that, but I need some time to paint. I would like to continue art classes like the ones I had in Mexico before we left. I would also like to have time to go to museums and galleries." *There. She had said it.*

"Of course, my dear!" said Mr. Harding. "That can be arranged. Margaret would you please call Ed Chase. He can advise us as to the best place for Clara to start. Don't worry dear Clara, you will continue painting," he added. "I have also been thinking that you need to have your own money to spend. Every month you will receive an allowance, enough for your expenses. I hope this is acceptable," he finished with a smile.

Clara got up and kissed him on the cheek. "Thank you, Uncle Spencer!" He was surprised by this expression of gratitude and love. "Thank you, Aunt Margaret!" she said and kissed her too. Embarrassed, Aunt Margaret quickly added: "I will find out when we can see Mr. Chase." At the back of her mind she believed that this was a waste of time. Clara would soon be married to one of her friends' sons. She had already planned her course of action.

The next morning Clara woke up feeling optimistic. She opened the curtains of her window and was astonished by the view. The big avenue was covered with a blanket of snow. A few carriages pulled by horses were travelling slowly and there were no motorcars on the road. She had never seen so much snow this close. She had only seen it from a distance covering the peaks of the Popocatepetl and the Ixtacihuatl volcanoes in Mexico. This was exciting. She got dressed to go outside. Aunt Margaret heard her opening the door.

"Have you got your coat and gloves, Clara? Be careful, it will be slippery."

"Yes, Aunt Margaret," she answered hurriedly as she walked out of the apartment.

"Good morning!" Clara greeted the doorman.

"It's a cold morning, Miss. Mind your step!" he said.

Clara took in the marvelous sight. She walked slowly for a couple of blocks and every so often she stopped to contemplate the ice glittering on the trees with the help of the early morning sun. This light was different. Maybe latitude and altitude had an effect on light. The streets were silent as few people were walking. Closer to the park the streets came alive with children coming out ready to play in the snow; Clara was cheered up by the sight of them. Full of energy she went back to the apartment and sat down to draw. Later, she would put down on canvas what she had just seen. She worked the whole morning without pause.

A few days later she was introduced to Professor Chase and under his tutelage she started art classes. Her days were spent drawing, painting and going to galleries and museums. She wanted to tell a friend about her activities. Roberto had written a postcard but there was no return address as yet.

One evening as they were having dinner, Aunt Margaret said: "I notice you are very busy with your art classes, Clara. Mrs. Sloan told me that you declined an invitation from Christine."

"Yes, I did. I had to finish an art presentation and couldn't go," replied Clara.

"She also told me that Curtis had invited you to a concert and you said you couldn't go. I'm surprised. I thought you liked concerts." Clara's aunt pressed on.

"I do, but just now, I have to dedicate more time to my art," Clara added.

"Art! Art! It's all I ever heard from your mother when she was your age. She fell in love with your father and just look where art has taken them."

"Margaret, please!" interjected Mr. Harding.

"No I must say it. If it were not for art, your mother would still be alive."

"Oh, Aunt Margaret, please don't …" and Clara couldn't finish the sentence. She stood up crying and ran out of the room.

"Margaret, why? That was uncalled for," said Mr. Harding.

"You spoil her. She is my niece and she should be thinking about getting married, not art!" Mrs. Harding was upset.

"No, my dear. I know she's your sister's daughter and because of that you may want for her what you think is good and desirable. But her life in Mexico was different. It will take her time to adjust to a new way of life."

"She never had it so good. She has a future here. Who do you think she could marry in Mexico? An ambassador?" added Mrs. Harding.

"Forgive me, Margaret, but I do not want to continue this conversation. I would like to think that it didn't happen at all. I must talk to Clara now." Mr. Harding stood up from the table.

"Go, go talk to her! As if she would care."

Mr. Harding knocked on Clara's door. He was very upset at his wife's outburst.

"Come in," said Clara between sobs.

He sat at the foot of the bed and waited for Clara to stop crying.

"I'm sorry for that, Clara. Please forgive your aunt for what she said. She is upset. Believe me, all she wants is the best for you. As you know, we lost our daughter several years ago to rheumatic fever. Your aunt has never recovered. Then she lost her only sister, your mother. She embraces social activities with a passion. I believe she does that in order to hide her sadness and not to feel the emptiness left by these enormous losses," Uncle Spencer said.

"But, why did she say all that?" Clara said.

"Because after the death of our daughter, the death of her sister and of your father was devastating. She wants to protect you from anything that may give you pain and sorrow. Please try to understand her."

"Uncle Spencer, I like her and I'm aware of what she does for me, but you and I, both know, that I don't like parties that much. I don't like to go out with people who talk about other people, or about what someone is wearing. I really don't care. I try to be polite and participate but it is all so foreign to me…"

"It's good to meet people your age, Clara," he said.

"I know. I would like to meet other students and talk with them. I like some of the people who are studying art with me. We don't talk much because we have to concentrate on our work, but I'm sure they must be interesting. And, Uncle Spencer, I don't want to get married. At least, not yet," she ended.

"Very well, my dear. I understand." He held her hand between his own big ones.

"Please Clara, don't be sad. We love you very much." He stood up and let himself out of the room.

He loved Margaret and would have liked her to think as he did, but that was impossible. She had built a wall of calculated planning around herself that could seldom be shaken by emotion. He was content to see that all her social activities kept her away from depression.

He himself had learned to put aside all thoughts about their daughter. She was only ten when she had taken ill. Kathy would be now the same age as Clara. He often imagined how it could have been with her around. They had gone to Mexico partly to get away from memories, but now, back in the apartment where she had grown up, her presence surfaced constantly.

Spencer Harding had put great effort to make a success of his business in New York and then in Mexico and was making good money investing in new industries. That, in a way, prevented him from dwelling on the past. He was content to have his niece living with them and felt they should spare no expense to make her life enjoyable and productive.

He went into the kitchen to make some tea. Although they had a maid, he preferred to do some things by himself, as when he lived alone in Philadelphia, years back. He brought the tea to their bedroom and poured it slowly.

"Do you remember when we first met, Maggie?" he said pulling her tenderly towards him.

"Yes, Spence," she responded with a soft smile. "Such a long time ago…"

"No, not that long, dear! The river is still there and the metal benches along the walkway still welcome people like you and me. And I still love you as I did then."

"Oh Spence, I'm sorry! I don't know what's wrong with me."

"I know what's wrong, my dear. You care and you worry."

"I remember your boss telling me to take it easy, not to worry so much."

"Good old Mr. Lansdowne. He was right! And he wanted so much for me to marry you. He felt we were made for each other."

"He's dead now!" said Margaret sadly, "and so is our Kathy."

"My dear," Mr. Harding embraced his wife gently, "we were blessed with her life for some years. We will never forget her, but we are here, now, maybe for a reason."

"Are you trying to tell me that Clara is that reason?"

"Perhaps, Margaret. Maybe if we open ourselves to her love and affection we will find happiness again."

"Oh Spence," she replied leaning her head on his shoulder, "perhaps."

CHAPTER EIGHT

On the second day of Roberto's trip across the Atlantic the weather, which had been for the most part foggy and cool, suddenly changed. The fog-whistle stopped and the ship travelled at good speed. But during the night heavy winds started to blow and the sea became choppy.

"We're approaching a storm," said the captain at breakfast. "There's nothing to worry about as long as you stay inside. The waves can get pretty high and everything will become slippery. No walking around the decks, please."

All five passengers listened attentively. They looked at each other wondering if anyone was nervous. They didn't know what to expect. A few minutes later they all walked to their cabins hoping for the sea to calm down. Roberto had never been in the open sea. It's enormity filled him with respect, bordering on fear.

Around three in the afternoon the winds got stronger and the waves got higher.

Inside his cabin, Roberto could barely make out through the porthole what was happening outside. His view was only of water constantly hitting the glass and his interest in the view didn't last for long as he soon became dizzy and nauseous. He crawled to his berth and stayed there for a long time. He had known about sea-sickness but had no idea how debilitating it could be. He couldn't even stand up.

When he had been a young boy, he had devoured the novels of Emilio Salgari that depicted the adventures of the corsairs travelling on the high seas, surmounting enormous dangers and surviving deadly storms. But had never imagined sea sickness and although he was worried about a shipwreck, after a while his mind could only muster one thought, the need for the malaise to stop.

Outside the decks were being hit by thirty-foot waves and the rain pelted relentlessly. The captain and his crew were on the strictest standby in case of damage or emergency. The dining space was empty and little food was consumed for a day and a half.

On the fifth day after sailing from New York, the ship finally entered peaceful waters. The passengers emerged from their cabins, their faces still pale and tired but relieved. The captain announced that the danger was over and it would be a smooth trip from there on.

A couple of days later the ship arrived at the Azores Islands. Mule carts and people could be seen descending the hills to greet the sailors. The parcels of land on Terceira were ploughed and looked ready to receive the seeds for the year's crop. For in this island, spring was already in the air. The women carried their baskets overflowing with goods, swinging their bodies and singing some popular tunes.

The passengers were anxious to set foot on steady ground. They disembarked extending their arms, feeling the sun on their faces and bodies and becoming talkative.

One of them picked up some soil and rubbed it on his arms and hands. It felt good to be alive!

Roberto looked at the land for a few moments. He knelt and then rested his hands on the ground, letting its generosity flow through him. Yes, he loved the land, the soil and its boundless productivity. He felt energetic, ready to climb the hills that surrounded the port. No more worries about having spent money unwisely and having to travel on a smaller ship.

A couple of hours later, crew and passengers sat at a wooden table, by the water, eating grilled fish, sliced tomatoes and freshly baked bread. The rough sea was forgotten and everybody talked animatedly enjoying the catch of the day and downing a welcome glass of wine.

"Now, this is life!" said one of the passengers raising his wine glass. "To the captain, the crew and to the people of Terceira, Cheers!" *Salud!* Said Roberto.

This was a celebration of life, of survival against the elements. A fisherman brought out an accordion and another one a Portuguese guitar. Soon the people who had been preparing the food, both men and women, joined in. It was a gift of music. The songs told stories of sailors travelling to far away places, away from their loved ones and their country. They spoke of *saudade*, the tragedy of human destiny and the loss of lives to the sea.

The place possessed a utopian quality. This area of the island with the sea to one side and the old town to the other felt like paradise with the view of the fields in the distance. Two of the passengers declared that they could stay in Terceira forever. It seemed like a perfect way of life.

During the night the ship crossed the Strait of Gibraltar and by the morning it was navigating in Mediterranean waters. A couple of days later the ship entered the port of Genoa.

The passengers and crew gathered in the dining area and the captain read from a Bible the gospel commemorating the birth of Christ. It was December 25th and this was the Christmas service.

What a strange moment to be on a ship, Roberto thought. Every person in attendance was grateful to be alive and for having arrived to Italy, their destination. A special dinner was served to celebrate Christmas and also the last night on the ship. As evening fell, the ship was greeted by the beautiful sight of the newly installed lights along the Genoa harbor reflecting on the water and lending a magical feeling to the city.

The next morning the dockhands were ready to disembark and unload the cargo. The crew stood at attention and the captain said good-bye to each passenger. The five of them descended the gangplank accompanied by the music of three *Zampognari* who played an old, Italian Christmas song on their bagpipes. "*Buon Natale!* Merry Christmas!" could be heard everywhere.

Finally Italy! Roberto would have liked to walk for a few hours and look at the splendid buildings that seemed to greet him at every turn, but he was assailed by an urgent desire to be in Milan. It seemed to him that he had been on a journey for a long time and he needed to start his new life.

He admired the imposing Brignole train station, with its renaissance arches and palatial appearance, but quickly followed the *facchino* who was pushing his trunk on a small cart and bought his ticket. "To Milan, please."

He sat down in the compartment and closed his eyes, waiting for the train to move.

CHAPTER NINE

Milan – December 1910

After the Azores, the cold weather was a shock. In front of Milan's *Stazione Centrale* there was a big park and it was covered with light snow. The carriages came around the park and stopped in front of the main entrance to pick up travelers. Although Roberto had felt sleepy on the train, the excitement of being in Milan dispersed any tiredness and, after placing his trunk in the baggage storage room, Roberto hurried out of the station and signaled a carriage to take him to a hotel.

The first impression Roberto received of Milan, a city in perpetual motion, was to stay with him for many years. Even though it was snowing, there was much movement, people walking briskly and streetcars ringing their bells as a group of young men swept the snow off the sidewalks. Travelling in the carriage he had the strange feeling of having been in the city before. It looked familiar, as if he might have dreamt about it. He was shaken. Maybe he just felt at home, his new home.

The next day he went to look for Maestro Stracciari's residence to try to set up an interview. The Maestro lived in a large apartment beside the School of Music, the place where he taught every day. Roberto rang the bell and waited. A doorman finally opened the door.

"*Si?'*

"*Buon giorno!* I'm looking for Maestro Stracciari. I have a letter of introduction. My name is Roberto Madariaga," he said handing the doorman an envelope and a visiting card with his name.

"Please wait here," said the doorman closing the door.

Roberto was suddenly invaded by incertitude. The next minute or two seemed eternal. *What would he do if the Maestro would not accept him or would refuse to even see him?* Finally the doorman returned.

"Follow me. The Maestro will see you."

"Right now?" asked Roberto.

"*Si, si!*"

At the apartment door was Maestro Stracciari, the singing master. He was a tall, heavy-set man with white curly hair and a white moustache. He shook Roberto's hand with gusto.

"It's always a pleasure to hear from Maestro Baldini. So you are Roberto? Baldini told me about you in one of his letters a while back. How is he doing?" The Maestro asked as he guided Roberto inside the apartment.

"*Piacere di conoscerla, Maestro.*" All what he had rehearsed in his mind was forgotten. "Maestro Baldini is well," he managed to say.

"Is this your first time in Italy?"

"Yes, Maestro.

Roberto was impressed by Stracciari's presence and style. Although in his seventies, he walked very straight and looked splendid in his vest and jacket and a wine color scarf. He held Baldini's letter of introduction with his left hand and touched it forcibly with his right index finger.

"Young man, opera is a discipline," he began. "The voice is a gift, but without study and training it cannot be good for opera. To follow that road you have to be prepared to study with dedication. Now, my good old friend Baldini has a good eye and ear for talent. I wish he were here, in Milan, at the *Scuola. Ci manca molto!* Yes, we have missed him ever since he left for Mexico." Stracciari's baritone voice resonated as he approached the baby grand piano that stood at one end of the room.

"Let's hear your voice, signor Madariaga. *Vediamo,*" said the Maestro, as he sat at the piano, ready to play. "First rule: always vocalize to warm up before you sing."

Roberto had thought that he would be given an appointment to come another day. This was wonderful but unexpected. As he started vocalizing his initial nervousness gradually disappeared. He looked around the room trying to construe Stracciari's personality from his furnishings and discover the secret of his successful operatic career.

It was an ample room, full of light that shone through the tall windows where the heavy curtains had been drawn back. It was a combination of music, library and living room. Behind glassed doors, protected from humidity and dust, were hundreds of musical scores and other leather-bound books. There was one table with a world globe, a sextant and a world map. Perhaps the Maestro had travelled around the world or simply enjoyed geography. There were also three framed poster *affiches* of the operas which had consecrated Stracciari as a great opera singer years before: *Rigoletto, Simon Boccanegra,* and *Don Pasquale.*

The room, like Maestro Stracciari, was grandiose but also orderly and warm. To one side of the Bechstein piano there were four chairs, four music stands and an additional stand by the curve of the piano, for the singer's use. A cello was resting on a special bracket close to the wall and a violin and a viola sat on top of a console. The bows were hanging from special hooks. This was a room dedicated to music.

After the exercises Stracciari said: "Would you like to sing a classical song or an aria? Do you know Tosti's 'Ideale'?"

"Yes, Maestro, I do."

The Maestro began to play "Ideale." Roberto looked at him and then concentrated on one point, breathing and singing carefully. He sang with his heart, feeling every word.

Io ti segui –I followed you like a messenger of peace… and ended with "a new dawn will shine for me."

When he finished, Maestro Stracciari was nodding his head as he played the last notes on the piano. Roberto waited.

"Bravo, Roberto! You have the basic tool. Your Italian pronunciation is good too. Now, you have to work. I will be glad to have you as a student. We can start just after *Capo d'anno,* on January 2nd. *Va bene?"* said Maestro Stracciari.

"Of course! Yes, Maestro. *Grazie Maestro!"* Roberto was elated. He couldn't stop smiling. He felt like embracing his new teacher.

"Now, where are you going to live? Do you have a place already?"

"No, not yet. I arrived only yesterday and I'm staying at the Albergo Rossi. I haven't looked for a place yet. I wanted to meet you first, Maestro."

"Well, I can walk with you to a *pensione.* The owner, Signora Corelli, is the widow of a good friend of mine. She may have a room available. You can talk with her and see if it is convenient for both of you."

While he walked with the Maestro, Roberto didn't feel the cold, warmed by Stracciari's caring attitude.

"There it is, across the street," said the Maestro. *"Buona fortuna!* I'll expect you then at ten o'clock, at my studio right after New Year's."

"Grazie tante, Maestro! Buona fortuna anche a Lei!" said Roberto.

"This is just the beginning," said Stracciari, "the rest is up to you."

Roberto crossed the peaceful street with a springing step. He was now a pupil of one of the best voice and opera performance teachers in Italy.

He rang the bell and was greeted by a small, bony woman who listened to him with a questioning smile, probably detecting his foreign accent. Roberto explained that he was looking for a place to stay.

"Adesso chiamo alla signora" she said, showing Roberto to a small parlor and signaling a chair. *"Un momento, per favore."*

Roberto sat down and looked around the room. It was not a large room but there was a black upright piano against the wall and above it stood a large engraving depicting the entrance of Catherine the Great into Moscow. Hanging also on the wall was a framed decoration medal with the coat of arms of the Kingdom of Italy. The floor was covered with a Persian carpet and the whole room spoke of culture.

"Buon giorno." A deep woman's voice greeted Roberto who was absorbed in his own thoughts. He jumped to his feet at the sound of her greeting.

"Buon giorno, Signora! My name is Roberto Madariaga. Maestro Stracciari told me about your *pensione.* That is why I am here," his words poured out like an avalanche.

"Piacere!" said Signora Corelli extending her hand. "I am Luisa Corelli."

She was a distinguished looking lady in her late forties or early fifties, almost as tall as Roberto. She smiled as she shook his hand. Her brown hair was combed back into an elegant chignon and all about her was pleasant.

"As of today, I'm a pupil of Maestro Stracciari, Signora," he added as way of explanation. "I was recommended to him by Maestro Giuseppe Baldini. He was my music teacher in Mexico."

"*Caro Stracciari.* How kind of him, to think of us. And Baldini… I remember him from years ago. So you come from *Messico?*"

"Yes, Signora. I have been travelling since the beginning of the month."

"It is a pity that the weather has turned so cold now," said Luisa Corelli. "I know that your country has beautiful weather."

"Not the north, where I come from, Signora. We can have very hot summers and cold winters. I'm sure I will enjoy Milan at any time of year."

"Do you think that you would like to live here, Signor Madariaga?" She asked.

"Your place looks wonderful, Signora and it's very close to the School of Music."

Luisa Corelli explained the cost and the meal services. Roberto sensed an approving gaze.

The house had three floors. The front was decorated with stone-carved architectural details on the portico, the window-sills and the second floor balcony. There was a garden at the back with trimmed hedges on three sides, covered now with a light film of snow. There were also some bushes and two cherry trees, all in a dormant state. Facing the garden, along the back of the house, was a veranda that extended the whole width of the house with a pergola, which in the summer would be covered in grape vines. Roberto was extremely pleased with the place.

She showed him the bedroom that would be his. "We're hanging new curtains and fixing things up a bit here. The room will be ready by the end of the week," she said. "Are you staying in a hotel now?"

"Yes, Signora. I arrived yesterday. I still have my luggage at the *Stazione Centrale.*"

"Well, that means that you require a room tonight."

"I can manage for a few days, Signora Corelli."

"*Ma no!* You shouldn't spend money unnecessarily. We can give you Cesare's room for a couple of days. He is one of my sons and he is still away in the army," said Signora Corelli.

"That's extremely kind of you! Are you sure it is convenient?"

"*Ma sicuro!* It's not a problem," she added. "Cesare will not be coming before *Capo d'anno.*"

After returning from the train station, Roberto was given Cesare's room. It was one of the two bedrooms on the top floor.

He sat in Cesare's room experiencing again the feeling of belonging that he had felt upon entering Milan.

Cesare's bedroom had just a few pieces of furniture, a bed, an armchair, a writing desk and a dresser. On the walls there were several charcoal drawings of mountains, maybe of the Alps or the Dolomites, and one large oil painting of a massive rock formation. There were a few books on the desk supported by a theodolite on one side and a stone carving on the other. From its window Roberto could see the roofs and chimneys of the surrounding houses. He liked the room but he especially liked Signora Corelli.

That afternoon Signora Corelli introduced Roberto to her only daughter, Amelia. As she came in, Roberto felt as if a luminous presence had entered the room. "*Piacere, signor Madariaga,*" she said in a low voice, extending her hand.

"Please call me Roberto," he said smiling. Amelia was about fifteen but nothing in her denoted the lightness of that age. She had the most expressive brown eyes he had ever seen and dark soft wavy hair that fell below her shoulders. Her beauty struck him.

Later in the evening, Roberto met Carlo, Signora Corelli's oldest son and two professors who also boarded in the house. Carlo was twenty-two and would soon finish his studies in economics and commerce. He was a self-assured young man with a sense of humor and appreciation for music. He kept abreast of economic situations around the world. The professors taught at the Institute of Banking and Commerce.

After supper they all sat in the living room.

"My mother tells me that you are a pupil of Maestro Stracciari," said Carlo.

"I will start studying with him after the New Year. I'm terribly excited about it."

"So, we may have an opera singer living in our home. That's wonderful!" said Carlo. "We all love music."

"I'm afraid I'm not an opera singer yet, I hope to be one, in the future," explained Roberto.

Out of the Chippendale armchair a soft voice was heard.

"Would you sing a song for us, please?" It was Amelia requesting it.

"*Cara, senti!* ... Maybe this is not the moment," said her mother apologetically, thinking that it was not polite to ask someone to sing on a first meeting.

Roberto had seen the piano that morning and was eager to hear its sound. He could play but he seldom accompanied himself and, also, he had not practiced in months.

"Please!" Amelia pleaded, joined by Carlo.

It was a friendly request. Roberto felt comfortable and willingly sat down to play as Carlo turned on the lights of the candleholders on both sides of the piano.

The notes filled the room as Roberto said: "Perhaps you have heard this Spanish song before. His voice started *Asomate a la ventana, ay, ay, ay...*" He sang softly and beautifully, a bit nervous about the effect his singing would have on the family. To his surprise, Carlo sang with him during the last part. They both smiled at the end, pleased with their duet.

"Bravo!" Amelia and her mother said clapping. "One more, please!"

"Do you know *Malia?*" asked Roberto.

"I've heard it but don't really know it," replied Carlo.

"Oh, please sing it! I love that song!" said Amelia.

And he sang as everyone listened enthralled. The two professors had entered the living room and Giannina, the housekeeper, stood by the door with tears in her eyes, not missing a single note. There was music in the house once again.

In the past, Amelia, who played the piano, and Cesare, her brother, who played the violin, had practiced together, but now he was in the army and Amelia felt that her solitary playing had become pointless. That night, after hearing Roberto and her brother Carlo sing, her enthusiasm was rekindled and she decided she would learn songs and arias to be able to accompany them.

Roberto retired to his temporary room that night feeling happy about everything: the people, the singing, the place where he was now living, his new teacher and Milan. He realized that nobody in this house had been surprised when he had said that he hoped to be an opera singer. On the contrary, here, singing was considered a desirable occupation. Late at night he wrote to his parents.

Dear Mother and Father,

I had a good trip from Veracruz to New York, met wonderful people and also had the opportunity to hear Caruso at the New York Opera House. It was an unforgettable performance. As for the Atlantic crossing, I can only say it was an enlightening experience.

Roberto proceeded to tell them all about meeting Maestro Stracciari and having a place to stay with the Corelli Family. He wrote to them about each member of the household and ended his letter with:

I hope you are well. I miss you all very much. As the New Year is about to start I have promised to myself that I will work hard to

make you proud of me one day. Please accept my love and respect.
I embrace you all.
    Your son Roberto.

Roberto closed the envelope and left it on top of the table to be mailed the next day. He hoped that his father would slowly accept his decision to come to Milan.

With the arrival of the morning, Roberto became eager to go out and explore the city. After having coffee and a brioche and spending what he considered to be a polite length of time at the table he said he was going out for most of the day.

"Later this evening, would you like to come with me and meet some friends?" asked Carlo.

"That sounds great! Thank you! I'll see you later then."

"Don't forget to wear your coat and hat, Signor Madariaga, *Fa freddo!*" said Giannina.

"*Va benne, grazie!* But please call me Roberto," he said to Giannina as he put on his coat and went out the door.

It was cold and the ground was covered with snow. Like everyone else, Roberto walked fast to try to keep warm. Soon he arrived at the Piazza del Duomo, the heart of Milan.

The Piazza was busy. Despite the cold, it was alive with the sounds of streetcars crisscrossing it and ringing their bells. The people waiting at different points stamped the ground and rubbed their hands as they looked out for the right tram to board. There were nuns shepherding uniformed children towards the cathedral, the pupils walked in pairs, talking and giggling in low voices. There were businessmen and office workers, some reading the newspaper and others talking. Although the ground was covered with light snow, there were a few young people riding bicycles, some even carrying bread and other goods in their baskets, which they balanced on top of their heads. The horse-drawn carriages that crossed the Piazza had to manage around streetcars and people. This was the *punto d'incontro* the meeting place, the heart of Milan.

From the far side of the Piazza, the view of the Cathedral was impressive, with its carved spires, its sculptures and its golden Madonna on top of the highest steeple. Roberto, putting aside the resentment that he had been harboring towards the Church and its role in the Mexican situation, decided to enter the cathedral.

It was dark inside but still its opulence showed at every altar and in the choir pews. He closed his eyes and let the feeling of gratitude envelope him. He gave thanks for all he had received, his life, his family, a new life and now the Italian family and the teacher who had accepted him.

He felt optimistic and he considered a good omen to be living on a street with an opera composer's name, Via Bellini. He started to fall in love with the city even though, at this point, it was damp and cold. Milan was not known for good weather, as Signora Corelli had hinted.

Roberto stood outside for a few minutes admiring the architecture of the Galleria Vittorio Emanuele with its enormous arches and surrounding arcades. Upon entering its grandiose covered space he was astonished. The light that filtered through the stained glassed dome and the four passageways gave the place a rainbow of color and a spectacular play of light and shadow. He walked through the place admiring the marble and granite designs and the mosaics on the pavement. The windows of the restaurants and offices rose about fifty meters high. It was a magnificent covered space and it bubbled with activity. People walked through it almost not noticing its magnificence. They were meeting each other for *pranzo*, a coffee or an aperitif. It felt wonderful to be part of that excitement.

The Milanese dialect, a version of Italian, was heard all over the place and some words were completely foreign to Roberto. Inside the Galleria he had his first Milanese Italian lesson: slow down, have an espresso, enjoy the *passegiata* and then go back to business. He discovered, inside the Galleria, the *Casa Ricordi*, the most famous music- editing house in Italy and spent hours leafing through opera scores. After being inside that place he could only think of opera and he directed his steps to the *Piazza alla Scala*.

He stood in front of the venerable theatre for a while. The Teatro alla Scala was closed, but he knew that its interior had been and continued to be the most famous stage for opera singers, conductors and musicians from all over the world. He lingered in front of its doors for quite a while reading the *affiches* of future performances. He wondered if one day he would be lucky enough to sing in this illustrious theatre.

The cold temperature got to him and he realized that it was time to return home for *pranzo*. Home, he thought, I have only been here three days and it already feels like home. The sound of bagpipes in the distance and the smell of roasted chestnuts filled the air. Those wintry smells and sounds were like an old memory of being at home.

CHAPTER TEN

Carlo and Roberto left the cold weather outside and entered the Cova Café, breathing in the wonderful smell of roasting coffee. It was crowded tonight and the mirror running the full length of the counter reflected the chandeliers and the busy waiters serving coffee and drinks to packed tables. Excitement sizzled in the air as patrons prepared to celebrate the upcoming year, hoping for happier times.

They walked between crowded tables until they found a place to sit and waited for someone to take their order.

"Roberto, cheer up! You looked preoccupied," said Carlo.

"This afternoon I read some news about Mexico and I'm worried about my family. The newspaper talks about army movements to control workers in the cities. The country is going through rough times."

"Some people believe that Communism is the only solution for the future, for all countries," said Carlo.

"I know something has to change, Carlo, but I'm not sure that Communism is the solution."

"Some professors at school believe that Marxism will take over Europe and America."

"I think the answer is education. Without it nothing works."

"On that we agree," said Carlo. They gave their order to the waiter.

"I want to see all people in my country able to read and write and do the basics of arithmetic, for starters. I want to see a more equitable society. Some of my friends think I'm a crazy dreamer, that this cannot happen."

"Then, I'm a dreamer too. I want to see every man and woman having a better life. There is so much poverty."

"*Gioventu! Sogni!* Youth! Dreams!" Mumbled the waiter as he placed the small glasses of grappa and the coffee on the table.

"To a better year!" Said Carlo

"To a good 1911!" Roberto raised his glass.

Glasses were clinking, people were toasting and the Café was bubbling.

When Carlo and Roberto came out the snow was falling heavily. They lifted their collars and pulled down their hats but stopped to buy some roasted chestnuts.

Grazie! Buon Anno!" The vendor said as he wrapped them in newspaper cones.

"You know, Carlo. I feel there's too much injustice in the world. Poverty could be avoided with some collective action, sharing."

"So far, injustice and poverty have been with us forever. But, we can't give up."

"In Mexico," said Roberto, I was beginning to feel out of place. People considered me a naïve fool."

"I would never think that of you. I may not know much about Mexico, but I do care. I care about poverty and injustice, no matter where it happens. Did you read the news of your country in the *Corriere?*"

"Yes, I did. The problem is that the articles are re-prints from Mexican news which often are lies," Roberto insisted. "Newspapers in Mexico are censored."

"Surely there must be liberals printing the truth. Perhaps some underground news?"

"Most probably, but how do I get that information?"

"Through your family," said Carlo. "Why not just ask them?"

"If they know, I doubt they will tell me." Roberto wasn't sure if he was getting colder because of the weather or because of the direction the conversation was taking. "My father and brother are extremely reserved and protective of my mother and sisters. I wrote to them but I'm not sure my father will even answer."

Carlo remained quiet and Roberto was grateful for his silence. He didn't want to explain the details of how he and his father had drifted apart.

They were getting closer to home and the snow was making it difficult to walk. The few streetcars around were making more noise with their bells than with their wheels, having trouble advancing.

Before entering the house Roberto asked Carlo: "Do you think I'm crazy studying to be an opera singer, the way things are now?"

"No. There's never the perfect time. I've always felt one has to have a dream."

"My father doesn't approve," lamented Roberto. "He'd rather I be a lawyer, like my brother and like him, but that's not what I want to do with my life."

"My father used to say that one has to have a dream, Roberto. His was cut short by death."

"That's sad! I'm sorry, Carlo! What happened?"

"He died in a crazy accident. It was nobody's fault. A streetcar went off the tracks and crashed against our motorcar. The chauffeur and my father were killed instantly. His dream, which was chemical research and finding new cures, died with him."

"Oh God! That must have been terrible for all of you."

"Yes, it was. I received the news while doing the military service. It was a most painful time. My mother was miraculously spared. She was beside him. The impact was on the driver's side. She was in shock and so was Amelia. My brother, instead, was angry at the train conductor, at the lack of regulations, at everything... In the end, we all had to pull ourselves together and carry on with our lives," said Carlo.

"I guess there's no other way."

"That's why we have to follow our dream, while we can."

"It's been good talking with you, Carlo."

"You're a friend now, like another brother, Roberto. Let's go in."

Amelia was sitting in the living room reading but the pages had not been turned for a while. She was thinking of past Christmas celebrations when her father was still alive and the house was full of activity with the cooking and baking and the decorating of the Nativity Scene. Her father would come in with a present for each one of them, including Giannina and would ask each and everyone to recite a poem or read a story and then together they would play and sing Christmas hymns and songs. It was the time of year they all looked forward to. Now, four years later, it was still hard to find the strength to celebrate the festivities. And for the past year and a half, Cesare had been away in the army. He was her friend, apart from brother, and her music partner. Together, they had learned to fill with music the vacuum their father had left.

Today, New Year's Eve, Amelia waited anxiously for the bell to ring and for Cesare to arrive. Everyone was silent after the mid day meal when, suddenly, the front door flew open and a young man's voice interrupted the quietude.

"Buon Anno a tutti!"

Signora Corelli ran towards the entrance and embraced the handsome young man who had opened his arms with a big smile. *"Mamma!"*

Carlo and Giannina followed suit.

"Cesare, Cesare!" Amelia's voice sounded joyful as she looked at her brother.

"Mia bellisima sorella! You have grown taller and more beautiful!"

"Piacere!" said Cesare as Carlo introduced Roberto to him.

"Altretanto!" Roberto said, wondering if it was really a pleasure to meet this bubbly young man who had disturbed the peace of the afternoon and had grabbed the attention of every person in the room.

The whole house was energized by Cesare's presence and Roberto felt a tinge of envy.

He heard him entering the kitchen. "What have you made for New Year's Eve supper Giannina?" He was lifting the lids covering the pots on the stove. "Ummm! What a wonderful aroma! And Ravioli! They look fantastic.

Roberto could see that Cesare enjoyed food a lot and being back with his family made him happy. His cheerfulness was contagious and the family as well as the boarders joined in the good spirits and laughed wholeheartedly at the hilarious stories that he told.

That evening Signora Corelli and Giannina served a wonderful meal starting with the ravioli.

"These are delicious!" said Roberto. "I've never had them before. What are they filled with?"

"Spinach and ricotta and Giannina's secret ingredient, a pinch of nutmeg," said Signora Corelli smiling. "I'm glad that you like them, Roberto!"

The meal continued with stuffed goose, vegetables and chestnut puree.

"What a feast this has been!" declared Cesare, eyeing his mother and Giannina.

"Bravo for the chefs!"

The dessert, the *torta di mandorle,* was so good that Roberto couldn't help himself and contrary to his usually reserved demeanor, he stood up and raised his glass for a toast: "Signora Corelli, Giannina, and Amelia, I saw you helping too, this was a splendid meal. Thank you so much for your hospitality! I should add that my mother would have loved the almond cake. A good year to everyone! *Buon Anno a tutti!*"

Everyone stood up: "*Buon Anno!* Happy New Year!" The glasses tinkled.

Later on, Carlo, Roberto and Cesare went out to join a group of friends from Cesare's Alpine company. The place was packed with mostly young men. They sat on benches that stood along the whole length of the place. In front of them were tables with trays of bread cut in smaller pieces. Some men dipped the bread in some steaming concoction with a strong garlic smell that the waiters kept bringing out.

"What is that?" Asked Roberto.

"That is *bagna cauda.* It keeps you warm in the mountains," said Cesare laughing. "Believe me, it's wonderful when you are cold –olive oil, garlic and anchovies. Try it."

Roberto tried a bit feeling doubtful. "Actually, it's very good," he agreed and ate some more.

Everyone was sitting elbow to elbow so conversations were shared and interrupted constantly. Accordion music started up and soon the alpine soldiers were singing mountain airs in two and three voices. Roberto was impressed by the ease with which they delivered the haunting tunes in perfect harmony. He joined in the singing with Carlo and Cesare and was enjoying himself immensely when from the other side of the table someone shot a question at him.

"Where are you from?" a man asked in an unpleasant manner.

"From Mexico," replied Roberto.

"*Messico ehh?*" Where everyone takes a siesta, *vero?*

"Not everyone," Roberto answered evasively.

"Mexicans are known to be lazy," the young man persisted.

"Stop it!" warned Carlo.

"I know because my father lived there," continued the man. He was quite drunk and determined to have an argument.

"I think I'd better leave," said Roberto standing up. The crowded room was almost silent.

But the young man was determined to fight and followed Roberto to the exit. As Roberto opened the door to leave, the man pushed him to the ground from behind and kicked him with his boot.

By this time Cesare was outside too, followed by Carlo.

"What's wrong with you?" demanded Cesare. "Do we know you? Are you a soldier?"

"No, and I don't want to be. You're a bunch of *vigliacchi!*" He yelled as he charged against Roberto once more.

But Cesare was ready and stood in between, receiving the full impact of the man's fist on his body. Some of the alpine soldiers came out and restrained the drunk who, suddenly, passed out in front of the entrance. Cesare was now sitting on the curb, recovering from the blow.

"I'm sorry, Cesare. Are you all right?" Asked Roberto.

"Yes, I'm fine. I apologize for the insults. I don't know who the man is or where all that came from."

"He's been coming around lately and drinking a lot," said one of the waiters who had come out. "Apparently he was rejected for the military service and he is resentful. I'm terribly sorry, gentlemen!"

"Are you okay to walk home, Cesare?" asked Carlo.

"Of course, I'm fine," he said as he stood up.

"Roberto!" he said opening his arms. "Carlo!" and the three young men embraced and walked home in warm camaraderie.

CHAPTER ELEVEN

With the New Year classes started and the *Scuola di Musica* came back to life with hundreds of students. Roberto started his classes with Maestro Stracciari. Every day he walked to the Scuola in the center of Milan and now, much of his time was spent in its buildings, which reverberated with voices and instrument sounds all the day and part of the night. Whenever he entered the school, he became enveloped in what seemed like a cacophony of musical sounds that seemed strident at the beginning and then they somehow came together and created a polyphonic harmony. In this magical place, Roberto studied with dedication, memorizing the music and lyrics of the operas that Maestro Stracciari had chosen especially for him. He was also learning to accompany himself at the piano in order to practice alone.

Roberto was a dramatic tenor and through the learning process his lower notes were acquiring a deep tonal quality that resembled a baritone register. Playing the piano, vocalizing, reading the full musical scores and singing every day for hours, left him exhausted.

Not only was the technique difficult, it was the interpretation of the arias that often drained him emotionally.

"You're portraying Des Grieux, a naïve student, remember," the Maestro would say, " he falls in love with beautiful Manon and ruins his life. But, pay attention, when he sings "Donna no vidi mai," he's blissfully in love and doesn't know what will happen so there's no sense of tragedy at this point of the opera."

"Right, Maestro," Roberto would reply and repeat the aria.

"Now, *Andrea Chenier*, is a different thing, altogether," the Maestro would say and Roberto would interpret the French poet and sing "Un di al azzurro spazio" and "Si, fui soldato," unleashing his hate and disgust towards the murderous abuses of the French Revolution. Roberto's emotion would surge with the last line –"… kill me, but leave me my honor." He dreamed of the day when he would sing *Andrea Chenier* and walk towards the guillotine with his beloved Maddalena de Cogny singing "La nostra morte e il trionfo dell'amor," –our death is the triumph of love.

Maestro Stracciari made him work hard and strive for better delivery of the arias every time. Roberto was also improving his French and was learning *Carmen*. He would strive to convey the desperate love and jealousy of Don Jose for Carmen, the gypsy. He found that singing in French required a different technique for pronunciation as the Maestro insisted that every word had to be clearly phrased.

All this was not only opera singing, but also a mind-expanding experience that drained all the senses and required tremendous concentration.

After a day of intensive opera work, Roberto liked to walk to unwind. Often he strolled along the *"naviglio"* –the ancient canal that traversed Milan, built during the twelfth and thirteenth centuries. Around the canal, he had heard more than once, an untrained woman's voice singing a mountain air, soon to be joined by other women who followed suit as they did their washing. That was a different musical experience but a very rewarding one too.

On market days the channels were crowded with barges carrying fresh fruit, vegetables and flowers. On Sundays, instead, people went to fish or to watch the rowing competitions. He and Carlo often went to see the rowing teams moving their oars in unison while people cheered and waved. The *naviglio* reminded Roberto of the river in his hometown, when as a child he had enjoyed the fun and carefree activities of fishing and hand-boat racing, before it had been rerouted.

Summer

At the beginning of the summer Cesare was discharged from his military service. He was keen about mountain climbing and bicycling and was now an "Alpine reserve soldier." He wore his insignia –a felt hat with a black feather- with enormous pride.

Roberto bought a bicycle and soon became a member of a small group that toured the northern part of Italy every weekend. Sunday afternoons saw Cesare, Carlo and Roberto coming home after a day and sometimes night of hiking, cycling and sleeping in the open. They went to places like Cremona, where Cesare bought a new violin, or the San Pellegrino Terme, where the wealthy English and Italians enjoyed the thermal baths.

They would leave the busy city behind and enter the world of agriculture in the cultivated tracts of land just south of Milan. There, the peasants moved their pitchforks and scythes back and forth as they sang their country airs accompanied by the soft wind that blew across their faces and bent the growing grain like a wave of green and gold.

The three friends were riding along the edge of a field one afternoon when they stopped to hear the singing and to rest. What a splendid sight it was! The sound of the workers' voices and the smell of the growing grain filled their spirits. They felt at peace and close to the earth.

"Imagine hearing this music in these surroundings," said Roberto as they ate the bread and cheese that Signora Corelli had wrapped for them.

"It's in our nature. We sing when we're happy or when we're sad," said Carlo.

"Look at that field! Pure gold! We'll have lots of bread this winter," said Cesare as he sat against a tree and stretched his legs.

"You know Roberto," said Carlo, "in the mountains we sing to fight loneliness and cold. The forest and the peaks are beautiful, the views are majestic, but even when the crevices in the mountains seemed to talk to us there is that deep silence that penetrates your mind and your senses. It's easy to become terribly homesick. Singing is one way of overcoming that."

"I know, in Mexico we also sing because of sadness or happiness." Roberto knew about loneliness and despondency in the mountains.

He closed his eyes and instead of the poplar trees lining the irrigation ditches he saw himself amidst the rock formations of the Sierra Madre Occidental in Chihuahua.

"*Buona sera!*" greeted the laborers who were walking at the edge of the fields, tools on their shoulders.

"*Buona sera!*" replied the three startled young men who had dozed off.

"*Che bel grano!*" said Roberto, recalling the bare land of northern Mexico. He had never seen fields of wheat such as these.

"*Eh, si lavora,*" –it's work, said one of them.

"*Buona raccolta!*" Carlo hoped they would have a good year.

"*Grazie!*" replied the men touching their caps. They looked tired but pleased with themselves as they made their way home from working in the fields.

"It must be grand to be a farmer," said Roberto. "Work the land and return home after a day of toiling, having a woman waiting with a warm supper and love."

"You're a romantic, Roberto," replied Carlo. "The *contadini* can barely survive. They really work for the landowners and they get paid very little. But, believe me, this will change in time."

"I would prefer to live in the Alps and be a mountain guide," said Cesare.

"An alpine guide, Cesare? Are you crazy? It's so dangerous."

"I know but I love the mountains. There's nothing else that I would prefer to do."

"Please don't tell mother! She was so worried when you were away in training," Carlo warned.

The afternoon fell away as they talked and dreamed of the future.

The heat and humidity in Milan that summer made everyone dream of cool places. Roberto thought that the dry heat of northern Mexico was hard to take but he found the humidity quite oppressive. He was happy to hear that the family was organizing a day trip to one of the lakes and that he was invited.

On Sunday all the family went to Lake Como by train together with some aunts, uncles and cousins. It was a big outing. The young men, mostly dressed in white linen suits and the women in fresh looking white blouses and long skirts, boarded the train in a talkative mood. Some women were wearing broad-brimmed hats adorned with flowers. The little boys in their sailor suits looked out the train window expecting to see the lake at any moment. Lake Como was a summer recreation place favored by the wealthy residents of Milan and Bergamo and by many English and German tourists. A picnic though could be enjoyed by anybody.

"There it is!" cried the children as the train approached the small station and the lake came into sight. The group got off the train leaving behind the smell of engine smoke and encountering the fragrance of the viburnum and the flowering baskets that adorned the passageway to the park surrounding the lake. Loaded with picnic baskets, blankets and umbrellas they walked briskly looking for a pleasant spot to deposit their load under the shade of an oak tree. Other tourists followed with porters who carried their luggage to the elegant hotels spread along the banks of the lake.

As the Corelli group got closer to the park they heard a band playing. The children ran towards the promenade where young people fitted with roller skates whirled around in front of the lake. It was such a clear morning that the mountains and valleys surrounding the lake could be seen in the distance.

"It's beautiful!" said Roberto leaning against the stone balustrade that ran along the promenade.

"The rowing competition is starting," shouted the children also running towards the balustrade.

Cesare and Roberto would have liked to be out on the lake pulling and pushing oars at full speed, but they were content to cheer on their chosen team. Signora Corelli was talking and laughing happily with her cousins, savoring the freshness and the beauty of the place.

After the race was over all the family rented roller skates and glided in pairs around the terrace accompanied by the music. The children also in roller skates made a long snake-like chain and skated expertly between the couples making them laugh. The band played Schubert's "Rosamunde" followed by Italian waltzes.

Young Amelia and her brother Cesare whirled around in their roller skates laughing and trying to avoid the children's serpentine.

Later, they all sat down in the park and enjoyed the fresh bread and cheese with *pepperonata, polenta fritta* and more cheese with fresh fruit.

"Giannina," said Cesare, "these *cenci* melt in the mouth. Nobody can make them better." *Cenci* was one of Giannina's secret recipes.

She labored over the dough for hours and that resulted in the lightest of fritters, which she dusted with powdered sugar.

Everyone thought these were the best ever.

The murmur of the conversation was hardly audible, allowing the rustle of the leaves in the wind to make music of their own. Lake Como was a lovely place and Roberto was grateful for this family that had opened their home and heart to him. They looked so happy together. Signora Corelli who smiled as she watch her children -Carlo who was the same age as he, and Cesare and Amelia who were radiant in their youth and gaiety. Roberto noticed that Signora Corelli's eyes had a remote expression and she was wiping a tear. Maybe she was remembering other times, here at the lake when her husband, Edgardo, was still alive. On the train, Carlo had told Roberto that the family used to come to the lake every year in the summer when he was a young boy. *Signora Corelli must miss her husband very much.* Roberto thought *and she must feel lonely, even if she has her sons and daughter.* He noticed Amelia's eyes looking in the distance and, when she became aware of his glance, she immediately lowered her eyes. She was a beautiful and gentle girl.

CHAPTER TWELVE

"To be a well-rounded musician, along with singing and build-ing an opera repertoire, you should study composition. It is important, Roberto." Maestro Stracciari believed that musical training had to be as complete as possible. He also believed that to play an instrument just for enjoyment was a blessing. "You will think opera, breathe opera and hear opera inside your head all the time. That's the way it is. It becomes a full-time obsession."

"I understand, Maestro, but the time has come for me to find a job to support myself as soon as possible," replied Roberto. "I may not have as much time to study."

"Couldn't you ask your father for help?"

"No, Maestro, I couldn't do that."

Roberto knew he couldn't ask for help from his father and the money he had arrived with was almost gone. Carlo suggested a banking clerk position but there was a long list of applicants and he decided to look for other kind of work. In the end, Roberto found a position as a draftsman in a factory that built machines.

The mechanical and construction drawing he had done in high school suddenly came in handy and he enjoyed the work. It allowed his thoughts to stray into music while his eyes and hands concentrated at the task before him. His days were so full between work and music classes that he seldom arrived home before ten o'clock at night. Giannina prepared a small bag with bread, cheese and whatever was available, to take and eat between classes and work. Gone were the bicycle trips with Carlo and Cesare. But one thing he never missed was the Sunday meal. Signora Corelli and Giannina made special efforts to have all the family and the boarders, -the two professors and the American man who worked at the United States Consulate- together on that day and everyone was keen to be present. Carlo and Cesare would come back from their cycling excursions just in time to wash, change and sit at the table. When the weather was warm enough, the meal took place on the veranda where the atmosphere was casual. Everyone sat at the long table outdoors and felt free to converse.

"Professore Gozzano, we have heard that you have written a play. *Come mai*? Said Signora Corelli in a friendly voice.

"Too kind, Signora! I'm only trying to put some thoughts in words," he answered.

"Mario believes that through a piece of theatre people can better understand what is happening in the country," said Professor Segni. "We get tired of repeating ourselves in class, always talking about political and economic problems but nobody seems to listen. Through a play people get informed about things in an entertaining way. And Mario is, indeed, a good playwright."

"Thank you, Giovanni!" said Professor Gozzano. "My purpose is to expose abuse of power, government corruption, colonialism. It upsets me to observe that we don't learn from our mistakes. Animals learn from only one experience. Humans do not. Countries get conquered, then they fight for independence, then they fight internally because of religion or ideology, always at the cost of thousands of lives. And having seen what has happened in the past, the next group repeats the whole process again. What for? To gain a few acres of land to cultivate?"

"No, of course not! All of that is done for monetary gain. What do you think, Carlo?" asked Professor Segni.

"That's right, Professor, history keeps repeating itself. There is profit in arms, in food distribution, in army uniforms, all the things needed during wartime," said Carlo.

"… and we just want to live in peace," added Cesare with a benevolent shrug.

Roberto was quiet. He looked at Mr. Allen, the American official who hadn't uttered a word during the conversation. Roberto couldn't help but to think about the way Mexico had lost a good part of its territory to the United States. It had been called "The First American Intervention" and it had its origins in the "Manifest Destiny" –the belief that the United States had the right to expand their territory throughout the American Continent. The Mexican-American War had taken place from 1846 to 1848. It had started with the annexation of Texas and had ended with the loss of Alta California, New Mexico, part of Utah and Nevada. In the end Mexico had lost fifty five percent of its territory. The Mexicans considered this war an abuse of power and it would not be forgotten for centuries. Roberto loathed any abuse of power, at any level, but he decided to remain quiet out of respect for Signora Corelli.

Cesare came to the rescue. "Amelia, do you talk about these things at school?"

Amelia was brought back to the table by the sudden question. She had been day- dreaming, fantasizing about that Sunday in Como and Roberto.

"Not really, we just observe with our geography teacher, how maps keep changing," she managed to answer.

"That's so telling," said Carlo. "If you look at an atlas of the African continent, you'll see that it has been divided, piece by piece, among the European countries. It is shameful."

"The official philosophy behind that..." said Gozzano sarcastically, "is that we, Europeans, are bringing to them our 'great knowledge and civilization' while in reality we are exploiting their minerals and taking away their riches."

Everyone was silent now.

"There must be some good things happening in the world," said Amelia.

"For sure! Have you heard that Marie Curie has won a second Nobel Prize?" said Roberto, knowing that Amelia was interested in science and hoping that this would stir the conversation away from politics.

"Oh yes! Our teacher has been talking a lot about Marie Curie. What an amazing woman! She's my inspiration," said Amelia. "I would like to be a chemist too."

"So you like chemistry, Amelia?" said Cesare. "I was never any good at it."

"This year our chemistry lessons have been practical. I've enjoyed them from the start," she continued. "At times it can be difficult to remember all those formulas and we have to consult our manuals but we are conducting experiments and I find the work exciting."

"Your father studied chemistry at the University of Bologna. Did you know that?" Said Signora Corelli.

"But, of course I know, Mamma. Maybe I will study there."

"They may not accept women," said Carlo.

"Well, then I will go to France. At the Sorbonne they do," replied Amelia.

"*Brava Amelia!* That's the way to talk," said Gozzano. "I hope you become a chemist. Italy needs scientists."

"Chemistry! My little sister! Incredible! I always thought that science and art required different abilities. You are an artist at the piano, Amelia!" Said Cesare.

"She is! But you're wrong, young man," said Professor Segni, "music and science go well together."

During the conversation, Roberto found himself admiring Amelia. She was finding the young woman more engaging and attractive. She was full of surprises.

"What do you think, Roberto?" asked Cesare.

"I think you have a brilliant sister, Cesare," replied Roberto, looking at Amelia.

"*Grazie,*" said Amelia feeling suddenly uncomfortable about being the center of attention.

"*Signorina* Amelia," Professor Gozzano said, "I respect anyone who wants to pursue knowledge. Best wishes in your studies!" He lifted his glass of wine.

Everyone was smiling as they went into the house. Signora Corelli put her arm around her daughter's shoulders and brought her close to her. It had been a special afternoon in the end.

Amelia slept soundly that night and when she woke up she remembered the dream she had had –working inside a huge laboratory among many scientists, all men, who labored over microscopes under the benevolent gaze of her father. She didn't tell anyone about it, but she was sure that this was a message for her.

CHAPTER THIRTEEN

Almost two years had passed since Roberto's arrival in Milan. His music lessons and his work had found a rhythm in his life. He kept in touch with his family through the overseas post, his mother gave him news about his father and sisters, and his brother about the political situation, at times out of date but always interesting. He also kept in touch with his travel friends, Clara Gillespie in New York and Mr. Stevens and his wife Francisca de Leon in Madrid. The couple often wrote to him and gave eloquent reviews of their performances in Spain.

After Italy declared war on Turkey in September that year, the economic situation in the country deteriorated. 1912 was coming to an end in a most dispirited manner. There were constant strikes taking place in Milan and political meetings sprouted at every corner. The professors living at the Corelli residence were worried but abstained from having heated discussions. The family was aware that Cesare could be called up to serve at any moment. They waited with mounting apprehension but Cesare was not called up despite the fact that, towards the end of the conflict, some Alpine regiments were sent to Lybia –the land in question.

Food costs were on the rise and although Signora Corelli made every effort to stretch the budget to the maximum, the professors and Mr. Allen had to increase their monthly payments for the board. Roberto was unable to increase his and was feeling much discomfort at his inability to pay more.

So when Maestro Stracciari presented to him the possibility of singing in Church for a memorial service, Roberto was happy to accept.

"There will be economic remuneration and it's good exposure," said the Maestro.

"Thank you, Maestro! What a great opportunity!"

Roberto, together with other students sang Rossini's "Petite Messe Solennelle" at the church of Santa Maria delle Grazie.

He was able to give some extra money to Signora Corelli, which made him feel better but, for the first time in his life, he was constantly faced with the possibility of not having enough money to live and considered terminating his music lessons.

However, as a result of the ceremony, he was asked to sing at weddings and funerals, which eased his money worries. Many nights as he was falling asleep, exhausted after a day of work and intense study, Roberto dreamed of the operas he would love to sing in the theatre. He imagined himself as Mario Cavaradossi, the painter in love with Floria Tosca. Singing this role was one of Roberto's deepest aspirations. He yearned to sing ...*E non ho amato mai tanto la vita!* "Never have I loved life as much!"

His thoughts about love were often related to the opera roles. He wondered if falling in love would make him sing with more feeling. Clara, his first dream of love, was far away and he was not sure what it was that he felt for her. Perhaps it had been just a magic moment. Perhaps love would never come his way. Perhaps it was better to live love through opera.

Roberto opened the letters now with apprehension, fearing bad news. The New Year had brought more economic hardships in Italy and political turmoil in Mexico. But in Spain his friends William Stevens and his wife Francisca de Leon seemed to be encountering success.

He was standing at the entrance of the house reading their letter, when Carlo walked in.

"Carlo, listen! My friends in Madrid are opening a theatre and they are asking me to sing with their company. They are going to stage the zarzuela *Marina* and they are asking me to sing the tenor role for ten performances.

"That's wonderful!" said Carlo shaking his hand. "I'm so happy for you!"

Signora Corelli was already at the landing, with Amelia, wondering what all the commotion was about.

"Mamma, Roberto is going to sing in Madrid!" exclaimed Carlo.

"Bravo, Caro Roberto!" said Signora Corelli.

"Auguri!" said Amelia smiling. "Roberto is going to sing in Madrid," she told Cesare as he walked into the house.

"That's great! You'll see. Once you have been heard somewhere else, you may find yourself in demand," said Cesare knowingly. "Most singers, artists and writers become famous when they are away from their own country."

"I have to make plans! Get ready! Study the music! And, answer to their offer." Roberto was excited. He immediately wrote to the Stevens' to accept their offer and to thank them. He decided to wait until after the first performance to tell his parents.

For the next two weeks Roberto walked on air. He studied every nuance of the interpretation. Maestro Stracciari guided his pupil through the *zarzuela,* and made Roberto polish some arias and songs. Perhaps they could plan for some recitals later on. Some evenings Roberto reviewed the music with Amelia, Carlo and Cesare.

At work a new general manager, Signor Fausto Tozzi, had been appointed and was annoyed about Roberto having obtained un-paid absence for three weeks from the previous manager.

"I don't know if there will be a job for you when you return," he said.

"I will complete all the drafting before I leave. There will be no items pending, Sir," Roberto replied.

"Well, we'll see when you come back. I may have other work for you," said Tozzi.

"Other work? Why?" Asked Roberto.

"We will talk when you return," Tozzi said.

Roberto was disconcerted but did not let the thought of a new job take over his mind. He concentrated on the music and the performance.

"Signora Corelli, I will be away for about three weeks. I will be back at the end of the month," said Roberto.

It was Sunday and they were having *pranzo* in the dining room. It was still too cold to eat on the veranda. The conversation was animated and for a while, at least, the family and their boarders managed to keep the troubled world at bay.

"Madrid! Wonderful city!" Said Mr. Allen, the American board-er. "You see people dancing in the streets day and night."

"Surely not at this time of year!" said Carlo.

"Oh yes! You can always count on Madrid for late suppers, dancing and guitars," confirmed the American.

"I'm so happy for you, Roberto! You'll be famous!" said Amelia.

Roberto smiled. Amelia was turning into a beautiful young woman. Her dark eyes had a touch of sadness and, once in a while, Roberto had noticed them looking at him with a glimmer of ten-derness. This made him uneasy because he didn't know what it meant.

"Well, *Buon viaggio!*" said one of the professors, shaking Roberto's hand.

"Buona fortuna!" added the other professor.

Roberto shook hands with everybody.

"A domani," said Signora Corelli.

"Arrivederci!" said Amelia. "Come back soon!" Next day she would go to school early and Roberto would have left for the train station.

Amelia

Every evening Amelia sat at her desk and wrote poetry. Today had been cold and foggy like that February day when her father had died. She opened a flat box and took out an old photograph of her parents, her brothers and herself. It had been taken just before Christmas of 1908. With a pastoral background painted on the wall, the photographer had pretended that it was a spring day. Amelia remembered that it was so cold that she had not wanted to take off her coat and gloves. Whenever she looked at this photograph she was grateful to have it. It was the only photograph she had of her father with the family.

There was a knock at the door. She closed the box and wiped away her tears as her mother entered.

"Amelia, aren't you tired?"

"Oh Mamma!" she replied trying to hide her tears.

"I know what you are thinking Amelia. Five years ago tomorrow, your father died."

"I don't know how you can take it, Mamma! I feel so sad!"

"Life continues *mia piccina*. You and Carlo and Cesare are my whole life now," said Luisa. "I'm thankful that I have you."

Amelia felt her mother's comforting embrace. She admired her outward strength but suspected deep sadness and enormous nostalgia for passed times. *Five years...* she could only imagine how much her mother missed her father. She would always remember the way he reached out to touch her mother's hand at the table. The way he said her name and touched her face when he left to work in his laboratory. Even with a full house, themselves and the boarders, Amelia sensed her mother longed for her husband's opinions and conversation.

"I'm sorry Mamma! It must be so hard for you!"

They remained embraced for a long time. Amelia was almost asleep when she felt Luisa helping her to undress and put on her nightgown, just the way she had done when she was a little girl. That was comforting.

The next morning Roberto left for Madrid in the midst of tremendous excitement but during the train ride, he suddenly worried. Had he acted rashly risking the loss of his job? He didn't like the new manager at work and he perceived the feeling was mutual. He had made a commitment of what he wanted to do in the future, so why was he perturbed by his own decision? This was a great opportunity and he would make the best of it.

His doubts disappeared altogether when he was warmly greeted at the train station by Francisca and Mr. Stevens. They accompanied him to a small hotel close to the Plaza del Sol but would not allow him to go to sleep.

"Life starts at midnight in Madrid, Roberto! We are going to eat now!" said Francisca.

"But first, we are going to see the theatre," said Stevens. It was only a couple of blocks away and when they arrived, Stevens proudly opened the back door. "What do you think, Roberto?"

They walked around the scaffolds and screens until they were standing in the middle of the stage and looking at the absent audience. In just a few days people would be filling the seats and the balconies and galleries expecting to be captivated by the power of music.

"It's wonderful! Also scary!" Said Roberto.

"It will be fantastic!" Said Francisca. "Come Roberto, I will show you something."

And walking out to the front of the theatre she said: "There! What do you think?" He was speechless as he saw his name on the billboard behind thick glass, at the main entrance.

All the faces of the people he loved came flooding into his mind. *This is it!*

"Come now, let's go for a good Spanish meal." Roberto was tired from the trip but he let himself be pulled to a *tasca* within walking distance from the theatre.

"You can always count on good food in this place," said Stevens, as he opened the restaurant door.

The room was smoky and crowded. Men stood along a counter drinking wine and talking excitedly. The Stevens and Roberto were escorted to the dining room where the atmosphere was quieter and an older man was playing a guitar. Roberto was thankful for the subdued music. And that evening, just as Francisca had predicted, he learned that Madrid lived at night.

The days of rehearsals went by quickly. Theatre people worked in the afternoon and evening so Roberto spent the mornings enjoying the city.

"Tomorrow evening the future of this theatre will be decided," said Stevens.

He walked around the place, checking the drop curtains, the stage sets and the seating areas. Finally he sat down to hear the dress rehearsal. The hammering had stopped and the music was starting.

"Everything will be fine Billy," said Francisca. "Please stop fretting like that. You're making me nervous."

"Sorry, my love!"

"Luckily, on opening night he is usually calm," said Francisca to Roberto.

"I can understand being nervous. He's not the only one," said Roberto.

But opening night was not to have a smooth beginning. The weather had turned colder and it was snowing. People were late arriving and the orchestra conductor had taken ill. William Stevens had to step in and conduct the orchestra himself. The performance was delayed. But these difficulties only helped to fuel the enthusiasm of the musicians and the singers. Their commitment and cooperation turned the evening into an unparalleled performance full of artistic vitality. The audience loved it. The principal performers were called back to the stage several times. Finally the curtain came down and Stevens asked the orchestra to stand up to receive a final round of applause.

Back in his dressing room, Roberto was exhausted and elated.

The door opened and Francisca walked in: "We did it!" she exclaimed, followed by Stevens who was still so wound up he could hardly talk.

"Unbelievable! You people were great!"

"Thank you, Maestro!" Said both singers in unison. Roberto hadn't known about Stevens' musical skills and was extremely impressed.

"You were absolutely fantastic, Billy! You saved the night!" Said Francisca kissing him.

"Well, the show must go on!"

They had performances for five days in a row and rested for two. On the following Tuesday, when Roberto was having a coffee and reading the paper, he came across an article about Mexico. *February 9ᵗʰ, 1913. The President of Mexico, Francisco I. Madero and Vice-President, Jose Maria Pino Suarez, have been arrested and put in prison. Conflicting reports. Fighting on the streets. Food and water shortages in Mexico City.*

Roberto was in shock. He had been so involved in his singing debut that he had not read the newspaper for days. He went to the Mexican Embassy but could not get any information. The officials were as bewildered as he was.

Would it help his family if he returned? He would have enough money at the end of the performances to pay for the passage. He kept singing at night and wondering what was the right thing to do. But his anxiety turned to dismay as the news arrived to Europe. *A coup d'etat took place in Mexico. General Victoriano Huerta, who had traveled to Mexico City to control the army, has become the new president of Mexico. On the 22nd of February, President Madero and Vice-President Pino Suarez were murdered as they were transferred to jail.*

The new presidency gave an account of the events that nobody believed especially the governor of the State of Coahuila, Venustiano Carranza. He did not recognize General Huerta's government and decided to fight him. The revolution continued with renewed force. Different alliances were formed and thousands joined Carranza's forces condemning Huerta's actions and rejecting his government.

The feeling of success was dampened by the news. Roberto completed his contract and realized that there was nothing he could do to alleviate the situation of his country. Francisca and William were supportive but realistic.

"This situation has come, Roberto, because people in Mexico want a radical change. Nothing will ever be the same. You must face that fact," said Steven.

CHAPTER FOURTEEN

W hen Roberto returned to Milan a telegram from his brother was waiting for him.

Mother passed away February 24. Burial has taken place. Father begs you to remain in Italy. Letter follows. Francisco.

Although Roberto knew that his mother was ill, her death caught him unprepared. He was heartbroken. Even if he had travelled to Mexico immediately after the Madrid performances, he would not have made it in time to see her again. All those evenings of music with her mother at the piano came to mind. He regretted not letting her know that he had finally performed in a theatre thanks to her unconditional and loving support.

Signora Corelli suggested to him that he could have a small church ceremony but Roberto rejected the idea. It took days for Amelia to convince him to have a mass for his mother.

"She was a devout Catholic, wasn't she?" Amelia asked.

"Yes, she was," Roberto had avoided that thought.

"Then do it for her. Sing for her during the mass and try your best to pray," said Amelia kindly.

He noticed how she had changed in the past year. She was sincere and direct. Roberto felt embarrassed about his behavior and made arrangements for a memorial service. Amelia and Giannina adorned the small chapel of *Sant'Aquilino* with white flowers. The Corelli family, Giannina, the professors and Maestro Stracciari attended the evening mass. Amelia read a short prayer that she had written in which she thanked God for the life of Maria Eugenia Pugibet Madariaga, Roberto's mother.

During the mass Roberto sang Gounod's "Ave Maria" and Jean Batiste Faure's "Crucifix" together with Carlo. Those words *"vous qui suffrez, venez a Lui"* felt like a presage of things to come. He thought about his mother's kindness and love for the whole family and for the people she came in contact with during her life. The ceremony restored Roberto's peace of mind and made him feel closer to his father.

"Amelia," he said as they came out of the church, "I want to thank you for your sympathy and for your persistence. You have taught me to open my heart and my mind. You are a kind and courageous woman. Thank you!"

That night Roberto wrote a very long and compassionate letter to his father. He could imagine his father's pain filtering through his strong, unbending façade.

Two weeks later, Francisco's letter arrived.

Mexico City, March 1ˢᵗ 1913
Dearest brother,

This is a difficult letter to write but I will attempt to tell you what happened at home and in the city.

February was a bad month. There was fighting on the streets between the rebels and the government army. No public services were available and the dead bodies were left on the street. It was chaos. I was trying to break the barrier of silence that had come between Father and me in the last while. We were sitting in the living room and could hear the shelling fire getting closer. Father was silent and I, instead, was ranting about General Huerta. I was saying that nobody could believe that a mob had attacked and killed Madero and Pino Suarez. That it all was the work of a traitor and a killer and his name was General Huerta. Father asked me in strong terms to stop and never to talk with anyone about that matter again. People were killed or imprisoned for less. He was visibly worried. I could not help but think that something serious had happened at the Ministry of Justice.

Do you remember how he would point out the deficiencies and lack of honesty of Diaz's government? That's all gone. He doesn't talk about the government. He has been at home for several weeks and so has another well-known jurist, you remember Aaron's father? I'm afraid that Huerta found their presence a hindrance to his plans and both were asked or ordered to stay home.

Suddenly, as I was talking, there was a big blast. We ran towards mother's bedroom. Teresa, who was by her side, was shaking. Mother was perfectly still. Maybe she had died before the blast. Father knelt by her side while bricks fell off one corner of the room. The library had been badly hit. Father asked me to call the doctor. The telephone line, which had been installed recently, was dead. I ran outside, through the back door as a wall collapsed in the patio. In the distance, I could see a barricade close to the Alameda, where some of the cannons were being fired. I finally arrived to Dr. Ocampo's house. He followed me as we scurried from one corner to the next until we got home. Father was still kneeling by mother's side. Our sisters were there too, crying inconsolably. As you can imagine, Father was devastated. We all are.

At least I can tell you that mother did not seem to be in pain during her last days. I think she knew that the end was coming and she was serene about it. She was talking very little but she expressed her love for all of us and asked me to tell you that she was confident you would achieve your dream.

The burial took place the day after in the French Cemetery. It was a short, sad ceremony accompanied only by the sound of firing guns in the distance.

Without his work to distract him, Father is finding her death almost impossible to bear. Our sisters are trying their best to be supportive and to keep the house in perfect order. I think Father would prefer to live in his beloved town in the north but to go back there would be impossible now, both for economic and for safety reasons.

Please keep writing to us. Even if your letters arrive with great delay, we wait anxiously for them.

We embrace you with our great affection.

Your brother, Francisco.

The letter from his brother left Roberto with disquietude – sadness caused by his mother's death and apprehension for his father's condition. In a short period of time his father had had too many losses. He had left his beloved town in the north of Mexico. He had been somehow banished from the Supreme Court and now had lost his wife, his trusted and beloved companion. Roberto knew his father would be shattered and probably felt defeated. He promised himself to work doubly hard and make him proud.

The Madrid experience and the death of his mother changed everything for Roberto. He became more serious but also more confident in his singing abilities. He took every opportunity to observe and learn from other singers. He was able to go to a memorable performance at the *Teatro alla Scala*. Together with Carlo, he sat in the very top balcony, barely able to see the singers but their voices soared with clarity to the heights of the theatre. All through the opera Roberto lived inside the character and a second before every moving passage or an aria, a difficult cadenza or an emotional phrase, his heart would stop for just a second as he waited for the joy to come. At the end of the performance he was exhausted from the contained energy.

One day, as Maestro Stracciari and Roberto were completely absorbed singing the duet from *La Forza del Destino,* "Solenne in quest'ora," they were surprised to hear a single burst of applause behind the door, followed by a knock. They both turned around and in walked the famous opera singer Gianni Seneschi with a big smile and wide-open arms.

"Maestro!" he exclaimed.

"Gianni, *che piacere!*" Stracciari was delighted to see his former pupil, now in his fifties, whose elegance had not diminished with age. "This is Roberto Madariaga one of my pupils."

"Piacere signor Madariaga!" Said Seneschi shaking Roberto's hand.

"It's an honor to meet you, Signor Seneschi," said Roberto awe-struck.

"That was a superb rendition. I can see the maestro is making you work hard."

"Thank you!" replied Roberto. He couldn't think of anything intelligent to say to the singer. He could see that Stracciari was extremely pleased to see Seneschi and perhaps wanted to terminate the lesson for the day. "Maestro, if you wish, I can go now and see you tomorrow."

"Thank you, Roberto! Is that all right with you?"

"But, of course, Maestro!"

Roberto shook hands politely and left the room. He closed the door but didn't go very far. He was sure that in a few minutes the famous tenor would sing and he waited in the corridor hoping that the singing would start soon and it did.

Seneschi had one of the most beautiful voices Roberto had ever heard. He had listened to some of his records but the voice, in person, even behind a closed door, was magnificent. Time flew by as Roberto listened, sitting on the floor outside Stracciari's door, dreaming of future performances. He could have stayed longer but he had to get to work.

That afternoon, while he was doing machinery drawings, the general manager called him to his office.

"Signor Madariaga," he started addressing Roberto in an official manner. "I need someone in another area of business in which the company is now involved. I believe you are the right person for the job."

"May I ask what kind of work it is?" said Roberto.

"Well, it involves inventory control and distribution," said Signor Tozzi cautiously. "Our company is expanding into distribution of hospital equipment and medical supplies. We may also need to distribute arms and I know you have accounting training," Tozzi added.

"Arms?" said Roberto.

"Well… maybe. The Lybian campaign made it evident that we need to improve our defense arsenal and one way or another, this is a real opportunity for you, Madariaga."

"But, Signor Tozzi, this position will require many hours of work every day and I take music lessons every morning. I can only work half days," replied Roberto.

"The pay will be much better," said Tozzi.

"I really appreciate your considering me for the position, Signor Tozzi, but I cannot accept," said Roberto.

"Well, it's your loss, I don't know how much longer the company will be needing drafting work," said Tozzi.

"I'm truly sorry, Sir," Roberto feared he would be fired on the spot.

He walked out of Tozzi's office with a heavy feeling. He was perturbed by Tozzi's words and the shocking possibility of manufacturing arms. Roberto didn't want to go back to accounting work. His experience at the mine had taught him about greed and he sensed it strongly in this man. He was always polite whenever they met in the corridors, but Roberto didn't like him.

People called Tozzi a *bon vivant* and a user. Always elegantly dressed, he ate at the most expensive restaurants often accompanied by a much younger woman. He was known to be shrewd and heartless in business. Roberto just hoped to maintain his drafting position until another singing contract like the one with the Stevens came his way.

That evening, when he arrived home, he found Amelia and Cesare in the living room playing a piece by Schubert. Roberto sat down quietly and listened. He was worried about his job and the music helped him to drift away in happier thoughts.

"You must listen to this," said Cesare. "My sister is playing better every day."

Amelia was shy about playing in front of others. At first her hands were trembling but soon she was involved in the music and could think of nothing else. As she finished a Schubert's Impromptu, she lowered her hands to her lap and bowed her head. As if exhausted, but it was a moment full of emotion.

"That was absolutely beautiful, Amelia!" said Roberto.

"Didn't I tell you?" said Cesare.

"I have been practicing this *Romanza*," said Amelia, trying to diffuse the intensity of the moment. "Would you like to sing it, Roberto? Cesare, would you like to try the violin part too?"

They all looked over the musical score for some minutes.

"Let's try it," said Cesare.

Cesare and Amelia played the introduction. It was Paolo Tosti's song "Vorrei Morir" ...*I would like to die at sunset when the sky is serene...* Roberto sang. It was a sad song, which made everyone think of death. At the end, Amelia stood up and walked quickly out of the room, almost bumping into Carlo who was standing by the door.

Roberto shook his head. "That song is too sad."

"At this time of year Amelia becomes extremely sensitive about death and loss," said Carlo, "and she told me that she saw a workers' protest today and the guards were extremely aggressive."

"They are getting more belligerent every day," said Cesare.

"Striking workers are gathering at every street corner. Professor Segni was right when he said that the war with Turkey would bring economic disaster," said Carlo.

"Not everyone is suffering," interjected Roberto. "Signor Tozzi, the new general manager, said today that the factory is expanding into medical equipment and arms.

"You see? That's exactly what war means," added Cesare, "the rich get richer!"

"What's all this excitement about?" said Signora Corelli entering the room.

"Nothing, *Mamma*, just young men voicing opinions," said Carlo flashing a look at both Cesare and Roberto to keep quiet. He didn't want his mother to worry. And the thought of armament would instill thoughts of war again. He knew that food was becoming so expensive that when Giannina came back from the market every day she complained about the rising costs.

Roberto was now fearful of losing his job and considered that soon he would have to end his music lessons. Although Tozzi had said to him that the factory was expanding he had laid off some employees. Roberto expected the worst was about to come.

A week later he entered Stracciari's music room feeling that most probably he would not be coming to his classes for much longer. But the Maestro greeted Roberto with open arms.

"I have wonderful news for you!" He could hardly control his excitement. "Seneschi is going to direct several operas this coming season and he wants you to try for the tenor role in them." Stracciari had tears in his eyes. *Sono tanto felice* Roberto!

"Oh Maestro, I can't believe it. It's fantastic news! Thank you!" exclaimed Roberto.

"No, don't thank me. It was a lucky break that Gianni heard you sing that morning.

He is determined. He wants to see you tomorrow and hear you again." Maestro Stracciari just couldn't stop talking.

"What operas is he planning to produce?" asked Roberto. "Do you know, already, Maestro?"

"*Traviata, Andrea Chenier and Tosca,* which you know but we must work," said Stracciari as he approached the piano. "Please take out the music. We will commence immediately, first with *Traviata.*

Roberto found it hard to do his drafting work that whole week. He couldn't stop thinking about the wonderful direction that his life was taking. He would have liked to work all day long in nothing but music and acting. Seneschi came every morning to hear him. He was a perfectionist and he made Roberto work on every movement as if he were in the theatre. "Emotion, of course! But great control, always."

The arrangements were made and Seneschi finally told Roberto the details –when opening night would be, how many performances would take place and how much money he would be paid. Roberto was finally going to be able to live from music.

Then came the other part.

"What do you mean you're leaving?" said Tozzi, when Roberto tendered his resignation. "I have offered you the chance of a lifetime. This company is going to grow. You'll see."

"I'm sorry, Signor Tozzi, this singing opportunity is what I have been waiting for.

This is my dream, what I have always worked for."

"And how long will your dream last? Four, six months?"

"I hope for many years," added Roberto.

"Well, we may see you here again. It happens, you know?" said Tozzi. "I like opera too. I may even go to hear you sing."

Roberto wasn't sure if Tozzi was being sarcastic, but decided to be positive.

"Well, thank you! I hope to see you there, Signor Tozzi."

CHAPTER FIFTEEN

Roberto opened the door to the Corelli's house and in full voice started singing: *Un di felice eterea...* Signora Corelli, Giannina and Amelia, who were in the kitchen preparing *cannelloni* and chatting animatedly, stopped. Roberto walked in with a big smile.

"I have a big surprise...!" he said, "I'm going to sing *Traviata* in four months, followed by *Andrea Chenier* and closing the season with *Tosca*," his face beaming.

"*Lo sapevo!*" said Giannina smiling, as she continued spooning the filling on the pasta strips laid out on the kitchen table.

"Oh Roberto! *Che meraviglia!*" said Signora Corelli, wiping her hands on her apron and going to the sink to wash them.

"That's fantastic! I'm so happy for you!" said Amelia turning around. She stood in front of Roberto, her hands full of flour not knowing what to do. Roberto embraced her.

"Thank you for believing in me!" He said.

"Maestro Stracciari must be delighted," said Signora Corelli kissing Roberto on both cheeks.

"Oh yes, he is very happy. He finally has me singing opera in Milan!" said Roberto.

"Your mother would be so proud of you. I'm sure she will hear you from heaven," continued Signora Corelli. Roberto was now part of the family and held a special place in her heart.

"I wish she were alive," said Roberto. "She always loved *Traviata*. Her own mother was from Provence in France, so she always related to the aria "Di Provenza" and adored it. Of course, it is the baritone who sings it. Still…"

"And who is going to sing that part?" asked Amelia.

"A famous Spanish singer will sing the part of Giorgio Germont and a well known Hungarian soprano will sing Violetta. They will ensure that the public comes. I will be the beginner," Roberto replied.

"This is so exciting! And when is the opening?" Amelia asked.

"In September. Opening night is the 15th. What a coincidence! The proclamation of Independence in Mexico is celebrated on the night of the 15th of September and the next day is a national holiday. Maybe it's a sign, maybe it means something."

That night Roberto wrote to his father and brother to tell them that he was finally going to sing opera in Milan. The next day he went to the Italian Maritime Company to find out how much a first class ticket from Mexico to Genoa, would cost. He wanted to invite his father to come. Not only could he see his son perform the role of Alfredo Germont, but he would also be able to meet the Corelli family.

A month later he received a letter from his brother. Every word in it was a premonition …*Father is delighted with the news. He even considered crossing the Atlantic to see you and attend your performances, but his health has deteriorated. The doctor says that he suffers from cardiac insufficiency and the trip could prove fatal. Since mother's death his will to live has withered away and the political unrest and the abuses of power he has witnessed, have shattered his love for the law and his trust in its efficiency.*

Very soon I will be going to work in Washington, so father has accepted the idea of living with Teresa. He loves her little son, Memo, and gets along well with Justino, her husband. Natalia will be married in December and she will be moving to Monterrey with her new husband, Diego. He has been offered a position with the new iron and steel company. She was very worried about Father staying alone when I leave for Washington. So living with Teresa and Justino is a good solution. They have built a separate apartment for him where he can have his library and a small office where he can meet his friends from the Faculty of Law.

Please don't be disappointed because he cannot come over. We will be with you in every performance with all our hearts and minds.

Your loving brother, Francisco

Roberto could not hide his disappointment. He had always felt that any good thing is usually accompanied by a measure of woe. However, he came to terms with his family's absence and concentrated in his studies and rehearsals. This opportunity could mean the development of his career as an opera singer and he wanted his performances to be perfect. With Maestro Stracciari he practiced over and over the delivery of the arias and with Seneschi he rehearsed the complete operas, the acting and the stage movements. He was meeting people in the music and opera world and he was listening and learning.

He had no time to go out with Cesare or Carlo and their friends, so he was almost unaware of the social unrest that was surfacing within the various political groups in Italy. It was only after an attempt on King Vittorio Emanuele II's life that he realized that Italy was showing the signs of an impending revolution. People had been shot by police and agitators arrested.

Then, as if responding to all the European unrest, Germany declared war on France. It was the end of July 1914, just a few weeks before the opera's opening. In Milan there were continuous meetings of groups, which supported Italy's intervention in the conflict and of groups that backed neutrality. By August the United Kingdom had entered the conflict too. It was difficult to think that life would continue its normal course and that the art world would not be affected.

On September 15th the Corelli family, Giannina, the professors and other members of the extended family took their seats in two first-floor boxes of the theatre. Maestro Stracciari and a colleague, Maestro Ravello and his family joined them on the next box. Tozzi, Roberto's former employer, was also in the theatre, imposing and evident. He kept looking around with his opera glasses admiring the women in attendance. Everyone was elegantly dressed and the men bent their heads politely to greet the ladies in the audience.

The printed opera programs were the proof that Roberto Madriaga was starting his career as an opera singer. Amelia read over and over the short biographical sketches below the photographs. Kovanskaya, the soprano, had already ten successful years of singing and so had Garcia, the baritone. Tonight, all eyes and ears would be upon Roberto.

The first violin stepped in and the whole orchestra tuned up. The conductor walked to the podium and the people applauded. Then silence. The stringed instruments delivered the haunting notes of the *Traviata's* overture –a prelude to the tragic story. Amelia placed her hand on her mother's arms as the curtain opened.

On stage, a party is taking place in Violetta Valery's apartment in Paris and a friend introduces Alfredo Germont to her. Very soon in the opera, Alfredo is persuaded by his friend to make a toast –*a brindisi*. The festive atmosphere and gaiety of all those present is contagious and the moment finishes with the high note of a cheerful chorus.

When Roberto started singing *"Un di felice eterea mi balenasti inanzi..."* Amelia could hardly contain her tears as she heard his voice singing precisely what she felt for him: "... and since that day, love has lived in me... cross and delight..." Her heart was so full of love that her eyes could not leave his figure on stage. It was a revelation to her that the emotion she felt could be expressed so well through an opera. She could never be that eloquent herself, but there he was, in front of her, the man she would love forever.

When Violetta in her aria repeated Alfredo's words, Amelia felt she was living that life. She accepted the fact that Roberto still considered her a young girl, but maybe one day... The opera was a mirror of life. Alfredo does not recognize the sacrifice that his beloved has made by leaving him. His father finally tells him the truth, but it is too late for Violetta... *e tardi!*

Violetta's last aria "Addio del passato" was delivered by the soprano in a most dramatic manner and Amelia thought *If only Alfredo had understood why she had left him, if only his father had told him sooner...* Amelia understood that many unnecessary tragedies in life happen because of misunderstandings and silences imposed by pride and propriety.

As the curtain closed and Violetta lay dead in her Paris apartment, Amelia's eyes welled up for the courtesan's tragic life. It took all of her willpower to suppress her sobs, but once she had regained composure, she went backstage with her mother to see Roberto.

There were big line-ups to congratulate the singers and to have the programs autographed. Delivery boys with large baskets of roses were trying to make their way to the dressing rooms. Maestro Stracciari stood at the entrance of Roberto's room.

"Luisa, *che piacere!*" The Maestro said to Signora Corelli, as they approached. Then added: "Amelia! My God, you have grown! Your father would be so proud of you and your brothers. He was a good friend of mine."

"I know, Maestro. We hear about you all the time through Roberto," she replied.

"I'm very glad to see you, Federico! It's been some time," said Signora Corelli. "I cannot thank you enough for having sent

Roberto to our house. It has been a pleasure to have him stay with us."

Amelia could not have agreed more. She also knew that Roberto had re-united the family through music. Without knowing it he had made them go back to their old tradition of playing and singing together. And now he had finally achieved success as a newcomer into the opera world.

"We have prepared a small celebration. It's tomorrow for lunch, at our home. Would you like to join us?" Said Signora Corelli to Stracciari.

"Thank you, Luisa with pleasure," replied the Maestro.

Amelia entered the room together with her mother, Giannina, Carlo and Cesare amid a whirlwind of compliments and congratulations. Roberto, beaming, shook hands and embraced people, thanking them all.

"Maestro Stracciari, all this is because of you," said Roberto putting his arm around the maestro's shoulders.

"No, it's your voice, your dedication and a bit of good luck," he said smiling. "I only assist and guide."

"Oh, Maestro…!" Words could not express what the pupil felt for his teacher.

By the time Roberto was able to overcome his emotion the room was crowded.

"Did you like the performance, Amelia?" he asked.

Amelia, who had been almost in trance since the end of the opera, was suddenly shaken out of her reverie. "Oh Roberto, it was so beautiful, so moving…" she couldn't finish. She embraced him hastily trying to hide her true feelings.

"Well, let's all go and toast to our great singer," said Cesare. "Tomorrow we'll eat but tonight we'll have some champagne on me."

"*Va bene! Andiamo!* Let's go!"

As they came out of the dressing room, Fauto Tozzi approached Roberto. "Congratulations Signor Madariaga! That was very good!"

"Thank you, Signor Tozzi!" replied Roberto.

"This is Signor Tozzi, the factory director," explained Roberto, introducing him to the Corelli's and to Maestro Stracciari. "Thank you for coming, Sir."

"I like opera," said Tozzi. "And I like to see beautiful women, too," he added as he looked appreciatively in the direction of Amelia and Signora Corelli.

Roberto cringed when he saw Tozzi's gaze. It was a disquieting moment but Cesare had already taken Amelia's arm and was walking out of the room. Amelia was looking in a different direction and did not notice Tozzi's look.

The musical and theatre season had started and the café/bars were bubbling over with activity. The city was once again vibrating with artistic excitement. Germany was at war with France and England but in Milan people were enjoying the glow of the chandeliers and the limelight. Higher prices didn't seem to affect the restaurants and bars tonight. They were well attended.

During the next few months Roberto enjoyed the feeling of wellbeing that accompanies all great achievements. He was finally singing opera for a living. Every time he entered the stage his knees would tremble for the first few seconds, but the nervousness would soon give way to a sense of confidence that he had now acquired. He enjoyed the stage but more than anything else he found enormous satisfaction in knowing, that he had done a good job and that he had sung the opera true to the composer's wishes. His teacher told him so, whenever he felt he had accomplished that. Seneschi was delighted with Roberto and with his own career as a director.

Amelia would have liked to go to all the performances but that was not possible. And she could not go back stage to see Roberto, as it would have been improper on her part. She rejoiced in his triumphs and listened with all her heart to his interpretations.

"Andrea Chenier" had been an enormous success. Roberto had transported himself to the French Revolution and denounced with eloquence the abuses of power and the cruelty, singing masterfully and walking to the guillotine accompanied by his beloved Maddalena de Cogny.

When the opera ended the singers were shaking from the effects of performing this tour de force. Roberto could not hide his happiness at having achieved his dream. It had taken time and hard work but he was ecstatic with the outcome. Every time, when he came on stage, he renewed his determination "to give the best performance of his life."

Once, late at night, he had stayed longer in the theatre just to breathe the scent of the stage. The place was now dark but he still could hear the echoes of the drama in his voice as he said farewell to life and to his dreams, while waiting for the firing squad to come. That night he had sung *Tosca,* the opera that he had dreamt of singing on a stage since he was a teenager. He couldn't stop the music from sounding in his brain, although all that surrounded him was the quiet stage. In the distance, the sound of the streetcars halting and starting filtered through the sets, still on the stage. He thanked life for the gift of voice that he had received and for the incredible opportunity that he had been given to study with Stracciari and the magical arrival of Seneschi. He gave thanks for the Corelli family that had become like his own and for his parents who had instilled in him their love of music and opera.

CHAPTER SIXTEEN

I t was the spring of 1915. The opera season was about to finish.
Roberto had completed his first opera contract and had received
letters from his family, from Clara Gillespie and from the Stevens
congratulating him on his achievement. Amelia was about to complete her studies and was hoping to enter the Scientific Institute
in the fall to study chemistry. Carlo was working in the Bank and
Cesare was apprenticing in a newspaper.

Life was good inside the house but outside there were strikes
affecting the public services and the population was angry. The
disturbances that had erupted the previous year in Milan had now
expanded to other cities and had increased in frequency and number. There were groups actively seeking a socialist government that
would not participate in the international conflict and there were
also the *irredenti* agitators wanting Italy to enter the War to recover
the lands lost to the Austro-Hungarian Empire.

Luisa Corelli was trying her best to keep the routine of family life unaltered. She encouraged weekly musical evenings sometimes attended by cousins or friends. Poetry and play reading had

been added to the activities. Cesare was now a proficient violinist. Roberto and Carlo were the singers and Amelia accompanied them all at the piano. She was the backbone of the group. One evening as she was accompanying Roberto singing *Mignon's* "Elle ne croyait pas," Giannina looking at them said to Luisa: "Signora, they look so good together."

Giannina's words shook up Luisa. She always saw her daughter as a very young girl and avoided the thought that she was becoming a woman.

Amelia was a sensitive and reserved young woman. Some afternoons before the other residents returned home, she sat at the piano and played and sang by herself. Luisa listened from other parts of the house as her daughter sang Gastaldon's "Musica Proibita" "...*vorrei bacciari I tuoi capelli neri...* -I would like to kiss your black hair!" She sensed the longing in her daughter's voice and she worried. One night she sat down and said: "The song you were singing is beautiful but love is not always that romantic. Love can hurt and make you suffer."

"I know, Mamma. Love brings pain. But is there any harm in dreaming?"

"I guess not," replied Luisa, wishing Edgardo, were alive to talk with their daughter.

Lately, Amelia, as most young women in the country, had been excited by the exploits of the poet Gabrielle D'Annunzio, flying his small plane all over Italy. His message directed at all the Italians but especially the young, exhorting them to be proud and to bear arms against the Austrians. Luisa was worried about the effect of the poet's actions.

"But Mamma, his poetry is beautiful and inspiring," said Amelia.

"I know, *Cara*, he is a great poet, but his work is like an ember. It can suddenly ignite and become a fire. We need peace, not war.

"Mamma, things are getting bad for Italy," Cesare interjected from the armchair where he was reading. "D'Annunzio is trying to get the government's attention. I think he is right. If nothing is done, Italy may end up being Austria's footboy again." These last words were interrupted by the sound of the front door opening. Carlo, usually calm and contained entered the house in an agitated state.

"Italy has declared war on Austria!" he exclaimed.

"About time!" Cesare closed his book and stood up.

"*O Dio!*" Said Luisa Corelli.

"What was that?" asked Roberto coming into the room.

"Here, look at the news!" replied Carlo hitting the newspaper with his hand. They gathered around him and read: *L'Italia dichiara la Guerra.* La Stampa di Torino gave the details.

"Yes! I say that we cannot allow the Austrians to continue their advances. We don't want more Triestes!"

"*Santo Cielo*, Cesare! Do you know what war really means?" asked Signora Corelli.

"Yes Mamma, it means fighting, it means we will show the aggressors who we really are."

"But it also means destruction, loss of lives, tragedy. A peaceful solution would be better."

"Not any more. We need to fight them. War's the only way!" Cesare's voice was rising. "D'Annunzio is right! We must offer our lives for our country and do it fearlessly."

"I don't think Italy is in any position to enter the war," replied Carlo, "the economic situation is already disastrous. We have enough conflicts right here. Why should we get involved in more? What do you think, Roberto?"

Roberto scrambled for words. "I prefer finding peaceful solutions. In a war nobody wins …and I'm against bearing arms."

"A pacifist! We don't need that now! I'm going to Piazza Duomo," exclaimed Cesare rushing out of the room.

Suddenly the room was strangely quiet. Amelia noticed her mother was trying to control her tears.

"Oh Mamma, don't cry! He becomes too passionate about this," said Amelia putting her arms around her mother.

"I worry about him, he can be so impetuous!".

Roberto stood up. "I'll go and talk to him,"

But Cesare was gone. They all heard the front door open and close. The news had left every person in the living room speechless. Their thoughts were in turmoil.

People were walking to the center of town avid for more news. A strange murmur came from the Piazza Duomo and voices in unison could now be clearly heard all over the city: *"Viva la Guerra! Viva la Guerra!"* "Hail to war!"

The Corelli family sat at home in silence everyone immersed in thought.

Roberto broke the silence and said to Carlo: "I'm sorry to have said what I said so bluntly."

"To Cesare war is an adventure. Challenges revitalize him and he will do his best," said Carlo. "A peaceful existence is not enough for him. Like you, I also feel it's always better to find solutions. However, in this case, there's nothing we can do. The future has been decided. Most probably I will be called to arms immediately."

"That's too bad, you were planning on marrying Eva, or not?"

"Yes, I was. But now everything will be postponed."

"Wouldn't you marry her before you go to the front?"

"No. That would be unfair. Times are going to be hard enough," said Carlo. "I'll visit her later this evening. She must be worried."

Crowds gathered in many towns to hail the government's decision to enter the war. In front of the King's palace the people saluted the Queen and the princesses. The young girls waved happily to the young men who were going off to defend their country.

At home, Amelia and Signora Corelli were silent but Giannina could be heard murmuring: *"Ma che disgrazia!* What a disaster!"

She kept drying her eyes, fearing the worst, causing the other two to shiver.

Roberto was disturbed. Although he had seen more and more restless people gathering to support Italy's intervention in the war, he had thought it would not go through. Yet now Carlo and Cesare, his two friends, would be called to arms. Was peace so very wrong?

"Maestro, why do you think this is happening, when Italy is in such economic straits?" he asked Stracciari the next day.

"My father used to say: 'man cannot live long without fighting.'"

"I don't understand why countries fight for a piece of land. The defeated will never be happy and they will fight again, or live with resentment. Why can't they reach an agreement that satisfies both sides?" said Roberto.

"I guess the answer is greed. You see Roberto, you and I don't understand war: but we understand the tragedy of war. Men are either fighters or dreamers and we belong to the second group."

"But Maestro, history tells us that nothing comes out of war, except death."

"I know, but don't forget that there will be people who will reap huge profits. There is money to be made in war...But enough of war! Let's do something beautiful with music. And they sang the duet of *La Boheme*.

A few days later Carlo Corelli was mobilized with his company to the zone of Bolzano. As they departed, pushing their bicycles loaded with their sleeping blankets and their packsacks, the people lined the streets and cheered them. Everyone was smiling and wishing them good luck. The alpine soldiers wore their uniforms and their famous hats with pride, showing their determination to fight for their country.

Signora Corelli embraced her oldest son willing herself not to cry. She knew that Carlo was careful and levelheaded in his judgments but she knew that in war survival is also a question of luck.

Amelia hugged her brother and joined the others on the street applauding and waving. Carlo smiled courageously. He had not told his family that he was in love with Eva. Only Roberto knew how close they had become. Now all the plans that Carlo and Eva had made were postponed or… forgotten.

Roberto embraced his friend: "*Coraggio, Carlo!* Courage! Take care of yourself!

They all waved at him as he turned the corner together with the others. Eva blew a kiss to him chocking back her tears.

Following the walking soldiers were the vehicles and the horses that would move the arms and supplies into the mountains.

When Cesare's orders arrived he was ready. He couldn't hide his enthusiasm, although Amelia had asked him to try, because it was hurting their mother.

"I can't help it. I feel ready for battle. I feel it in my bones."

"I'm going to miss you so much, Cesare! Who will play the violin with me?" She then pulled a tiny leather bag out of her pocket. "This is for you. It's the *Madonnina.* She will protect you." It was a small gold medal of the Madonna that stands at the tip of the highest steeple in the Cathedral of Milan.

"*Grazie,* Amelia! I'll be back. We will defeat them. You'll see!" He assured her as he embraced his sister and then turned to his mother.

"Mamma! No matter what, I will love you always. Please don't worry about me."

"*Mio figlio!*" Said Luisa Corelli with a sigh. Such zeal to fight worried her. "Please take care of yourself! Be cautious!" She kissed him on both cheeks and blessed him.

"*Attento al nemico!* Mind the enemy!" Said Giannina, embracing him and knowing Cesare would always go forward, no matter what.

They saw him carrying on down the front steps of the house entrance with an eager stride as if he were going off on an exciting excursion in the mountains. He was to take the train from Milan to assemble in Bologna with the rest of his company. Roberto accompanied him to the station. In the train station the atmosphere was festive.

They embraced as Roberto said: "Take care, my friend!"

"Of course! *Ciao* Roberto! Cesare replied and rushed towards the train.

"Cesare, over here!" a young soldier called and Cesare disappeared into the sea of uniforms that were filling the train.

Women young and old were crying. The young men, instead, were excited about going to war. As the train pulled out of the station the voices of the alpine soldiers could be heard singing: *"Sul capello, sul capello che noi portiamo.."* On the hat we wear there's a black feather. It's our flag to fight the enemy in the mountains..."

CHAPTER SEVENTEEN

Carlo

A month later, Carlo, along with many others, was trudging along the steep trails of the Dolomites, pushing cannons and wagons loaded with supplies. Other men were towing mules carrying sacks and rolled up blankets, while still others hauled in unison enormous parallel logs from which trench mortar bombs hung, tied with ropes. They resembled pallbearers, carefully transporting their burden of death. On both edges of the road the soldiers on foot joked with them as they passed them with their own load of hand weapons. The view of the mountains and rock formations inspired reverence but also apprehension. They would be climbing them but also fighting from them.

Every evening after the troops ate and drank some wine, the alpine group would sing. Both groups, the *alpini* and the *bersaglieri,* sat side by side surrounded by the wagons, trucks, mules and the trench mortar bombs, while their voices filled the rifts and cliffs of the mountains with music full of longing. They were united in a deep sense of self-protection against the invader.

Very often Carlo wondered what would happen if the enemy joined in the singing. Maybe the words would be meaningless to them, but the music would move their hearts. But then... they were the enemy.

In other areas of the country civilians were actively involved in the construction of railway lines to assist the troops in the war effort. Passenger cars were converted into first aid clinics and some cargo cars were armed with cannons against the new menace, the air raids. The majority of the railway cars however, were used to carry men, arms and ammunition to the fronts. Most of the fighting lines were in the mountains so the final hauling of arms was done by men, mules and, in some cases, cable cars.

Cesare

From Bologna Cesare boarded the train bound for Pordenone with many other alpine soldiers. Nothing else was said to them and despite the fact that they had some idea of what was waiting for them, they all talked animatedly. The thought of fighting in a war was a challenging adventure. They played cards, told jokes and finally fell asleep. When the train stopped and they knew they had arrived at their destination, it was not where they had thought they were going. The place was not familiar to any of Cesare's group. They all jumped out of the train and lined up for inspection, eager and proud.

Along with infantry soldiers and *bersaglieri*, the *alpini* assembled outside an old farm building that was now the regimental headquarters. The valley with its group of houses and its chapel looked like many mountain towns, peaceful and friendly. After they ate and received their orders, their long walk began.

Cesare was now a lieutenant and, as they marched up towards the ridge that would be their starting point, a feeling of wellbeing came over him —that sense of peace and harmony that he found in the mountains. Soon they were climbing up a hidden path between firs and pines. As all other regiments, they also carried supplies and arms with the help of carts and mules. When each company located its position, the groups separated to carry out the work they had been assigned. They dug trenches, built latrines and established camps with a kitchen area as instructed by their superiors. They located strategic points to place the armaments, inside tunnels and corridors created by the rock formations.

Cesare felt his spirit strengthened by the mountain air and the spectacular landscape. The evergreens showed their new growth. The mountain peaks were still topped with snow and the men worked with enthusiasm and prepare themselves for battle.

I feel good here. He wrote to his mother who read the letter to Amelia, Giannina and Roberto. *As you know, I love the mountain air and the magnificent landscape. We are working hard preparing ourselves to defend our country. I'm now a lieutenant and I hope to do a good job. We have established our camp now and every evening when the sunlight hits the peaks of the mountains, this earth becomes heaven. I like being here.*

My love to you, Amelia and Giannina.

Your son, Cesare.

Roberto was pensive as Signora Corelli folded the letter. He avoided looking into Amelia's or Signora Corelli's eyes. He had read the papers that evening and the news from the front were disheartening. The month-old letter was almost disturbing in its optimism.

The battles had started almost immediately after the positions were established in all fronts. Both sides followed a pattern of attack –first the shooting, then the shelling and then the firebombs. Sometimes the fighting ended at the point of a bayonet. Positions changed on a daily basis advancing or retracting only a few meters at a time. These first battles were disastrous for the Italians.

One evening, as Luisa Corelli was in the living room writing to her sons and waiting for Amelia to come back, the doorbell rang and Fausto Tozzi stood at the entrance.

"Signora Corelli, good evening!" he said in his most respectful manner.

Although Luisa Corelli was surprised at such unexpected visit, she replied politely: "Signor Tozzi, please come in."

They sat down and Fausto Tozzi continued: "I've heard that your two sons are at the front. Do not worry about what the newspapers say, I'm sure they are going to be fine," he said in an all-knowledgeable tone. "And Signorina Amelia? And Signor Madariaga, is he still here?"

"Yes, they are well. Thank you," she replied as the front door opened and Roberto walked in.

"Oh, Roberto, how are you?" said Tozzi standing up and extending his hand.

"Signor Tozzi! Good evening," replied Roberto, shocked to see Fausto Tozzi there and surprised at his sudden friendliness.

"I was asking Signora Corelli about you," he said. "Remember what I told you a while ago about the company? Well, it has grown and needs someone in the supply distribution area and you, Roberto, would be perfect for the job. I'm afraid everything will change and the opera season will be cancelled this year. So, think about it."

Tozzi stood up without giving Roberto a chance to reply.

"Signora Corelli, Roberto, *Arrivederci!* Remember, young man, things are different now and we all have to adapt." Tozzi put on his hat and inclined his head ceremoniously.

He must know something I don't, Roberto thought.

As predicted by Fausto Tozzi, everything changed in a few months. All efforts were concentrated on the production of arms and the gathering of supplies for the front.

Tozzi had become a big supplier to the Italian forces and his company now encompassed the production of arms and munitions and the distribution of medical equipment and supplies.

In most Italian cities the Lyric Opera Season had been so affected that performances were reduced to a minimum or cancelled. A disheartened Seneschi announced to Stracciari and to Roberto that he would not be producing any operas in the next season.

Surmounting his pride and disregarding his misgivings, Roberto went back to work in Tozzi's medical and supplies company. No more designing or drawing, his job was now inventory control.

Every day large numbers of stretchers, hospital beds, operating beds and surgical instruments were sent to the front together with the medical supplies that were assembled in the laboratory. To control the equipment leaving the warehouse was not difficult but it was almost impossible to verify the receipt of the shipments by the countless country hospitals that had been established in barns, country houses and tents close to the fighting lines. The staff was so busy with the wounded that paperwork was neglected. Roberto noticed that Signor Tozzi didn't think that control outside of the warehouse was important. The shipments left his company and got paid by the government. If someone else re-sold the goods on the black market that was not his problem.

CHAPTER EIGHTEEN

Some evenings when Amelia came home, a sense of emptiness invaded her. It was quiet without her brothers who had been gone since May of the previous year. The American had also left Milan and only the two professors and Roberto were boarding. He was still practicing with Maestro Stracciari and working long hours and there was little time to sing at home in the evenings.

Amelia had noticed that with her brothers' absence and one less boarder the family income was depleted and she decided to look for a job without telling her mother.

She had given up her dream of studying chemistry, for the time being, so she had been delighted to find a job in a pharmaceutical company laboratory. She was assigned to assist two chemists. Very often she found herself looking through a microscope and felt she had fulfilled her dream, partially. When she told her mother about her work, Luisa was almost pleased.

"But I thought it was necessary to study first, Amelia, and I wanted you to do that."

"They need help, Mamma. And, I'm learning a lot."

"But, your studies…"

"Maybe later, when the war is over, Mamma. Don't worry!" She was happy to help her mother now. While doing her work, Amelia often envisioned her brothers at the front climbing mountains but she pushed away any thoughts of battles and visions of wounded soldiers. She didn't know exactly where Carlo and Cesare were stationed but the reports about the battles were distressing.

The New Year had come and gone without much celebration. All thoughts were fixed on the battlegrounds. Food shortages had contributed to the low spirits amidst the population. Italy was mobilizing great numbers of men from all levels and ages to the front. The war effort kept growing and the results were doubtful.

The long-awaited spring finally came.

"Food is scarce," said Giannina. "There are almost no vegetables and only fruit preserves for sale."

"Mamma, we should plant some vegetables in the backyard. In a few months we could have fresh turnips, carrots and maybe tomatoes."

Roberto who was in the next room overheard the conversation.

"I couldn't help hearing what you were saying, Signora Luisa. To plant vegetables is a good idea. I can help. We can do that tomorrow, Amelia, if you wish."

The thought of working with Roberto cheered Amelia. "We can plant onions and cauliflower, too."

"Onions are easy to find," said Giannina. "Think of other vegetables, things that we like to eat and that grow fast like chard, spinach, herbs and maybe tomatoes, also roots like carrots and beets."

The next morning, a Sunday, Amelia and Roberto went to Piazza San Nazzaro to buy whatever seeds and vegetable plants they could find. They were thrilled with what they found and if they had had more money they would have bought enough seeds for a park.

"Where did you learn to prepare the earth like this?" asked Amelia as she observed the way Roberto was digging in the garden and mixing the soil.

"As you know, I grew up in a mining town with limited amounts of good soil, but every year the river left behind a layer of humus that people carried in pails to their houses to enrich the soil in their gardens or to grow vegetables. That was the only way to cultivate something. Some people had small plots by the river where they grew corn, which was harvested before the river flooded. Agriculture in that area of Mexico is difficult if not impossible."

Giannina came out to the garden, hands on her hips: "You people seem to enjoy this work. Who could have guessed? The pianist and the singer," she added jovially.

"I see why some people like working the land," said Amelia. "The feeling of the soil in my hands is refreshing and knowing that something may grow out of it, is comforting."

"Working in a closed space such as a factory can be jarring –all that noise," said Roberto. "Planting, instead, is a quiet occupation. I imagine where you are working is quiet too."

"Yes, I enjoy the place very much and I love the work. What I don't like is coming out at closing time and finding all these people crowding around the entrance reading the lists of casualties that are posted every evening. I am always scared to look."

"If something happens, the family is informed first."

"I know. Still..." "These seeds feel very light," said Amelia changing the subject. She was finding it hard to talk about the war and to think about her brothers at the front.

"They may not be as fresh. It's hard to tell, but we will use them too."

"Look at those rows! They're beautiful and to think that they'll give us vegetables in a few months..."

"Yes, I hope. Planting is satisfying and rewarding," said Roberto.

They were kneeling on the ground and perspiring heavily, their brows covered in beads of sweat. The smell of spring earth filled the air and Amelia looked up as she felt Roberto's hand brushing hers. She trembled from the effect his touch had on her and immediately straightened her back. Their eyes met and, for the first time in a long time, Roberto felt something like desire. He looked for a moment into the eyes of the young woman kneeling beside him and realized that something magical had happened. He was shocked and stood up immediately to diffuse the intensity of his feelings.

"We need to put some water right away," he said as he walked briskly towards the garden tap.

Amelia looked in his direction wondering if he had felt the way she had. She needed to say something. "You seem to know a lot about planting, Roberto."

He also wanted to talk and put the moment at the back of his mind. "When I was a boy I used to help Don Panchito, who was the gardener and keeper in our house in Santa Rosalia. He taught me all I know about plants and horses," Roberto said and busied himself for quite a while carrying pails of water and watering the plants.

"Planting gives me a feeling of hope," said Amelia as she stood up. "Look at the cherry trees. My father planted them the spring before he died and they are giving us fruit now."

"They're lovely, especially when in bloom," replied Roberto.

"These trees mean a lot to me."

"I know they do, Amelia."

Dusk was falling and it was getting cool.

"Well, we did it! Now, let's go in," said Roberto.

Giannina called for supper. "I have made a good, hearty soup for you, *Signori contadini*," she said happily to the "farmers." Seeing the rows of future vegetables had made her optimistic. The trees and shrubs were starting to bloom and there was a promise of new life sweeping over like a mantle of hope.

As they were sitting at the table, Roberto said to Signora Corelli and Amelia:

"I have something to tell you." The two women stopped eating and looked at him, as he continued. "I have volunteered to work in the *Treni Sanitari* and the ambulances helping move the wounded away from the front."

"Oh Roberto, why do you want to do that? You don't have to," said Amelia.

"Yes, I do! Please try to understand. I cannot continue to remain on the fringe. This country, my chosen homeland, is in the middle of a war and although I'm against war I can help those who have to go to war. It's something I just have to do."

Amelia felt a heaviness of heart that didn't seem to lift. Everyone would be gone now. And, after what she had just felt kneeling beside Roberto, his departure would be tragic.

"I hate war! Why did we have to declare war?" She said almost crying.

"Countries have to make decisions and those decisions affect their citizens," said Roberto calmly.

"I just think of all the people that suffer and die unnecessarily," said Signora Corelli.

"I know," continued Roberto. "I feel sad about this. But when a government sets out to destroy the sovereignty of another country, their culture, their language… the attacked country has to respond. Most of the time, the people who have to go and fight don't even know the reason why the others are the enemy, when only a while before they were good neighbors. When the war finally ends and the tragic losses and the deaths are counted, few know what the war was about."

Amelia was silent as she listened to what Roberto was saying. Signora Corelli knew that it was useless to plead. "When are you starting?"

"Right away. I will be on first aid training with the Red Cross every day for ten days and then I will leave for the front. I have informed Signor Tozzi already. He is quite unhappy but, as he told me a while back, this is war."

"And your singing career?"

"Maestro Stracciari knows my feelings and Seneschi doesn't think that much will change for a while. He has not been able to get the opera season organized even for the year after. Maybe singing will have to wait."

"Please promise me that you'll be careful," Amelia urged him.

"I promise you that."

Amelia knew she would miss Roberto even more than her own brothers. Lately, his presence had become indispensable to her. That night she cried until she fell asleep.

Roberto said goodbye to Maestro Stracciari and promised to stop by the school of music if he was ever in town.

"*Attento col nemico e con la voce.* Be careful with the enemy and with your voice," said the maestro embracing him.

"*Maestro! Grazie di tutto!*" Roberto had a big knot in his throat.

"*Buon ritorno!*"

Roberto completed his training and when he came out a few days later, he was wearing the armband of the *Croce Rossa*.

As he walked down the street he felt the urge to help the wounded soldiers at the front and, for the first time, he thought he understood Cesare's eagerness to go to war.

CHAPTER NINETEEN

Amelia

The heat and humidity in Milan were suffocating. Amelia, Signora Corelli and Giannina longed for their Sunday excursions to Lake Como. But everybody was struggling to survive and there was no money to buy train tickets or go for picnics. The carefree, joyful summers were gone. Amelia was glad that she had planted the vegetables in the garden with Roberto. They were a happy reminder that magical moments could happen.

Every evening she went out with Giannina to pick whatever was ready for eating. The tomatoes and carrots had yielded enough to make a few jars of sauce and although they ate only pasta or polenta every day, they considered themselves quite fortunate.

"Aunt Lina is coming to live with us," announced Signora Corelli one morning.

"Aunt Lina? Oh Mamma, she's such a difficult person! I love her but... to live with us...?

"She has no one to take care of her. She is old and forgetful, Amelia. She is a widow and now she has lost her only son to the war."

Amelia was thinking how could they take care of her when lately they had barely enough for themselves. "Of course, Mamma! I'm sorry for being so unkind. I didn't mean to be."

She was on the verge of tears. Too many things were happening all at once. She had been working all this while in the laboratory, enjoying the quiet work when, without warning, the staff was transferred to another building. The two biochemists were sent to the pharmaceutical part and she was transferred to the same company where Roberto had worked for Fausto Tozzi in the distribution of armament and medical supplies.

She was trying to be strong but she was finding it hard. She longed for the quiet of her space along the laboratory table where the excitement was created by the small staff formulating theories or writing up the results of their tests. Now her work consisted of putting together first-aid boxes and assembling medications for the field hospitals. She had to prepare the lists for the accounting department to submit the invoices to the government. She found some relief by thinking that Roberto or someone like him would use the supplies to alleviate the suffering of wounded soldiers. She understood the importance of the work but she was not happy about the change.

More than the noise and the change of tasks, what she found disquieting was Signor Tozzi's frequent presence in the office. He was now the director of all these companies under the same roof and was always walking around looking elegant and observing the process. Often he came too close to her trying to strike up conversation. One day he had invited her to a concert which she declined saying that she couldn't leave her mother alone with the caring of her aunt. How long would she be able to stand her ground? She needed the job, but she had no intention of going anywhere with the man.

The professors at home referred to Tozzi's business as "Tozzi's amassment."

"How his company has grown in these terrible times, should be up for scrutiny," said Professor Segni.

"And who do you think would be courageous enough to stand up to him and his government contacts?" replied Professor Gozzano.

"I don't know; plenty of ideas but nobody to carry them through."

Amelia knew that whatever monies she brought home from the job were greatly needed. She felt uncomfortable with Tozzi's attentions but she couldn't talk about the situation to anybody, least of all her mother. She would want her to leave the job immediately.

In order to get to the pharmaceutical office every morning, Amelia had to walk along the corridor that stood in the middle of the large cavernous structure that housed the armament factory. There was a railroad track in the middle running the full length of the place. On both sides of the track there were hundreds of women bent over the task of filling belts and disks with ammunition. There was only a handful of old men and some underfed youths. Everyone concentrated on the work, as the supervisor walked up and down the aisles checking productivity. Nobody complained about the repetitiveness of the job while they were inside the structure. This effort was for their country.

Two or three times a day, the railway cars came in to be loaded with arms, medical equipment and supplies by a handful of men. This was the only moment when the workers could see that there were still a few young men around. At those times the noise inside the factory was deafening, sometimes aggravated by the pounding of rain on the metal roof.

As the weeks and months passed, people talked less and thought more. Few had received letters from the front and when the lists of dead and wounded men were posted at the entrance of the factory, everybody crowded around them, their hearts in their throats.

The professors' comments had a ring of truth. Tozzi was becoming richer and more powerful while thousands were dying at the front. They had called him a profiteer and a heartless vulture. His quiet insistence made Amelia tense but she was busy enough during the day to keep him at bay. Often during the evening, her nervousness expressed itself in uncharacteristic impatience towards the old aunt living with them.

Amelia was considering looking for another job when suddenly Tozzi announced that he was going on a trip to visit hospitals around the front.

The professors were unexpectedly called to arms and with their departure the house became extremely quiet. Money was tight and the news from the front scarce. Each woman was privately worried and did not want to upset the other two. They maintained a form of composure that was only disturbed by the old aunt's complaints. Nobody talked about the war or about shortages and Giannina found it hard to cook with the scant food available to them.

"When are we having some meat?" ranted Aunt Lina.

"No meat, Signora, only pasta or polenta," answered Giannina.

"Cara Zia," said Signora Corelli, "there's a war. Remember?"

But Zia Lina was barely aware of where she was and complained constantly about the food, the lack of sugar and of coffee. Signora Luisa, Giannina and Amelia were at the limit of their patience.

The house was silent that evening except for the aunt's grumbling, which was upsetting the others. Amelia couldn't take it any longer and started to play in order to muffle the sound of Aunt Lina's complaints. To everyone's surprise the old aunt calmed down and stopped pestering Signora Corelli. From that day on, Amelia resumed her playing every evening, bringing a measure of relief. There was no news from Carlo, Cesare or Roberto and mother and daughter fought hard to hide their fears.

Amelia was walking down the factory's corridor one evening, immersed in thought, when she noticed a young boy bent over the fitting tables. She thought he was sleeping but when she got closer she realized that he was trying to push the last of the ammunition in a firing belt. He seemed to be making a big effort and his body was tense. He looked pale and his eyes were heavy with sleep.

"Ti senti male? She asked thinking that he looked weak.

"Sto bene," the boy replied.

"It's time to go home," Amelia continued. The factory was almost empty.

"Yes, I'm sorry, Signorina!" he said rubbing his eyes and looking around the factory, putting on his jacket.

"It's cold outside. Don't you have a coat?"

"I'll be fine, Signorina. Don't worry." He tried to smile to show that he was strong but Amelia was too attentive not to notice the quiver in his voice.

"Where do you live?" She asked.

His deep dark eyes clouded with tears and his jaw started to shake.

"My father was called to arms last year. My mother and I tried to keep the farm going, but the crop was poor and we could not pay. We were sent out of the house. We came to Milan and she found this job. She worked until last month but then she got sick. She couldn't come and told me to take her place and do the work."

"Is she better now?"

"She's dead, Signorina." At this point his voice broke down. "She was buried by the Red Cross."

"I'm so sorry!" Said Amelia putting her arm around his shaking shoulders. "Let's get out of here. We'll go home. Giannina will give you a big bowl of soup and you'll feel better."

The boy could not have been more than twelve or thirteen. It was bitterly cold and his jacket was too light for the low temperature. Amelia took off her scarf and gave it to him.

"No, no Signorina!"

"Please! I don't want you to get sick."

The streets were nearly empty and only a few people were walking hastily, their faces hidden by their scarves and hats. Upon turning on to the *Viale* they were hit by the smell of roasted chestnuts.

"Let's buy some!"

"But Signorina…!" He couldn't finish the sentence; Amelia was already buying the chestnuts. She was reminded of years back when she was walking with her father and they had stopped to buy some *castagne*. As Signor Corelli was about to pay, he noticed a poorly dressed child looking on, avidly, as the vendor put the chestnuts in a small bag. "Would you like some?" Signor Corelli had asked.

"Si, si!" was the child's reply.

Signor Corelli had bought another bag and given it to the boy.

"Grazie Signor!" The boy had simply said and had run away with his treasure as Amelia's father smiled. He always took time to smile. Most men his age did not smile or talk with the children, but her father did. He talked and listened to what they had to say. She knew her father had been a kind man and she still missed him.

"Here, have some," Amelia said, turning to the boy and offering the warm paper bag with the nutty delicacies. "What's your name?" She asked him as they walked and he cracked the shells eating the chestnuts with visible delight.

"Campobasso, Renato," he replied between bites.

She saw that his shoes were too big for him, but he was trying to keep up the pace that Amelia was sustaining to keep warm. She hoped that her mother would not be upset at her bringing the boy to their house. Her beautiful welcoming smile had a veil of sadness these days. She was worried constantly about her sons.

As they entered the Corelli house, Amelia and the young boy were greeted by the smell of pasta and beans soup and the energetic voice of Giannina.

"E chi e questo giovanotto? Who is this young man?" She asked noticing the famished face.

Giannina directed him to the washbasin and handed him a piece of soap and a towel. He washed dutifully and waited for instructions.

Signora Corelli entered the kitchen. She was surprised to see the thin boy standing shyly by the pantry.

"Buona sera!" She greeted him.

"Buona sera, Signora," he replied.

"Mamma, he is Renato Campobasso, he has been covering for his mother at the factory. I brought him over tonight to have something to eat."

"Bene, bene. Sit down. Welcome, Renato." Signora Corelli said automatically.

While Renato ate avidly Amelia and her mother went out of the room.

"I felt sorry for him, Mamma. His mother died a few days ago and he is alone. His father was sent to the front and he hasn't heard from him. Can he stay here tonight?"

"Yes, Amelia. He can sleep in one of the empty rooms tonight. But tomorrow I must go to the shelter and find out what should be done," said Signora Corelli.

"You won't take him to the orphanage, Mamma. Will you?"

"No, of course not. But we cannot keep a child in our house without advising the authorities, Amelia. He may have other family. We must do what is right."

"I understand, Mamma," replied Amelia, aware of her mother's anxiety.

Giannina came to the rescue. "For now, I'll take care of him. First, he needs a bath and clean clothes. Then we will see."

The young boy, Renato, confided to Amelia that no money had been paid to him yet. He had tried to ask Mr. Donato, the administrator who was acting in place of Mr. Tozzi. However, Mr. Donato would not see him. Amelia decided to take the matter into her hands and went to talk with the factory administrator.

"Signor Donato, this boy, Renato Campobasso, covered for his mother while she was sick and then she died. He tells me that he has not been paid for the weeks that he worked in her place."

"Signorina Corelli, the child is too young and he should not have worked here, in the first place. I can't afford to be fined by the inspectors."

"I see the situation and he will not come back to work. But I respectfully ask you to please pay him what is due to him. You must understand that he has no family left. His father is at the front and the boy has had no news from him," added Amelia.

"Signorina, this is not your business. Why are you getting involved?"

"Because I believe, Signor Donato, that he is entitled to his mother's pay, since he did the same job. Nobody told him that he couldn't work."

"Well Signorina Corelli, I cannot do anything about this. And I advise that you keep all this to yourself," the administrator added with annoyance.

"This is extremely unfair," said Amelia as Signor Donato turned around and walked towards his desk. "How can you do this?"

"Signorina Corelli, I certainly can! Even better, you don't need to come to work as of this moment. Look for another position somewhere else. I don't need a communist in this place. It's enough with the ones on the streets."

"Communist? What do you mean?"

"We have nothing more to talk about, Signorina. I have work to do." And in so saying he stopped looking at her and concentrated his attention on the stack of papers on his desk.

Amelia stood there in disbelief. She had just lost her job in her search for justice.

She walked out of the place not knowing how she was going to face her mother with the news.

She wandered through the snow-covered streets trying to think of something. It seemed that everything was going wrong. That winter she had seen children who looked about twelve years old or even less cleaning the snow off the streets. Why had Mr. Donato refused to pay the boy? She had heard that in the countryside there were children working with their mothers making rolls of barbed wire for the front. What made the factory any different? Amelia was distraught. Now she needed to find some work right away. Any work. She stopped at the pharmacy a few blocks away from her home. The owners had known her father and maybe they could help her find a job.

"Buona sera, Signor Morgatti!" Amelia said as she closed the door of the apothecary behind her.

From an early age she had been fascinated by the place –the glass containers aligned along the shelves with their mysterious contents marked by names written on stickers in beautiful, large script and the scales on top of the counter. There also was the big logbook where everything was written down.

"Signorina Corelli, how are you?' replied Morgatti. "It's good to see you. How is your mother?"

"She's well, thank you!"

"What brings you here? I hope you're not sick. Your Aunt?"

"No, Signor Morgatti, nothing of the sort. I was wondering if you know of any job or if you could use my help in the pharmacy."

"But, aren't you working at the pharmaceutical company?"

"Not as of today," she finished, almost afraid to be heard.

"What happened?"

"I will tell you, Mr. Morgatti, but not right now."

"Bene, Signorina. Actually, I could use some help every after-noon and evening. I cannot pay very much though. You know how things are... these days.

"What will I have to do?" Amelia asked.

"You will write down the orders and mixtures in the log, to start with. Once you gain some experience, perhaps you could do additional work," said Morgatti, kindly.

"Oh, grazie! Signor Morgatti!" Amelia felt like embracing the man.

"Your father was a good friend. I often think of him. His experiments and his work alleviated much pain and suffering. Well…! When can you start?"

"I can start right now, if you want me to," replied Amelia without flinching.

"Why not? I could use the help right away."

Amelia couldn't believe the outcome of that horrible morning. This was a miracle. And at the back of her mind was the realization that she wouldn't be seeing Signor Tozzi anymore. Signor Morgatti explained the workings of the pharmacy and Amelia proceeded to hang up her hat and coat and put on the white apron and white cap she'd be wearing in the pharmacy. She washed her hands thoroughly and with reverence opened the logbook. The lines and columns became poetry.

All through the afternoon she wrote down names of balsams, inhalants, potions, tonics and poultices. People came in and spoke with Morgatti. Some had medical prescriptions in their hands and others just asked for remedies. She was so involved in her work that the hours passed unnoticed. When Morgatti announced that it was time to close, Amelia was surprised. Now she could face her mother.

"A domani, Signorina Corelli!

"Till tomorrow, Signor Morgatti and thank you very much."

Luisa Corelli had gone to the government offices to find out what she could about Renato's family. Two weeks later the reply had arrived from Pavia. His father had died at the front and, as far as the landowners knew, there was no other family that could take the boy in. So Luisa, Amelia and Giannina decided that Renato could live at the house, at least until the war was over. Renato went to school every day and in the evening he delivered medicines for the Morgatti Pharmacy. When Amelia was too busy in the pharmacy and could not return home in the early evening, he would read to Aunt Lina.

One evening Luisa heard Renato crying softly. He had been reading De Amici's *Cuore* to the old Aunt and one of the stories had touched him. The Corelli family had given him shelter and love but he missed his father and mother deeply.

"May I come in?" said Luisa, knocking on his door.

"What did I do to make them die?" was his anxious question.

"Renato, you did nothing. I know it's difficult to accept death," said Luisa placing a hand on his shoulder. "But we learn to live without the people we love and we go ahead."

"But why did they die? Could I have done something?"

"Of course not, Renato. We would like to have an explanation for death, but there's none. We live and we die. Life isn't fair. It takes away good people, young and old," Luisa paused. "I know we cannot replace your father and mother but remember this is your home and you can stay with us for as long as you wish. We all care a lot for you."

"*Grazie!*" Renato replied deeply moved. He was only thirteen but he realized that he had found the next best thing to his parents. Amelia, Signora Luisa and Giannina were now his family. Aunt Lina, in her confusion, thought that he was Giannina's son who lived in the United States and kept asking him about his life there. Amelia and Luisa took care of the boy guiding him and helping him with his studies and Giannina took him under her wing teaching him most of her cooking secrets.

Renato was an example of the harvest of war.

CHAPTER TWENTY

At the beginning of his voluntary service, Roberto was assigned to the hospital trains. These trains were furnished with first aid equipment and travelled back and forth between the front and the big cities where the hospitals tried to cope with the large number of wounded soldiers. But as the city hospitals became crowded the government installed emergency country hospitals close to the front.

At first, Roberto was sent to Padua. From there he was constantly moved to smaller towns close to the front. There he provided first-aid treatment to the wounded and then moved them in the least painful way towards the various hospitals in the cities. But as the fighting intensified the wounded had to be treated inside the trains and in tents. The first aid workers were not able to place them in city hospitals.

"*Documenti!* We need documents" urged the medical supervisor.

"They are going to Bologna."

"Bologna? Impossible! They can't take them there. No more spaces in the hospitals."

"Fast! Come on!" They could see the man was bleeding heavily.

"Dio! Oh God!" Uttered the young soldier searching with his hand for his missing leg.

The orderlies had nothing to ease the pain. They applied bandages to stop the bleeding but nothing else was at hand. Roberto ran towards the railway station to try to get more supplies. He almost knocked over an elegantly dressed man who stood in the middle of the platform.

"What on earth?" Shouted the man.

"Sorry!" Said Roberto hurriedly.

"Roberto? It's me, Tozzi."

"Signor Tozzi, I apologize, I have to get some first-aid supplies."

"There are no more bandages," shouted one of the carriers coming out of the building. "They are out of everything."

"How is it going, Roberto?" asked Tozzi as he pointed to his own insignia.

"Colonel Tozzi! Sir, I'm sorry! We're having a difficult time. There are no medical supplies. Things are getting worse by the hour, as you can see."

"What am I to do?" retorted Tozzi, making a hopeless sign with his hands. "I send what the government asks for. I don't know how they distribute the supplies." But Roberto knew that Tozzi was aware of every movement and had absolute power over the supplies and their distribution. He just chose to close his eyes.

"With due respect, Colonel, we could use more first aid supplies and food."

"Well, my orders are to hold on to the food and supplies for bad times," said Tozzi. "After all, this is war, not a picnic."

"These are bad times, Sir, the worst," replied Roberto. "We don't have medical supplies, nothing to relieve pain. The soldiers are hungry and have no ammunition. How can they sustain?"

"They don't have to sustain, they have to attack. They are a bunch of lazy, disorderly cowards," argued Tozzi.

"Sir, they have no ammunition. How can they attack?"

"With their bayonets!" answered Tozzi.

"Sir? Colonel," said Roberto as he saluted and hurried away from the platform before he'd do something that he would regret. He was shaking with anger. He couldn't believe what Tozzi had said. His cruelty permeated his polished demeanor. How far could he go? Probably very far! He had friends at all levels of government and no shortage of money.

Roberto walked to the back of the station and leaned against a wall bending his head.

"Cigarette?" offered another first aid worker.

"No, thank you!" replied Roberto. He was infuriated. No matter how much he tried to stay away from Tozzi, the man always reappeared unexpectedly at the top and in control.

Carlo

It was now late autumn and the evenings were getting cold in the mountains. The war that had been expected to last a few months was now in its second year for the Italians. The rumors were that the soldiers were ill equipped and that the government was not providing enough food and munitions for them. The offensives had to be conducted climbing the mountains while under direct fire and with little armament.

In some areas of the front line, the fall had come like every year and the valleys had rendered excellent fruit crops.

The shelling from the Austrian side stopped and some alpine soldiers went down from their strongholds to the empty town and enjoyed the fruit. The town had been evacuated and only one or two farmers had stayed in the hope of converting the fruit into money to be able to move away, far from the front. But the soldiers had little money. They were stationed up in trenches and *caserme* excavated in the steep, rugged rocks and were only trying to forget the war for a few hours. The autumn rains had drenched their duffel coats and their blankets provided no warmth. Only exhaustion enabled them to sleep. Life had been constant misery and suffocating in its closeness, when they had to sustain the presence of death companions in the trenches until the first aid carriers arrived to remove them.

Carlo was hoping to shake off the feeling of despair that had plagued him in the last while. He attempted to write to Eva and to his mother but he couldn't concentrate.

"*Signor Capitano*, do you want to come with us to the *casa rossa?*" asked the sergeant.

"No, no," answered Carlo as he pretended to write.

"You're too much in love. Not good for you. Soldiers need relaxation."

"Truly, no thank you," replied Carlo, trying not to sound impatient. The men were happy to have some time away from the shelling and go to the barn provided by the government, that doubled as a bar and brothel. "Enjoy yourselves!"

To go and drink with women who were desperately trying to sound happy would depress him even more. Life had been dismal in the last while. There had been several days with almost no food. The men, short in ammunition and strength had defended their posts bravely, only to find at the end of the battle that their small victory had cost the lives of many comrades.

The Austrian offensive had been relentless and although Carlo's group was partly protected by the rock formations, they had been ordered to come out and charge against the enemy. The sound of the grenades and bombs exploding as they advanced blindly, grated on their nerves. They only hoped to strike the enemy before they were killed.

Some got entangled in the barbed wire that lapped at them like a merciless wave of thorns. They screamed in pain and if they couldn't cut the wire fast enough they fell over the razor sharp spears receiving frontwards the relentless impact of the enemy machine gun fire. The sight was enough to immobilize the steadiest of soldiers. At the end of the attack the results were disastrous and the number of casualties was appalling.

The whole thing is madness. Carlo reflected on the trust that they, as soldiers, had deposited in their superiors and how harsh the discipline had become –anyone suspected of desertion was shot by the military police without court martial. The commanders gave orders from a distance, unaware or indifferent to the conditions that the men had to contend with. They were unconcerned about the futility of gaining a few meters of terrain.

And in the cities the situation was getting worse. Carlo had received two letters from Eva that had left him with an uneasy feeling. Anti-war demonstrations had paralyzed Milan for several days and there had been riots about bread distribution. It was evident that the government had underestimated the cost of the war in lives and money and its effect on the economy.

The alpine voices were almost silent. Some angry men had put new words to their songs –words that ridiculed the generals and the orders from the high command.

"Don't think so much, Signor Capitano," said the sergeant finding Carlo still awake when he returned.

"This war was to be over in a year. Just look at us now," said Carlo somberly.

The sergeant was smoking a pipe and the sharp scent of the tobacco reached Carlo's nostrils. It was good to smell the smoke of tobacco instead of the fumes of burnt gunpowder.

CHAPTER TWENTY-ONE

Cesare

When Cesare had arrived with his company hauling mortar cannons, machine guns and ammunition, it had seemed impossible that the enemy could cross the mountain range or the river. The alpine troops had rolled out barbed wire around the brush and dug trenches. All of these obstacles and the rock formation would offer protection from shells and cannon fire.

Cesare had embraced the idea of battling in the mountains because he was to be surrounded by the natural beauty of the area. Many nights he had sung the alpine songs together with the rest of the company, harmonizing and dreaming of love and honor.

Now, two years later, Cesare stood in his army helmet with his rifle slung over his shoulder. The forest of spruce and fir directly in front of him was a wasteland and smoke was filtering up between jagged tree trunks that stood like spears ready to rip through the sky. The villages perched on the mountainsides were now abandoned and their chalets and chapels half-destroyed. The bramble and brush were now cinder and ashes.

Cesare's eyes saddened. All the beauty of this place had vanished. His nostrils flared at the smell of the burning forest below. Narrowing his eyes he tried to detect enemy movement on the other side of the river.

"Anything moving, Signor *Tenente?*" whispered one of the men called Baretta.

"Nothing." Cesare shook his head, tormented with the agony of waiting and guessing when the attacks would start.

"It's too quiet, but they're there… the bastards!" said Baretta.

"For sure."

"Do you think they are tired of fighting?" asked Baretta.

"They must be."

"Then, why do they continue?"

"They don't have a choice," replied Cesare. "Like us."

But what was the point? The land was useless now. Cesare had stared all afternoon at the valley down below, now full of craters.

"*Café e pronto,*" the camp cook's voice was heard saying.

"I'll bring you some, Tenente," said Baretta. He left and returned with coffee, hard bread and cheese.

"Baretta," said Cesare as he sipped his coffee. "What did you do before the war?"

"I used to make cheese, ricotta and pecorino."

"Really? Where are you from?"

"Busetto. *Conosce?* Ever been there?"

"Of course! Verdi's birthplace!"

"Small place," said Baretta. "Not too many people know Busetto. How come you do?

"I used to bicycle around that area with my brother and a friend. We went to Brescia, Bergamo and even Cremona, where I bought a violin."

"A violin!" exclaimed Baretta excitedly. "Do you play, Tenente?"

"I haven't played for a long time," said Cesare, "but, yes, I do play."

"Good! I may accompany you on the accordion, when we return home, Capitano."

"Yes, that would be nice, Baretta."

The two men fell silent. Baretta thought about his town. Cesare thought about the Saturday nights when he played the violin, with Amelia at the piano and Roberto and Carlo sang. Those times seemed so far away and so long ago.

Two years of fighting on a daily basis had eroded any sense of wellbeing. His company had fought from the trenches and from the *caserme* where they had felt unbeatable at the beginning. But the mortars and the artillery had hit them hard and the fall weather had left them cold, wet and edgy. Winter was around the corner. Now, their officers had warned them about surprise attacks. Small enemy groups silently had stormed two alpine posts and while the troops were involved in returning enemy fire, they had thrown hand grenades and gas bombs inside the trenches with horrible results for the Italians. The attacks had been fierce and unexpected.

Cesare and his group were worried. The heavy fog was making it impossible to distinguish any movement and the light rain masked the sounds of steps. Four soldiers who had been playing cards were now quiet. Cesare and Baretta walked back and forth silently patrolling the sleep of their companions, making an effort to hear every sound in the mountain and feeling quite vulnerable.

Suddenly there was coughing and shouting in the gallery behind the rocks.

Cesare and Baretta ran to the entrance.

"What's happening?" Cesare shouted as he entered the protected area trampling over blankets.

"*Dio Aiuto!* God! Help!" Men were convulsing as Cesare and Baretta tried to pull them out in the open.

"*Fuori!* Out! Get up! Out! Out!" shouted Baretta.

Cesare tried to pull another man out of the *caserma*. His eyes were watering and soon he was coughing violently. He could see

Baretta shaking uncontrollably, but couldn't move to reach him. Cesare realized that it was gas and that he would not be able to help the others for much longer. As he pulled out another man his body collapsed and he fell to the ground.

After a few minutes all coughing had stopped. The place was silent and the killing gas had done its deadly deed.

Roberto was assigned now to an area close to the mountains where the bigger houses and the barns had been turned into country hospitals. These *ospedaletti* provided medical care for seriously wounded men who could not be moved anywhere else. Many were just waiting for death.

"Slow down," said Roberto to the other carrier. "We must try to avoid any bouncing of the stretcher. He's in terrible pain," he whispered as he nodded towards the man they were carrying.

"We can't cope with so many," said one of the nurses as they entered the *ospedaletto.*"

"What do you want us to do?" answered back one of the bearers.

"Stay calm," said Roberto.

"How can I?" The carrier answered. "Just look at that!" he added crying at the sight of a wounded soldier whose legs were severed. There were moments when the emergency staff could not handle the sight of the dismembered bodies.

"Come on," said Roberto taking him out of the *ospedaletto.* "Let's get something hot to drink. You're freezing!"

It had been a hard day. The two doctors and the nurses could not treat so many wounded men but Roberto and his team could not stop to consider that, they just kept arriving with their despairing loads.

"Sometimes I try not to see," said Roberto to the other carrier. "Because if I do, I could end up screaming, cursing the war and the generals... everything. But that doesn't help the wounded. We have to instill hope. They are terribly scared already."

"Is that why you sometimes sing to them?" Asked the carrier.

"I guess so. That's the only thing I can give apart from taking them away from the battleground," said Roberto.

"I'm sorry, I just couldn't take it any longer this evening," said the carrier as they entered the small building where the indefatigable Red Cross volunteers served soup and coffee.

"You have had a difficult week," said one of the volunteers. "Sit down for a moment and have something hot. This rain can make you cold to the bones."

Roberto had heard that newspapers had reported the Italian army as having broken through enemy lines during October, but that was not evident to anyone close to the front; at least not in the area where he was posted. The *infermieri*, as he and his first aid team were called, had been going up the mountains without rest and a high percentage of the soldiers they had carried back were dead. There were so many that a group of soldiers had been ordered down from their posts to dig graves for their fallen comrades. The burial grounds kept growing and lines of crosses stood like sentinels guarding the resting place of the soldiers –the last chapter of their story.

It was a rainy afternoon when Roberto walked towards the place where the chaplain had arranged a table to carry out a funeral service for all the dead soldiers. The sound of shelling and explosions could still be heard in the distance.

"Could you please sing something for these men," the Chaplain said as he finished the last prayers and stood in front of the lines of freshly dug graves. Roberto's voice soared under the light rain as *Dona Nobis Pacem* spread its message. In groups, the alpine soldiers joined in the singing of the old hymn. To say goodbye to the fallen comrades they sang *Il Testamento del Capitano*. The doleful voices resonated through the cliffs and bluffs of the Dolomites followed by the sound of shovels and falling earth.

Before sunrise Roberto and his team started their work again. The rain had stopped but the early morning was heavy with fog. A light wind brought a foul smell that made Roberto think of rotten fruit. Strange that after so many days of heavy fighting, the sounds of shelling and firebombs had stopped. Perhaps the enemy was too tired to attack. The troops would be sleeping heavily after days and nights of continuous battles.

Roberto and his team walked up the mountain in silence. He was thinking about the suffering he had witnessed in the last while. The days and nights they had spent carrying men to the medical posts. At times they could not differentiate between humans and matter. Between the mud and the pieces of rock and shrapnel and the limbs that sometimes were scattered on the ground. They had loaded limbless bleeding bodies onto their stretchers, unable to distinguish the living from the dead, except for the agonizing groans. He often had to make a tremendous effort not to emit a cry of horror when a soldier was so hurt that he wished him death. He then tried to sing a peaceful song to ease the soldiers' pain and to choke the hatred in his own heart. He understood less and less the need for war. He knew that the country hospital was running out of supplies, especially morphine for the dying soldiers. There was no means of alleviating pain.

Despite their weariness, Roberto and his group plodded up the path to the trenches and the *caserme*. There was an eerie silence –no moaning or shouts. At this hour, with the heavy fog and without their calls for help, it was difficult to locate the wounded. He walked carefully in case there were sleeping soldiers. He tripped over someone on the ground and expected to hear a groan or an angry voice. But there was only silence. His heart was pounding. He entered the gallery behind the rock formation following the steps of the carrier in front and bent as he felt a human form on the ground.

"Fuori! Out! Get out!" The first carrier shouted. Roberto pulled himself up from the ground and backed out of the gallery feeling his mouth and throat burn. He staggered into the open air

coughing and vomiting. He leaned against the outside rock, sliding to the ground.

"Stand up! Keep your head away from the ground!" Roberto could hear someone shouting as he continued to cough violently. They all had a sudden urge to lie down but the carrier who had stayed outside shouted forcefully: "Stand up, for your life! It's gas!"

Once they had calmed down, the carrier who had not entered the gallery said: "There's no movement inside, looks like nobody is alive in there."

All the carriers were still standing against the rock when daylight uncovered the magnitude of the tragedy. The men on the ground were motionless and quiet. Now the carriers had to enter the gallery to take out the rest of the men. The only way was to use their military caps as breathing masks. They wetted them with their own urine, put them in front of their nose and mouth and entered the *caserma*. They worked in silence for a long time pulling the bodies and placing them in the open. Roberto proceeded to check for any sign of life. There was none. Then, as they were leaning against the rock to recover from the effort, every carrier heard Roberto's hoarse scream:

"Cesare! Cesare, no!" He was shaking a soldier lying on the ground.

His dear friend was on the ground with his right hand holding the top button of his tunic as if he were trying to pull it open. Roberto could only imagine what his friend had gone through during the last seconds of life. Tears were running down Roberto's cheeks thinking of Cesare and his company confronting the silent killer.

He thought of Signora Luisa and Amelia getting the news of Cesare's death. *What a waste! What a terrible waste! Damn this war!*

Roberto took hold of himself. He embraced his dead friend and kissed his forehead. The carriers were shocked at the sight of some of the contorted bodies and at how close their own end had been. Although they had sore throats and could hardly talk they continued to move bodies down the mountain for the rest of the day.

They had been told that later that day, the neighboring alpine company had mounted a ferocious counteroffensive against the enemy. They had run up the mountain with hate-filled hearts shouting *"Maledetti!"* They screamed against the Germans who had now joined the Austrians on the eastern front. Emperor Franz Joseph had forbidden the use of gas by his troops but by now all armies were using it. That attack offered no consolation to Roberto and his group.

At the end of that terrible day the doctors in the country hospital forced all the carriers to rest. They were sick and had great difficulty breathing and swallowing. The doctors diagnosed "Acute Bronchitis and throat infection." Roberto could not make himself heard so he asked for a piece of paper and pencil and wrote: "I want to be present at my friend's burial."

An English chaplain who had just arrived in the area to help asked if Roberto would sing an Italian hymn for the dead soldiers, but although he was present, he couldn't sing or talk. The service was carried out with the English chaplain reading and then singing "The Lord is My Shepherd."

For a couple of days Roberto and his team rested on cots in the open, well covered with blankets. As they got better they returned to their dismal work with hoarse voices and weakened bodies. Roberto kept hoping to wake up one morning and hear his normal voice, but this was not happening. His voice continued to be hoarse and often he would suffer from coughing spells. People were getting used to his rasping voice but he couldn't get used to it and he was desperate to sing again.

CHAPTER TWENTY-TWO

Amelia

Signora Corelli was given the news of Cesare's death in person, by an officer. He had brought with him the insignias and other personal belongings. Signora Corelli couldn't utter a word while the officer was there, but the moment she closed the front door she couldn't contain her pain. Her handsome and cheerful young son had been killed in his beloved mountains. Giannina embraced her as Luisa Corelli sobbed uncontrollably. "Oh, my son, my Cesare!"

When Amelia came home that evening Luisa managed to control her grief but something seemed to have died inside her. She saw the devastating effect that the news had on Amelia. Her daughter had cried for hours over Cesare's alpine hat and his belongings.

"She did not protect him, Mamma!" she exclaimed as she took the small medallion of the *Maddonnina* that she had given to Cesare; the little leather pouch still intact. "Why? Why him? Damned war!" She said sobbing.

Her brother and best friend was no more. She loved her brother Carlo very much but between Cesare and her there had been a quiet understanding. They both had felt that emptiness that their father's death had left. It was with Cesare that she had let out her sorrow, unchecked and raw. He had done the same with her, thus the special bond between them.

"He fought for us and for our country, my child!" Said Signora Corelli that night, when she was able to say something. "He will always be with us."

"Who will play the violin, Mamma?"

"Oh, my child!" said Luisa Corelli embracing her daughter suppressing her own grief.

Both women forced themselves to continue with their lives but there was an evident lack of purpose in their daily activities. Only Giannina kept the home in order, forcing them to eat regularly and protecting them from further anxiety. Renato tried to be quiet and inconspicuous. He imagined his presence would make them sadder. Amelia noticed his reticence and tried to reassure him. She also mustered the strength to continue her work at the pharmacy. Signor Morgatti was understanding and was great moral support to her.

But Luisa Corelli could find no relief or consolation. In spite of Giannina's efforts and Amelia's loving concern, Luisa was retreating into her own separate world. She was now distant with the friends and family who had come to visit her. She was almost uncommunicative. She was not able to shake away the feeling that all this was a nightmare and that soon she would wake up to the real world where Cesare was alive. Waiting for that to happen, she talked very little and barely answered when she was asked something. She had not reacted when Aunt Lina had died. Amelia and Giannina took care of everything. Luisa's condition was now a serious worry for them.

"I think we should ask the doctor to come and see her," said Giannina.

"I will go over to his office today, Giannina," said Amelia, hoping that the doctor wouldn't charge too much.

"We'll find some way of paying him," said Giannina reading Amelia's thoughts.

After careful evaluation the doctor recommended for Signora Corelli a fortnight of rest and treatment at the thermal waters center of San Pellegrino.

"How much would we need to pay, doctor?"

"I'll try for the lowest rate," said the doctor.

That evening Amelia opened her little treasure box and got out a gold chain and a bracelet. She could get good money for them. With that she would be able to cover the costs of her mother's stay at the health clinic.

When Signora Corelli arrived at the Terme, she was put under the care of a nurse who helped people suffering from depression. A week later Luisa Corelli was integrated into a group of women who had lost their sons or husbands in the war. She was unresponsive at the beginning but some of the stories reached the depths of her generous heart and eventually she found herself giving support to others. Together these women worked out their deep sorrow, their pain and their anger.

When Amelia picked her up two weeks later, Luisa's demeanor was one of sadness, but acceptance.

"Poor Aunt Lina," she said then. "I wasn't with her, in her last moments. I never understood how much pain she went through when her only son died. No wonder she became bitter."

Aunt Lina had been dead for several weeks and although her temper wasn't missed, they all felt compassion for her.

"She's in peace now Mamma," said Amelia and perhaps with her son and her husband.

The reduced Corelli family found some consolation in Renato. He was a considerate boy but with him at home the economic situation was getting worse because he was a growing boy in need of food and clothes.

Amelia worked long hours at the pharmacy and the constant disturbances on the street kept her mother on edge until she was back home in the evenings. The currency had been devalued and most things were in short supply. Giannina, however, went to the market almost every day and observed that no matter the currency devaluation, there were always well-dressed women out shopping, accompanied by maids and chauffeurs. They seemed to have a lot of money to spend.

The Corelli house had no more boarders, the rooms were empty and the first floor had spaces that nobody was using except for Amelia, when she played the piano. There were no more visitors. No one had the time or money.

Amelia was surprised to hear Giannina say one evening: "Signora Luisa, why don't you turn the first floor of the house into a dressmaking workshop? You and I can become seamstresses. You used to sew beautiful gowns, I remember. I'm good at stitching and embroidering."

"Where do you get these ideas?" Luisa smiled.

"That's a marvelous idea!" Said Amelia who knew that anything that could infuse some interest in her mother's mood would be good.

"Well, I see all these well-dressed ladies at the market. No shortage of money. Even in these terrible times, they still attend balls and receptions. They have reunions and they dress up for all those occasions.

"Oh Giannina," said Luisa, "I don't think I have the energy to deal with those people."

"Yes, you do and you will when you become more fully aware of your financial situation," replied Giannina. During the time that Luisa had been shattered by her son's death, Amelia with Giannina's help had taken over the household accounts. To protect Luisa from worries they planned the purchases in the evenings, without telling her. But now, in Giannina's opinion, things had to change. Amelia knew that her salary was not enough and although she wished to protect her mother, she also wanted her to be involved in something worthwhile.

And so it was. Luisa, Giannina and Amelia made plans to open a small sewing business. The first floor of the house was converted into a dressmaking workshop of *haute couture.* For the first time in their lives, the three women spent hours looking at some fashion magazines that Giannina had bought at a substantial amount of money. She had said it was their investment. They created a comfortable and efficient environment. Renato proved invaluable bringing down the sewing machine and moving furniture. The dining room table was set up as a pattern drafting and cutting area. Amelia saw the change in her mother and was grateful to Giannina for her entrepreneurship.

At first, Giannina only told other housekeepers about the business. They could do alterations to dresses or make new ones. Eventually she invited the ladies to come to the *atelier* and look at the new fashion styles that women were wearing in the United States, in England and in France. The ladies had seen famous actresses like Mary Pickford and Lillian Gish in the movies and wanted similar outfits. Even in war, men and women of means followed the fashion.

At the beginning the women ordered simple garments but as they came to see that the two women were extremely good seamstresses they ordered dresses, suits and gowns of the latest Poiret styles. They brought their own fabrics –silk, wool, velvet and the new material called jersey, which they managed to buy through their husbands' connections.

Luisa and Giannina created garments, which were easy to wear. The clients found them comfortable and stylish. They wrapped themselves in the beautiful new dresses and suits when attending official ceremonies or banquets. Soon the workshop was busy and the couturier business started to grow.

Amelia helped in the evenings but, as the workload increased, Luisa hired two seamstresses. The women were happy to have a job outside of the munitions' plants.

The great pain of Cesare's death did not diminish but the women were busy trying to make a living and there was little time to be sad during the day. Only the night brought the darkness of grief.

CHAPTER TWENTY-THREE

Tozzi & Amelia

When Fausto Tozzi returned after a few months from his trip to the front, he was upset not to see Amelia in the offices.

"Where is Signorina Corelli?" He asked Mr. Donato.

"She's gone," replied the other curtly. "She had problems."

Tozzi didn't want to appear too obvious and decided to go to the Corelli house.

He was surprised to find a small *"Haute Couture"* sign beside the entrance. He rang the bell and was greeted by Giannina, who was not happy to see him.

"La Signorina Amelia?" He asked taking off his hat politely.

"She's not in," replied Giannina. "She's at work."

"At work?" Do you know where she works?" Tozzi asked trying to sound casual.

"No, I'm sorry."

"And Signora Luisa?" Tozzi persisted.

"She's busy with a client."

"I see you are now in the dressmaking business. Is it going well?" asked Tozzi.

"Yes," replied Giannina, becoming impatient, "even in these hard times some people have money to dress up."

"Kindly tell Signora Corelli that I came by." Tozzi said.

"Very well," Giannina replied curtly.

Tozzi had time to think. He had seen Roberto at the front and decided that the young man would never amount to anything. He was obviously not interested in money since he had opted to volunteer in the Red Cross instead of staying with him, in his profitable business. By the time he came back from the war, he, Fausto Tozzi, would have conquered Amelia's love. She was beautiful and reserved and he was looking for a change. He was tired of frivolous women who were mainly interested in his money. He wasn't looking for marriage either, just for a long, informal relationship. Why not?

A year and a half had passed since Roberto's departure. The Corelli family had received one letter at the beginning and then nothing else until about three months after Cesare's death. In that last letter Roberto had explained that by chance he had been present at Cesare's funeral in a cemetery close to Belluno. It was a warm letter in which he had expressed his deep sadness and offered his sincere condolences to Signora Luisa and Amelia. He had given some details about the ceremony but had said nothing about the manner in which Cesare had died and how he had found him. That was terribly painful and it could wait.

Amelia thought about Roberto constantly. There was only one photograph of Roberto with his family in the room that was still waiting for his return from the war. In the photograph he was a very young man. He probably looked different now, especially with the war. Amelia always cleaned the room and when she did she looked longingly at the beloved face for a very long time. She couldn't forget him.

There were two letters waiting for him one from his brother and one from his friend, Clara Gillespie. Amelia guessed that they probably had to do with the fact that the United States had declared war on Germany. It seemed that more countries were now involved in the conflict. France, England and Italy were waiting anxiously for the arrival of the American troops.

Every evening when she walked back home from the pharmacy Amelia glanced rapidly at the newspaper stands to find out about the front. It was on a cold and rainy evening when she walked across the Galleria Vittorio Emanuele, hoping to hear some cheerful music from the restaurants that were always well attended, when she heard people shouting: "Incredible!" "Shameful!" People were arguing and gesticulating as they read the newspapers. There was no music, only the sound of angry voices echoed from the beautiful walls of the Galleria. *Il Corriere* announced in big letters that the Italian Army had retreated from Caporetto. Amelia bought a newspaper anxious to read about the happening. As she was paying the newsstand attendant and was trying to read beyond the headlines, someone said:

"*Buona sera, Signorina Amelia!*"

To her dismay, in front of her was Fausto Tozzi, extending his hand and smiling with that calculated style that she so disliked.

"What a pleasant surprise to find you here," he added.

"Good evening, Signor Tozzi!" *Of all the places she could have chosen to buy a newspaper, she had stopped here...*

"Please permit me to accompany you home. People are quite excited about the defeat at Caporetto. The streets may become dangerous... you never know..."

Amelia couldn't say anything and just tried to walk as fast as possible.

"I see your mother has opened an atelier of *haute couture*. That must be a good business. Women always require beautiful gowns," he added lightly.

"Not all women, Signor Tozzi. Some are having an extremely hard time."

"Signorina Amelia, could I ask your mother if you might accompany me to the theatre? You could wear one of her creations. I have seen them now at receptions, quite a unique style!"

"You don't need to ask my mother, *Signor Tozzi*. She lets me make my own decisions. And I'm sorry, but I don't want to go out anywhere while the war is on. My brother Cesare died a few months ago and Carlo is still fighting at the front. Please forgive me."

"But life has to go on, *Signorina Amelia*."

"Maybe for you Mr. Tozzi, but for us life has changed. It can never be the same," she replied. They had arrived at her house and she opened the door without asking him to come in. "Good bye, Mr. Tozzi! And thank you for accompanying me home."

Amelia let herself in and closed the door behind her. She was shaking.

CHAPTER TWENTY-FOUR

The late autumn with its drizzle and damp cold drenched the exhausted armies in the mountains. But the Italian units, although greatly diminished in number and arms, found the spirit that would save them in the end. They had sustained tremendous battles and hand-to-hand combat had become a fierce and common occurrence. The dead and the seriously wounded were left at the mercy of the rain and the cold until the *infermieri* were able to transport them. Many soldiers were taken prisoner and shipped to camps in Hungary.

The Italians had fought alone against the Austro-Hungarian army, which was now strongly supported by the German army. After the disaster of the Battle of Caporetto when enemy storm troopers fired gas canisters and confusing orders caused a massive retreat on the part of the Italians, the government appointed General Armando Diaz. He was a well-respected commander who was able to instill faith in his soldiers. They fought the battles that followed with renewed strength and zealousness, bringing Italy ahead in the war.

The fourth Italian army staged a furious assault on the Grappa massif and was able to prepare the ground for the units that followed. The twelfth army, which was Carlo's division, fought their way up the Piave River and were able to cut off the Austrian communication, prompting the beginning of the end as the Allies finally sent their divisions to assist the front lines in northeastern Italy.

On the 3rd of November, Trieste fell to the Allies and the Austrian and German Armies started their retreat.

On the 4th of November of 1918 the Armistice between the Austrian-Hungarians and the Italians was signed in Padua.

On the 11th of November of 1918 the Armistice between Germany and the Allies was signed in Paris.

Soldiers of all ranks and companies –*alpini, bersaglieri, fanti* – descended from the Alps and the Dolomites and crossed the rivers in the thousands.

"La Guerra e finite. Andiamo a casa.!"

Yes, war was over and they were going home, after three and a half years of continuous battles and senseless destruction and death. The columns of men walked orderly trying to keep the pace but found it difficult to lift their feet with energy. No more was there the thunder of boots upon the ground that had been heard when they had climbed the mountains three years before. Now, with just shreds of leather left to them, the men trudged along the slippery, muddy road trying to muster enough strength to keep going. They were malnourished and only the thought of a bed to rest on and something hot to eat could infuse some hope.

The displaced farmers and mountaineers still alive, returned to their towns eager to find out the extent of the damage left by the war. They greeted the hungry soldiers with cheers and applause and ringing bells. It was at this point that the Italian divisions became aware of the enormous feat that they had accomplished. The town folk celebrated the end of the war by sharing whatever they had with the exhausted soldiers who, for the first time in months, were able to enjoy a restful sleep.

Bringing the last of the wounded to the country hospitals was an arduous task. The large number of soldiers moving through the same mountain paths made it difficult and slow.

Many of them were almost blind and walked unsurely, their eyes covered with bandages, and holding on to one another.

As he carried the men to the ambulances, Roberto could not silence his inner anger. *Would the powerful regret their actions? How many deaths had they caused on all fronts? What had they accomplished?*

Milan

Amelia was bent over the log book writing when, all of a sudden, the pharmacy windows rattled with the surge of sound and music coming from the street. Amelia looked up and Signor Morgatti stopped his work too. They looked at each other.

"What's that?" they exclaimed, as both rushed to the entrance and opened the door. Unbelievable.

People of all ages walked or ran waving Italian flags and chanting: "War is over! *La Guerra e finita! Viva l'Italia!*" Newspaper boys could hardly make their way to *Piazza Duomo* as men and women came out of stores and houses stopping them to buy *La Stampa or Il Corriere.*

Morgatti was already reading. "Signorina Amelia! It's over; the war is over!" He was so excited that he embraced her and danced in front of the pharmacy. What a joyful moment! Amelia was in tears as were many of the people walking by.

Motorcars, bicycles and open trucks moved slowly down the avenue filled with youths, women and children shouting: "Viva l'Italia! Viva l'Italia!" The children blew cardboard trumpets and whistles and the drivers honked their horns adding to the clamor. On a large cart pulled by horses there was a group of older men singing *"La Leggenda del Piave"* in perfect pitch. It was a huge victorious parade making its way to Piazza del Duomo.

"We're closing the pharmacy right now," said Morgatti. "You rush home Signorina, this is a historical moment!"

"Grazie!" said Amelia as she put on her coat and hurried out the door.

"Till tomorrow, Signorina. *Auguri!"* Said Morgatti as he placed the closed sign and locked the door.

Amelia almost ran home, cutting across the crowd that grew by the minute. The joyful voices echoed on the old buildings and the cobblestones of the medieval part of town. It was cold but the people were not only waving flags but also their hats, berets and scarves. They had waited a long time for this day.

When she finally arrived home, Amelia found her mother and Giannina standing at the entrance of the house mesmerized. People were pouring out from every house and every street corner to go to the center of town. When Luisa saw Amelia she opened her arms and both were locked in a long embrace, soon joined by Giannina. The three of them cried silently wishing this moment had happened before Cesare's death.

"Let's go inside," said Luisa. "I'm suddenly tired."

Amelia knew that her mother was experiencing mixed emotions, like her. They were happy that the war was over and that soon Carlo and, maybe Roberto, would be home, but Cesare would not.

"Mamma, we have to get ready for Carlo's arrival."

"Yes, my dear!"

"Well," said Giannina, "all this calls for a good dish of *pasta asciutta.* Renato should be home soon. Schools will be closing early today, for sure."

The whole country was energized by the news. Church bells rang non-stop during the day, for days, lending the cities and towns a festive feeling that could not be shared in the same way by the families of the dead soldiers or by the soldiers already back from the battle grounds who would be facing a life without limbs or sight or other disabling conditions.

Two days later a *Te Deum* was celebrated at the cathedral and all around the city the various churches and the synagogues opened their doors to people to give thanks for the end of the war.

"Should we prepare Roberto's room too?" asked Giannina.

"Yes, we can, but we don't know if he'll be coming back soon," said Luisa.

Amelia was quiet; they had no news from Roberto.

Soon after the celebrations several ladies came to the workshop. They needed new gowns. The President of the United States was expected to visit Milan after Christmas and the Mayor of Milan would be hosting a reception, a banquet and an opera performance at Teatro La Scala.

Luisa, Giannina and the two helpers, Loretta and Rosa, worked feverishly for days. It was exciting to have so much work and to know that the outfits would be worn for the special festivities.

They heard the firm steps at the front entrance. Their hearts stopped. The bell rang and Giannina ran to the door. Carlo poked in his head and said: "Is this the famous fashion design atelier?"

Giannina embraced him and signaled inside the room. Luisa was standing by the sewing machine looking at him in disbelief. She opened her arms, which filled in a second with the tall and now thin frame of her older son.

The built-up-tension of three years came out in a rush of emotion.

"Carlo! *Figlio mio!*" She said as tears rolled down her cheeks.

"Mamma! Mamma!" He cradled her tenderly.

"They didn't feed you well, I can see," said Giannina squeezing his arm.

"This my son, Carlo!" Said Luisa to Loretta and Rosa.

They both replied in unison: *Piacere!"* Carlo made his way through the tables and the sewing machines and shook their hands cordially.

"You go ahead Signora Luisa, please," said Loretta, "we will finish the last two dresses. Don't worry!"

Luisa and her son walked arm in arm into the next room that was used now as dining and sitting area. Carlo couldn't stop smiling.

"Mamma, it's so wonderful to be back home! The atelier looks fantastic! Are you happy with it?"

"Yes, Carlo, as happy as I can be. It has been a great economic help. It was Giannina's idea, you know?"

"Really? Giannina, you should teach at the Commerce School. It would do us much good," he added smiling. "Mamma, at what time does Amelia get home?"

"Not before seven. They are quite busy at Morgatti's these days."

"And you, Mamma, how are you really? I wish I could give you strength and wisdom but I don't know what to say. I was stunned when I received your letter telling me about Cesare. I was so sad! I often wonder how I made it back. So many men died. What a terrible waste of lives! At times I felt so angry... I was glad that Cadorna was replaced. General Diaz was good with the troops and King Vittorio Emanuele came around the front often. They were encouraging sights."

Luisa could not reply immediately. She dried her tears and shook her head sadly, Imagining the life that could have been if the war had not started.

"When Amelia comes back tonight tell her about the end, when you were sure that the war was over. I'm worried about her. She looks sad. I think she misses Cesare and Roberto a lot," said Luisa.

"Yes, Mamma, I'll talk to her. We'll talk about the future. Cesare would have preferred that."

"And what about you? What do you plan to do?"

"First thing, I will go to the bank and find out if they have a job for me. Once I know, I will decide."

"I hope you can find something. It will be good for you, my son. But, don't you want to rest for a few days?"

"No Mamma, not now. I can rest or take a short trip later, maybe when Eva and I get married, if she still wants me. You know Mamma, we wrote to each other often but we haven't been face to face in more than three years. Maybe she has changed and would like a different life. I know I have changed..." Said Carlo.

"We all have changed, my son, but if you love her and she loves you..." she added as she stood up and kissed him on the head. It was a miracle he was alive.

When Amelia returned from the pharmacy, the household was engulfed in mixed emotions. There were tears of joy, sadness and hope.

"Amelia, *Cara!* You look so grown up and so beautiful," Carlo said after a while.

"Oh Carlo, I'm so glad you are back!" She said still crying and hiding inside his embrace.

The evening at the Corelli home was full of tender and sad moments as they recounted their experiences of the past three years. Renato was introduced to Carlo. The young lad had transformed himself into a well-spoken youth who could assist in the kitchen and prepare a good meal out of very little. Giannina was responsible for that. She treated him like the grandson she didn't have. His son, who had gone to "America" and had married in New York, had two daughters whom Giannina had never met.

Amelia wanted to know about the front and Carlo tried to comply. He left out the painful moments. He talked about the bridges they had to build in haste to cross the Piave River –the old bridges had been destroyed by bombs. He told them about the Red Cross and their amazing work in the front.

Carlo knew that Roberto had been assisting with the dead and wounded but he didn't know that he had been present at Cesare's funeral. It was a very sad moment to imagine.

When they recovered, Carlo said to Amelia: "Tomorrow I'll walk with you to the pharmacy and say hello to Signor Morgatti."

"He'll be happy to see you, Carlo.

Emotionally exhausted the whole family went to sleep that night, thankful for having Carlo back at home.

As they walked the next morning, Carlo asked Amelia about her work.

"It's good. I like it very much and Signor Morgatti is a very kind person."

"But you wanted to study. I hope you can do that now, Amelia."

"I don't know... maybe I should continue working. I'm learning here too and I don't know if I have the mind to study for three years."

"Of course you do. We all are tired as a result of these years of terrible tension and economic stress, but studying chemistry was your dream and you should try to follow it," said Carlo. "Remember what Father used to say. As for the mind, you have it! For sure!"

"It's nice of you to think that, Carlo."

"Now, tell me, have you had any news from Roberto? I didn't want to ask you in front of the others, last night. Is he all right? Do you know?"

"He wrote to us saying that he was staying to work at the *ospedaletto* until all the wounded were in better condition or were transferred to permanent hospitals, but we haven't heard anything more.

"Are you disappointed?"

"What do you mean?"

"You know what I mean. I know that you are in love with him."

"But, is he in love with me?"

By the afternoon Carlo had secured a position at the Bank. They needed staff. He was in high spirits and went directly to visit Eva. Signora Rivarolo, her mother, opened the door.

"Carlo! *Che gioia!* Welcome back! Come in, please! Eva, Eva!" she called.

"Look who's here!" Carlo wanted to run up but waited at the bottom of the stairs filled with anticipation.

"Carlo!" Eva said lovingly as she came down. If he had doubts about her love, they dissipated when he saw her expression. She looked as lovely as ever, just a bit thinner, as he was.

"Cara! Mia Cara Eva!" My dear, dear Eva! You look more beautiful than ever!"

"Oh Carlo, my love!"

They kissed and embraced under the pleased smile of Signora Rivarolo. They would not have done that in front of her before but times had changed and she was happy for them. They went out of the house arm in arm and walked and talked and had coffee, still made out of roasted *cicoria,* and planned. By the evening they had set a date to get married and they were delirious with joy.

That evening when the family was together Carlo told the news. They were all happy for him. It would be a small ceremony and it would take place in May.

December was a busy month for the workshop. All the gowns on order were to be ready before the end of the month. President Woodrow Wilson was to stop in Milan for the New Year's celebrations before proceeding to Paris to sign the Peace Treaty.

On the 5th of January 1919, the whole of Milan poured unto the streets to cheer the American President and his entourage. People shouted calling him: "Saviour of Humanity," "Angel of Peace," and wished all blessings on him and his family.

The motorcade arrived to Piazza del Duomo, where Wilson, the man of the moment, waved and saluted the Milanese from the balcony of the Royal Palace. This was the largest and most spontaneous crowd ever to have greeted an American President. More than fifty thousand people waved and cheered for hours. It had been impossible for Carlo and Renato to get closer to the palace to catch a glimpse of the President and his wife and daughter, up close, but they were happy to have been there and to have seen them at a distance.

That night the American President, his family and dignitaries attended a Gala performance of the opera *Aida* by Giuseppe Verdi, at the Teatro La Scala.

The war was over but the economic situation in Italy was still difficult. The government had incurred tremendous debt to sustain the war effort. Food shortages continued, but there was much work in the medical and pharmaceutical fields.

One evening Amelia arrived home with exciting news. "Mamma, Signor Morgatti has offered me a full-time position at the pharmacy. There's a lot of work to be done for the hospitals now.

"That's good Amelia! That shows that your work is good. But, I've been thinking that you should go back to school to pursue your chemistry studies. Carlo and I were talking about that yesterday," said Luisa.

"Mamma, I want to help. I don't want to cost money," replied Amelia.

"My dear, we have the possibility at this moment. God knows what tomorrow will bring. Carlo and Eva will come to live here after they marry. That will be a great help. The top floor will become their apartment."

"But what if Roberto comes back? Where will he stay?" She said, looking at them anxiously.

"He can stay in my room," said Carlo. "I won't need it anymore."

"Maybe he will go back to Mexico," interjected Giannina.

"No, he won't go back to Mexico without saying good-bye to us, Giannina, said Amelia, almost in tears.

"Ehh! Who knows? War has changed everything."

"I will write to him and ask if he would sing at our wedding," said Carlo.

Amelia's expression changed. "That would be lovely," she said.

She was terribly sad that Roberto had not returned. She didn't know what to think. His last letter had given her so much hope but after that, nothing. She wanted to live again the happiness she had experienced during the few weeks before Roberto had left to volunteer in the front. She was scared because her father had died when she had felt closest to him and so had Cesare. Now she was fearful that she had lost the man she loved.

CHAPTER TWENTY-FIVE

The wounded were slowly being placed and the work was far from finished. Roberto had stayed in the *ospedaletto* close to Pordenone to assist the medical officer, Dr. Antonelli and his staff. The makeshift hospitals were still crowded with sick and wounded men and everybody worked to the limit of their strength. The war was over but for these men a private war continued.

In the country hospital Roberto watched the mutilated bodies in disbelief, trying not to think and hoping that whatever he was doing would relieve some of the pain. Yet it was nearly impossible to remain serene and untroubled. The chaplain came around to dispense the last rites to dying men, but Roberto could not bring himself to pray with him.

He couldn't sing either. His voice was mute. He had not been able to sing since the fateful morning when he had found Cesare and the members of his patrol dead from poisonous gas. That eerie silence still rang in Roberto's head.

With the winter season Christmas arrived, bringing a renewal of hope. Once more the *zampognari* played their bagpipes and recorders. Roberto remembered that he had heard the sound of these wind instruments for the first time in Genoa upon his arrival in Italy. So much had happened in those eight years. The voices rose from the small chapels in the mountain towns to celebrate the birth of the *Bambino Jesu* and it grieved Roberto not to be able to sing.

Spring 1919

After the country hospital work was finished and the sick and wounded had been transferred to official hospitals, Roberto arrived in Padua. He wanted to have a private consultation with Doctor Antonelli and ask his opinion about the sore throat, the hoarseness and the breathing problem that had not gone away. He had intended to ask him about it when they were in the country hospital, but there had been so much to do and the doctor was so overworked that Roberto had thought it inconsiderate to bother him with his complaint.

"*Professore, come va?*" Said Roberto as he entered the doctor's office.

"Roberto, *che piacere!* I thought you would have hurried to Milan after we closed our country hospital," said Dr. Antonelli, shaking Roberto's hand effusively. "I have missed your helpful hands."

"Thank you doctor, you're very kind. How are things with you?" Asked Roberto.

"*Bene, bene.* My wife is well, slowly getting over the death of our son."

"Your son? He died?"

"Yes, at Conca di Plezzo. I couldn't talk about it. How can we talk about a dead son or a friend when surrounded by dying men? You know how it feels."

"Oh *Professore,* I'm so sorry!" Roberto said, thinking that during those days Cesare's death had occupied his thoughts entirely and he had been blind to the deep sorrow that Dr. Antonelli was experiencing. "There was so little time to talk at the *ospedaletto...*"

"I guess we mostly talked about the conditions there, about the emergencies, about the lack of medication. Strange that we spent so much time working together but we seldom talked about ourselves. In those situations you get to know people on a different level, their ability to work under pressure, their energy, their compassion. Seldom do you get to know about their own lives, their feelings," said the doctor.

"I learned a lot about myself during that time. I learned to hate," said Roberto.

"Hatred doesn't cure the wounds or the damage, Roberto. It is more of a burden. We must do the best we can while we're alive."

"I guess you're right, Professore," said Roberto, making an effort to appear calm.

"Things here... well, they are not so good. Medical supplies are slow coming and medicine production is also slow. Some of our people did not return and we are short of medical staff. We don't know if they were killed or if they are prisoners of war. All this will take time to sort out. I believe that life will go back to normal but it will never be the same as before."

"I know doctor. Going through some of the towns I spoke with people who hadn't heard from their sons or husbands or brothers or friends. Maybe they will never hear from them. Lost or killed, unidentified. They may never know."

"War does that," said Dr. Antonelli. He now had a scar on his left eyebrow, caused by ricochet fire. "I made an agreement with God that if I survived all this I would continue to treat people and operate until the end, and I'm still here. But I would have preferred my son to live, instead of myself."

Both men fell silent. "Well," said the doctor, placing his hands on his knees and standing up. "Let's talk about other things. I imagine you're here for a reason. Do you want a job in the hospital? The door is open for you!"

"Not really, doctor. You probably noticed the change in my voice since I was sick in the mountains. I still have that cough and

I'm short of breath. Whenever I try to sing I get a sharp pain in my throat and almost always I end up coughing violently," said Roberto.

"Do you cough up blood?"

"At times."

"Let's see," said the doctor. He heard his lungs and then he pushed down Roberto's tongue with a flat rounded depressor. "Hmmm.., I'm going to hold your tongue with a piece of cloth. Just be calm." And a moment later, he added. "Finished!"

"*Allora Professore?* What do you think? Can you give me something that will improve the cough and stop the pain?" asked Roberto.

"I would like you to be seen by my friend, Dr. Sasso. He specializes in the respiratory system. Is that all right with you, Roberto?"

"Yes doctor, of course! Thank you!"

"Let's go down to his office. Come with me."

Dr. Antonelli and Roberto walked down the hospital corridors until they reached Dr. Sasso's office. They knocked and went in.

"Fortunato, good day! This is my friend, Roberto Madariaga. He assisted us at the *ospedaletto* and he seems to have some throat and respiratory problems. Would it be possible for you to examine him?"

"*Ma sicuro! Avanti!*" Come in, Signor Madariaga," said Dr. Sasso shaking Roberto's hand. "What seems to be the problem?"

Roberto explained his symptoms and added: "At first, I thought it was tiredness. We were working non-stop and the weather was bad in the mountains. I had bronchitis at one point. But I have been in the city for a few weeks now and it still hasn't cleared and I'm not able to sing."

Dr. Sasso washed his hands and proceeded to inspect Roberto's throat for a long time. He then listened to his chest and tapped his back and asked Roberto to breathe in an out several times.

Then he sat down to give his opinion.

"Your throat shows signs of burning and your lungs don't have a clear sound."

"Burning?"

"You mentioned that you sing. Is that right?" Asked the doctor.

"Yes, but I'm finding it impossible now," replied Roberto.

"Most certainly, it would be. Your larynx has suffered severe damage."

"I'm sorry! Could you repeat that?" Roberto almost jumped off the medical table.

"Roberto, just listen," said Dr. Antonelli who had remained in the room.

"Many unexpected medical conditions have arisen as a consequence of exhaustion and malnutrition during the war," continued Dr. Sasso. "But this is different. Were you exposed to any direct explosions or fire during the conflict?"

"Well, there was one day when the explosions were continuous and fire was around us as we were carrying the wounded, but no fire ever touched my head or chest."

"Were you exposed to gas?"

"Yes, but for just a moment."

"Go ahead," said Dr. Sasso.

"We were walking up the mountain early one morning. It was dark but we knew we had to move wounded men from a gallery behind the rock formation. When we went in there was only silence. We couldn't see anything. The carrier at the front started shouting to get out and we immediately went out. We couldn't have been inside more than ten or fifteen seconds," said Roberto shaking his head at the memory. "It was horrible! Minutes later I found my dear friend Cesare, lying on the ground dead. Everyone was dead!"

"I'm sorry about this," the doctor paused. "Unfortunately," he added gravely, "ten seconds of gas exposure can damage the respiratory system and from what I can hear when you breathe, your lungs may have suffered damage as they are not working at full capacity."

"That much I had suspected but what about the rest?" asked Roberto trying to control his impatience.

"A tiny amount of poisonous gas can do a lot of damage, longer exposure means death. Its use in combat is an abomination," said the doctor, avoiding the impending truth.

"How long do you think this condition will last?" asked Roberto.

"Signor Madariaga, unfortunately, this is a permanent condition," said the doctor patiently. "It may improve a little with time. However…"

"But that's not possible. I'm a singer, an opera singer. There must be a way, maybe surgery?" Roberto started pacing back and forth, his hands crushing an invisible enemy.

"*Calma Roberto,*" said Dr. Antonelli, as he put a hand on Roberto's shoulder.

"Signor Madariaga, you are a friend of Dr. Antonelli and I imagine he has also checked your breathing and he knows. That will probably improve in time, but I would be lying if I said that the throat and the vocal cords could go back to their original condition through some sort of treatment or operation. Maybe they will get a bit better, as the healing tissue forms, but they will never be the same. I am so sorry to have to tell you this!" said the doctor.

"Are you absolutely sure, doctor?" Roberto asked as he rapidly envisaged his dismal future.

"I am. But perhaps you should consult another doctor in Milan."

There was a moment of difficult silence in the room as the three men took in the meaning and the implications of the diagnosis. Finally, Roberto stood up to leave.

"Thank you, doctor," he said seriously, pulling out his wallet to pay for the consultation.

"No, please! Nothing at all!" Said Doctor Sasso gesturing to Roberto to put his wallet away. "I'm really sorry, Signor Madariaga." He shook his head as he went back into his office and closed the door behind him.

Roberto and Dr. Antonelli were silent as they walked back through the same corridors.

"What am I going to do, doctor?" Roberto finally said.

"Roberto," said Dr. Antonelli. "I know this is a shock for you. I can't begin to imagine what you feel, but try to calm down and think what you can do. I would like you to come and see me in a couple of days. We will talk. Remember that when life closes one door, it can open another. I really do believe that."

"Yes, Dr. Antonelli," said Roberto in a low voice but he wasn't really listening.

"Promise me that you will come," the doctor said as he opened the front door of the hospital and shook Roberto's hand. "In three days? Yes?"

"I will. I promise," replied Roberto rushing down the entrance steps not knowing where he was going or what he was going to do. He really didn't care.

CHAPTER TWENTY-SIX

The shock of the diagnosis left Roberto in an agitated state. He walked for hours in a daze, impervious to the stealthy glances of the people who could see the bewildered look on his face.

What am I going to do?

By the evening his despair had turned into an agonizing wish to die. When he was a teenager a friend of his had told him that he wanted to die and Roberto hadn't understood his feelings. He had talked with him until very late at night, hoping that his friend would change his mind. The next day his friend had left town and had never contacted any of his classmates again. Nobody knew if he was alive or dead and Roberto understood now.

The ghost of a dead opera singer kept coming to mind. What would his parents say or feel? They wouldn't know. They had died. Nobody would know who he was, except for Dr. Antonelli.

He arrived at the *pensione* where he was staying certain that his life was about to end. He lay down and begged for death to come. He closed his eyes and travelled to the distant past when he had decided to be an opera singer. He had gone against his father's wishes and had pursued that dream. It had not been an easy road but he had even had a taste of success. Now it was over. He had left the revolution and the fighting in Mexico only to involve himself in a bloodier and deadlier war in Italy.

For the next couple of days he scarcely moved inside his room. Still ready to die, he rejected the coffee that was brought to his door in the morning. He wouldn't even allow the chambermaid to come in to clean the room.

Nightmarish visions of innumerable dying men assailed his mind. They were desperately calling for help, while he looked on unable to move them or assist. Then he was marching to the guillotine trying desperately to sing the final duet of *Andrea Chenier* but no sound came out of his mouth. He would wake up covered in cold sweat and struggling to breathe.

The owner of the *pensione* pounded on the door and opened it.

"*Signor Madariaga, ma che cosa succede?*" What's happening? I'm calling the doctor, right away."

Roberto tried to make a feeble negative gesture with his hand, but it fell beside his body.

"Roberto!" Dr. Antonelli exclaimed upon his arrival, alarmed by Roberto's appearance and blank expression. "I'll take care of him," he said to the owner gently pushing her out of the room. He opened the window and rapidly gathered up Roberto's belongings, most of which were unpacked. He was still dressed as he had been when seeing Dr. Sasso.

"You are coming with me right now, Roberto!"

The doctor could see that the specialist's diagnosis had been a tremendous blow for the young man. How would it be for him to lose one of his hands? Dragging his feet Roberto got to the ambulance that the doctor was driving. He slumped on the seat and stared blankly out of the window while they travelled through the streets of Padua. Groups of men were laying bricks repairing buildings damaged during a bombing raid. The men stopped their work and waved at the doctor's ambulance, but Roberto was unmoved.

The hospital was still overcrowded, so Dr. Antonelli took Roberto to his home.

"The war is over, Roberto," he said as he drove. "We are alive and we have to rebuild our lives, refashion them and find alternate paths."

Roberto kept looking out the window thinking *I will never sing again*. He didn't have the strength to answer Dr. Antonelli. He just wanted to sleep forever.

"You must drink this," Dr. Antonelli said, putting Roberto into bed. Roberto complied out of respect, but could not bring himself to eat anything or to talk.

Signora Antonelli cooked every day but the appetizing smells did not change Roberto's demeanor. He was silent, almost morose. The doctor was patient. During the evenings he sat beside him and talked about his work in the hospital. He told him he was pleased that he was staying with them.

His wife was content to have someone to care for and to talk to, although Roberto wasn't always responsive. Signora Antonelli had asked him very gently about the places where he'd been, about the war, the battles and the wounded. And out of respect, but reluctantly, Roberto had talked about where he had been. In turn, he had learned about Dr. Antonelli's young son and about his death, which had left a terrible emptiness in the parents' lives. Why was he alive instead? His parents were dead and he didn't want to live now, not like this. He had carried so many men who had wanted to live... and had not.

One day, as Signora Antonelli was listening to the radio in her kitchen, the sound of Caruso's voice singing "Celeste Aida" reached Roberto's ears. He was sitting in the room he now occupied, looking out the window. Against his will his eyes filled up and his body started to shake. He was choking with tears and sadness and sobs.

Nobody had come to his room during those endless minutes or hours –he didn't know– when he had allowed his grief to pour out. All the operatic characters that he had hoped to sing one day marched in his mind like a procession of unattainable heroes. He knew that he had to let them go.

From that moment on, he listened to the doctor's words every evening when he came home and slowly his desire to live was restored. One morning he got up and asked Signora Antonelli if he could work in their garden.

For several days he raked, cleaned and dug, making the place ready for planting. The smell of freshly turned earth filled his damaged lungs. He then remembered the day when he had planted the vegetables with Amelia. The thought of her hit him like lightning, filling him with an indescribable sense of loss. He thought of the marvelous feeling of love and desire experienced that afternoon while he knelt beside her, aware of her beauty and of the love in her eyes. He desperately wanted to be by her side, but not like this.

He had not returned to Milan after the end of the war. He could not face the Corelli family and talk about Cesare. He didn't want to tell them how he had lost his voice and, yet his loss was nothing compared to Cesare's life.

While working in the garden his childhood enjoyment of the land was awakened. *Could he be a farmer?* What was he thinking? How could he buy the land? He didn't have a *lira* to his name. He was twenty-nine years old, his operatic career was over and he didn't have anything. How could he carry on with his life?

"How about becoming a doctor?" said doctor Antonelli one evening.

"A doctor? At my age?"

"Why not?"

"I'm too old, *professore.*"

"One is never too old. Look at me. I study and learn every day. And you? You're thirty years younger. You were good at the *ospedaletto* everybody noticed it. The nurses thought you were a skillful assistant."

"But I have no money, Dr. Antonelli," replied Roberto suddenly conscious that he had been living off the doctor's kindness. He urgently needed to find some work.

"You volunteered during the war and that could help us find a scholarship to cover the university fees. The hospitals are short of staff and the country is committed to training future doctors and surgeons. People of all ages are retraining in every field. What do you say, Roberto?" He gazed intently into the young man's eyes, hoping for an affirmative answer. "You could live in our house and help us with the garden, plant vegetables. You could also drive the ambulance when you don't have classes," the doctor went on. He was very fond of Roberto and it was good to have someone around to fill the vacuum his son's death had left.

"All this seems so strange, so different from the life I had planned for myself, Doctor, I don't know. I'm out of sorts."

"Look Roberto, most great things are achieved when we attempt what seems impossible. You may think that it's preposterous to study medicine at twenty-nine. But if you look at it from the point of view of a seventy-year old, twenty nine is not even half a lifetime."

"Do you really believe I could be a good doctor?" asked Roberto.

"I do, or I wouldn't be considering it, my son. You like to help people and you have what it takes. To remain calm in the face of serious injury or death is a rare quality. And to be able to go on when extreme fatigue hits is a discipline. You possess both. Maybe there is a reason for you to have ended in the *ospedaletto* working with me and the other doctor."

"You mean, like destiny?"

"Maybe…"

While he was caring for the wounded Roberto had thought many time that to be a doctor was a venerable profession and he had enormous respect for the nurses and for all the people who worked under those difficult circumstances. However, he was satisfied with his singing future and it never occurred to him that it could terminate the way it had. Everybody's favorite sentence at the front was: "When this war is over…"

"I'll think about it, Dr. Antonelli. I'm most grateful."

"Why waste time thinking about it Roberto? Why not simply say yes and do it?"

Then seeing a spark of hope in Roberto's eyes, he added. "You may have a good future in medicine. It's a different area of study, of course, a new field." Then the doctor added: "I guess you could become a different kind of opera musician, if you wanted, a composer, a director… But please think about this. There is a great future in the medical world and I would be terribly happy if you would become a doctor."

"Thank you, again, Dr. Antonelli." Roberto went out and walked for several hours. *Could he ever be happy in the opera world, without singing? He would not be able to coach the opera singers. He had not study composition and, he knew, that he liked to hear and interpret the music of others, he might not have any ability as a composer. He liked being with people. A composer needs silence.*

The next evening Roberto gave his answer: "I'm ready, Dr. Antonelli. I think I would like to be a doctor, hopefully a good doctor."

The doctor didn't waste any time.

"The important thing now, Roberto, is to study for the admission exams. The School of Medicine is one of the oldest in Italy and they receive many applications every year. It won't be easy. You must study diligently. I will leave the volumes I have on anatomy and physiology for you. Were you any good at chemistry? Refresh your knowledge. There will be long written examinations and endless interviews with many questions to answer. You will be asked to identify the bones, muscles and organs of the different body systems. You will have to name the chemical components of body fluids. I'll be here to help you with your queries every evening but it will be your effort and dedication that will get you through," said Dr. Antonelli. From that moment on he would adopt a professorial attitude towards Roberto.

"How much time do I have?" asked Roberto looking at the books that the doctor was placing on the table as he talked, positively excited at the prospect of having a new student in his life.

"Three months. No time to think about anything else if you want to be accepted."

Roberto had been depressed not knowing what he could do for a living. Now he had to study but he had no money. Maybe he could teach piano, or Spanish for a few hours a week, but who would have the money for that after the war? He had considered being a carpenter, since he knew how to do the drawings. He also thought about becoming an architectural assistant or a bricklayer. But his interest for anything had died with his voice. This was the first time that both his heart and his mind had become engaged. A medical profession was something that he would not have considered on his own, feeling it was completely out of reach due to his age. Dr. Antonelli had hit Roberto's poetic and productive nerve.

"I'll try my best, doctor. Thank you so very much."

Every day, early in the morning Roberto sat down to study at home. In the afternoon he went to the university library. He tried not to think about music and he made an effort not to listen when Signora Antonelli turned on the radio. He made big drawings of the body systems and whenever his mind began to wander, he forced himself to look at them and to memorize them. Sometimes in the evenings, he would walk around the park for a few minutes to clear his mind and think of other things. He had no money to go to a café so he hadn't made any friends. His whole being was now concerned with learning. Life was giving him this opportunity and he had decided to take it. Often he was tempted to walk by the Verdi Theatre but he forced himself to avoid the area.

"We'll be going to Milan," said Dr. Antonelli one morning, "a friend of ours has bought a motorcar and there's room for one more person, Roberto. Would you like to come with us and maybe visit your friends?"

"Thank you! Maybe next time," replied Roberto.

He still couldn't face the Corelli family. He needed more time and he didn't want to think about opera before the examinations. Besides, he was grateful that Dr. Antonelli had opened his house to him but he couldn't accept any more favors from them. He was now committed to this path and had to give it his very best effort.

A few days before the beginning of the exams he thought that he was having trouble remembering the medical terms and instead, opera arias kept intruding his mind. He thought he was going crazy.

When Dr. Antonelli returned from the hospital one evening, he found Roberto extremely agitated.

"What's wrong, Roberto?"

"I don't know professor. I'm having trouble memorizing. I feel sick to my stomach all the time."

"Hopefully it's only nerves and not something else. I've been told that some hospitalized soldiers in Milan are exhibiting disturbing symptoms. Let's hope it's nothing of the kind," the doctor said.

Finally the examinations came and Roberto completed the whole series. The experience left him exhausted but he had managed to finish. Now, he and Dr. Antonelli had to wait for the results.

What would he do if he didn't get accepted? Doubts started tormenting him. Then he would have to become an apprentice in carpentry or masonry. There was quite a bit of construction taking place in the city. He could go back to making drawings. Or, as a last resort he could retrain in accounting, for which he had developed an aversion. He now associated that work with disaster. To cope with those days of anxiety he went to an architect's office in search of drafting work. There were carpenters sawing and sanding long pieces of wood rhythmically. The smell of the shop was pleasant.

"We have some workers who don't read Italian. It would help them a lot to refer to tri-dimensional drawings with measurements. Do you think you can do that?" The architect asked Roberto.

"I can certainly try," replied Roberto. "I used to do drafting for machine building and I think this is similar."

"It will probably take you only one or two days of work a week. Would that be enough for you?" the architect asked.

"I'm waiting to hear from the university. I finished the entrance examinations a week ago but I won't have the results for at least six or seven weeks and, if accepted, I have to wait for classes to start. I could work until September, unless I don't get accepted. Two days a week would be perfect. I drive an ambulance on Fridays and Saturdays."

"Well, that sounds good. See what you can do. The pay is low these days," started the architect.

"Anything will do," replied Roberto, happy to be able to contribute something to the Antonelli household.

While barely enduring the passing of the weeks by working in the garden, drafting and driving the ambulance, Roberto received a letter from Carlo Corelli announcing his forthcoming marriage to Eva and asking him to sing during the ceremony. The request felt like fire on an open wound. He stood there, reading the letter without moving. He realized that deep in his heart he had harbored some unrealistic hope to be able to sing again. He had wanted to wait until that moment before contacting the Corelli family. Now he could not hide from them anymore. They were his closest friends, his family now, and they had opened their home and their hearts to him from the beginning. He had to face them.

Carlo's letter had taken more than a month to arrive. It had been sent to the *ospedaletto* in Pordenone and from there forwarded to the Red Cross. The wedding was in six weeks.

He sat down to write to Carlo. He told him that unfortunately he couldn't sing but that he would be honored to attend his wedding. He tried to sound casual about not being able to sing and concentrated his writing efforts on expressing his good wishes for their happiness and his love and friendship for the whole family.

With Carlo's letter he received a forwarded letter from Clara telling him that she would be travelling to Europe, mainly France, sometime during the summer. She would visit Milan during the trip. Her uncle would also be in Europe, doing special work for the United States government.

She proceeded to tell him that she had converted to photography, just by chance and had learned to do the whole process, from taking pictures to developing them to final prints. She had seen the work of incredible photographers and wanted to follow that path. She had landed an assignment to take pictures while in France, for a magazine. An unexpected piece of good luck, she called it.

She was now living with a woman friend in Greenwich Village thanks to a monthly stipend left to her by Aunt Margaret, who had died suddenly of a heart attack. Uncle Spencer still lived in the Park Avenue apartment and she was thankful that he had been given an important mission in Europe. It was keeping him busy and didn't give him time to dwell on the loss of his wife.

"I still paint," she wrote "but I'm now committed to photography." She also explained that she had the economic freedom to travel and that she hoped to see the world and take photographs for magazines and books. She expressed high hopes of seeing him in Italy and also of meeting the Corelli family.

Roberto felt good about Clara's letter. They had corresponded for several years until he had left for the front. He had thought she would marry one of her rich friends, but instead she had become an independent woman who was following a dream. He admired her determination and realized that she did not feel for him anything more than deep and sincere friendship and he had come to understand that he felt much the same for her.

A couple of days before leaving for the wedding, Roberto was surprised by Dr. Antonelli's unexpected return from the hospital in the morning. As he opened the front door of his house the doctor exclaimed at the height of excitement: "You made it, Roberto! They have accepted you!" He embraced him and kissed him effusively.

"Oh Professore! I can't believe it! Thank you! Thank you so much!"

"And another thing," Dr. Antonelli continued, "you are to enter straight into second year. You see? Your work at the front and all the studying bore fruit. It meant something. And there's even more, you will receive a scholarship that will cover your university fees for as long as you maintain a high level of achievement in your studies." Dr. Antonelli finished telling the news and slumped on an armchair smiling. At last, something great had happened.

Roberto's excitement was almost uncontrollable. He felt like jumping and embracing Dr. Antonelli. "Oh Professor, I'll never be able to thank you enough for all you and Signora Antonelli have done for me. You pulled me out of despair. Without you I don't know what would have become of me. *Grazie, grazie infinite!* I'm forever grateful!"

He couldn't say anything more. He had a lump in his throat. He would have loved to tell his parents about this, about human kindness in the middle of tremendous grief. But no one was waiting to hear from him. His brother had gone to the United States and his sisters were living somewhere in Mexico. Roberto hadn't had any news from them since his brother's last letter, forwarded by the Red Cross at the front, informing him about his father's death. He was painfully aware that during the war he thought about them as if they were part of someone else's life. Since the death of his mother and then his father, his brother and sisters seemed remote, almost belonging to another time in another world.

Roberto felt now strong and in high spirits. He had a long road in front of him. It was a new dream, a very different one. He was excited about his trip to Milan, to see his friends again. He wanted to see and talk with Maestro Stracciari. He was the one person who would understand his situation more than anyone else. He hoped that he was healthy and still teaching.

His thoughts wandered towards Amelia. He tried to picture her after almost three years away from her. He could not. Only her beautiful dark eyes, full of love, seemed to be imprinted in his memory.

CHAPTER TWENTY-SEVEN

Amelia

I n Milan, Amelia was thrilled. Aunt Lucia, her mother's cousin
was coming to visit them.

Lucia Russo lived in Bologna and for years she had been
running a small leather goods factory on her property. Like the
Corellis, Lucia was making a living by dressing up the wealthy. She
had been a widow for many years and she had no children. She
was a fun-loving and colorful person. They hadn't seen her since
before the war and Amelia adored her and admired her style.

"Why don't you tell her to bring some of her purses and gloves?
Perhaps she can sell them to your clients," Amelia said to her
mother.

Aunt Lucia had a casual but business-like attitude developed
through years of dealing with the men who cured the hides that she
used to manufacture her creations. She had a vibrant personality.

"I will write to her immediately," said Signora Corelli.

The household was getting ready for Carlo's and Eva's wedding. For the last month two carpenters and a plumber had been

working to convert the third floor into a separate apartment. The place was taking shape and Eva was there almost every day sewing curtains and embroidering linen towels. Due to shortages of the many things that normally would be purchased, they were adapting existing household items from her parents' house and from Carlo's mother's house as well.

They were exciting days as they transformed furnishings to suit their needs. Everyone was enjoying the process. Having little money had made them quite creative.

When Lucia Russo arrived the Corelli family knew that they were going to be in a whirlwind for a few days. She brought with her the energy of someone who has plans for every single moment of the day. She loved the *atelier* and spent many hours giving ideas to Luisa and Giannina to lend the place a touch of modernity. She was talkative and warm and had the ability to find solutions, even for minor things.

Every evening when Amelia came home, they talked for hours as if they were lifetime friends. Amelia guessed that probably Lucia was lonely and her constant activity prevented her from feeling sad. Her days were absorbed by her work and she loved it. She had brought samples of her purses, belts and gloves. Luisa's clients had admired them and had placed orders.

But apart from very active, Aunt Lucia was a dream of an aunt. She was caring and also stylish. She wore her clothes with magic. She made her own dresses, loose, soft and simple with delicate embroidered details around the neckline and the sleeves. Luisa and Giannina were inspired and decided to present new styles to their clients together with Lucia's purses and gloves. When Lucia departed a week later, Amelia felt that she had lost a sister, but Lucia would return for Carlo's wedding.

Amelia was about to leave the pharmacy one evening when the door opened and Fausto Tozzi entered.

"Good evening, Signorina Amelia, Signor Morgatti," he said politely as he greeted the owner.

"Good evening, Signor Tozzi," said Amelia, her spirits suddenly dampened

"What can we do for you?" asked Morgatti, who knew who Tozzi was.

"Actually, I was hoping to accompany Signorina Amelia to her house, if she's finished for the day."

Amelia thought of saying that she had work to do but she had already put on her jacket and her uniform was hanging in full sight of Tozzi.

"Thank you Signor Tozzi. I have to rush because my future sister-in-law is waiting for me to help her."

"We'll walk fast," said Tozzi as he opened the door for her.

"Till tomorrow, Signor Morgatti," said Amelia.

"Arrivederci," said Tozzi. Morgatti didn't answer. He was concerned about Amelia having anything to do with the man.

Amelia walked so fast that Tozzi could hardly keep up with her, but he didn't want to waste any time.

"Signorina Amelia, I want to invite you to the opera next week. La Scala is presenting *Il Barbiere di Siviglia*. It promises to be an exceptional performance. And... please call me Fausto."

"I'm sorry, Signor Tozzi, I can't do that." She was upset. "And I'm grateful for your invitation to the opera but I cannot accept. Please forgive me." They were already at the street corner of her house. She stopped and turning around, faced him. "Kindly understand that I cannot go out with you."

"But why, Amelia?" She noticed that he had dropped the "Signorina" and her anger rose.

"Signor Tozzi, I don't want to go out with anybody. I love someone else."

"Ma che centra? So what?" He replied.

"I guess you will never understand my reasoning Signor Tozzi. Good night!" She said and rushed into her house. She nearly slammed the door but didn't.

Carlo was coming down the stairs and saw Amelia leaning against the door.

"What is it, Amelia?"

"Don't go out now, please," she said.

"What's wrong?"

"Oh, nothing!"

"Please Amelia, tell me," said Carlo seriously.

"That man! Signor Tozzi. He keeps inviting me to go to places. I don't want to see him or talk to him. I dislike him. I'm almost scared of him," said Amelia. "Please don't mention this to mother, Carlo." Fortunately Luisa was busy in the workshop and had not come out to the entranceway.

"I won't. I promise. Let's go upstairs and talk," added Carlo.

Eva was upstairs arranging some linen and kissed Amelia.

"Hello, Eva dear!" Said Amelia with little expression in her voice.

"Are you sick?" Asked Eva.

"No, just a bit tired," answered Amelia

Eva excused herself and left the apartment to allow brother and sister to talk.

"Amelia," said Carlo, "have you made your application for the entrance exams at the university, here in Milan?"

"No, not yet. I'm afraid I'm losing courage. They may not accept me."

"Don't think that way, please. I have an idea. Why don't you apply to the University of Bologna? Women have studied there for some time. Students and professors are getting used to having women in their classes. They are more progressive. Bologna is a wonderful city and you could probably live with Aunt Lucia. She likes you a lot and you like her too. Don't you?" Said Carlo.

"I do. But do you think mother would like that?"

"We'll talk to her. She may even think it's a good idea for you to go to Bologna."

It was clear to Amelia that Carlo was trying to be a good brother. She had always seen him as much older and serious, very different from Cesare, but now she was aware of how much he cared for her.

Luisa was a bit reluctant about the idea. "Amelia is too young to go away."

"Mamma, Amelia is a responsible and mature woman. It may be good for her to be away from us for a while. She will grow intellectually and will meet other people. Her life here has been limited to us, and the pharmacy. She has no friends her age," said Carlo.

"I guess you're right, Carlo. I still think of her as a little girl."

"If she gets accepted in Bologna, she can live with Aunt Lucia. They like each other very much and, something else, Mamma, universities always welcome their alumni's children. Father would have liked to see her study at his alma mater. Don't you think?"

"Oh, yes! He would have like that. I want Amelia to have a profession. I was lucky to have been left a house by your father to be able to get ahead. I also thought, once in a while that I would have liked to work as a teacher, or a librarian."

"Oh Mamma, I never knew."

"Well, when I was young I dreamed of finding someone to love and marry and I did. I was lucky! My parents never thought otherwise. That was what one was expected to do. They were happy for me. After your father died and my parents had died too, I had to face the fact that I could only be a governess for little children in someone else's house. I was not equipped to do any other type of work. That's when I decided to convert our house into a long-term *pensione.* That allowed me to run the house with the help of Giannina and to be with all of you. But few women are given that opportunity."

"So, you won't mind if Amelia has to live in Bologna, will you?"

"I will miss her enormously, Carlo, and it will be difficult not to have her around, but I know it will be the best thing for her," said Luisa. "Thank you, my son, for talking to me about this. We'll speak with Amelia tonight."

That night Luisa, Carlo and Amelia talked for hours. Amelia was both scared and overjoyed at the prospect. Now she had to find out about the requirements and start studying for admission exams.

Signor Morgatti was all for the idea. He encouraged her and immediately offered to accompany her to Bologna, together with his wife who could visit her sister, who lived there. Amelia felt that things were falling into place and immediately wrote to Aunt Lucia. Her prompt response assured her of a place to stay during the three years that it would take to earn a chemistry degree.

She submitted her application and was given the examination date. It was to be in May, a few days before Carlo's wedding. She really had to study hard and would miss all the excitement of the final wedding preparations.

"Look Signorina Amelia," said Morgatti, "from now on you can sit in the back room and study every day. I can call you if I need your help. Otherwise, you should just study. You should review your biology too, as it is part of the science examination. You have been a good assistant and I want you to succeed. My brother, as you know, has returned from the front with a disability. He'll be unable to work at his former position, but we're going to see if he can help me here. In any case, you deserve this opportunity.

Amelia was grateful. She studied day and night. She felt tense but focused.

In the meantime, Carlo received the letter from Roberto but wisely didn't mention anything to Amelia or his mother. He quietly hired a violinist and a cellist to play with the church organist during the ceremony and continued with the final arrangements. If Amelia was wondering about a reply from Roberto to Carlo's request to sing, she never said anything.

Three days before the examinations, Amelia arrived in Bologna.

"*Cara!*" said Aunt Lucia when she met Amelia at the train station, "Welcome! Your room is waiting for you, ready with a desk and everything conducive to study."

"It's so wonderful to see you, Aunt Lucia! Thank you for coming to meet me!"

It was a lovely day so Aunt Lucia hired an open carriage to take them home with the luggage. Amelia was able to see much more of the city this time. When she had come with Mr. and Mrs. Morgatti, it had been raining. Today, the city looked lovely with its splendid medieval and renaissance buildings and its arcades. By the time they arrived at Via della Brania, where Aunt Lucia lived, Amelia was captivated by the place.

She only had the weekend before the exams so there was no time to visit the wonderful monuments and palaces. After a delicious *pranzo* Amelia and Aunt Lucia went out to have a coffee at a nearby café. It was crowded with people of all ages, all involved in animated conversation.

"This is Bologna, my dear. I hope you like it."

"I hope I pass the examinations, *Zia*. I'm terribly nervous."

"Just learn to calm down. Tonight I will teach you some deep breathing exercises. A woman physiologist from the university gave a conference on the subject a while ago. I attended out of curiosity but I learned some things. The ability to breathe properly has helped me all the way. It becomes part of daily life. I use it even more when I feel lonely or when I'm dealing with difficult suppliers or clients. It's a wonderful tool."

Lucia rapidly showed Amelia her small factory and introduced her to the glove makers and the tanners. Amelia would have liked to talk with them and linger for a while but she had to study.

Her room was comfortable and away from any factory noise. She was able to concentrate even when she was tempted to look out the window and admire the small garden at the back of the house where a magnolia tree was in full bloom.

On Monday morning she entered the University of Bologna examination room the size of which was terrifying. Rows of writing tables were arranged from one end of the room to the other with wide aisles in between. Every examinee was given a place to sit. A professor stood at the front and told everyone to be silent. The papers were going to be distributed presently and everyone had to keep them face down until instructed to start. Everyone was silent. Only the sound of the paper touching the wood could be heard. The professor announced that the exams would last approximately three hours. Every fifteen minutes he would be writing the time left on the blackboard. When he finally announced that the exam papers could be turned over, several tutors or professors started walking slowly up and down the aisles between the tables observing and monitoring every movement.

Amelia was petrified, as everyone in the room was, but after a moment she remembered to breathe as Aunt Lucia had showed her and then concentrated on her answers.

By the end of the morning people were leaving the room quietly until they reached the courtyard and then they let out their nervousness. When Amelia came out, students were talking in fairly loud voices. "That was some exam!" "Now we have to study for the oral tomorrow. Good luck!" Gradually the courtyard became empty as the last students walked away from the imposing building.

"How did you do?" Aunt Lucia asked when Amelia opened the door.

"I hope well, but I'm pretty nervous about tomorrow."

"Did you remember to breathe?"

"I did. And you're right! It works!"

"Well, you just do the same tomorrow, every time before you answer. Now, let's have something to eat."

Amelia realized that she was famished. She hadn't eaten anything the whole day. After dinner Aunt Lucia practiced with Amelia science questions and answers. When Amelia started to answer, her aunt immediately indicated. "Breathe! Breathe before you answer. Don't forget." She paused to hear Amelia's reply and then continued. "Do you feel the difference?"

"Yes," replied Amelia, "somehow that pause gives me the time to think clearly."

"Do that every time," continued Aunt Lucia. "Don't allow the examiners to press you into speedy answers. That's the most important thing."

Aunt Lucia kissed her goodnight and wished her all the luck in the world for the next day.

Amelia tried her best. The oral examiners did not give the slightest idea of how she was doing, not a single hint. They just asked the question and heard the answers. At the end, they just said: "You will get your results in the mail."

Now Amelia would have to go back to Milan and wait for the university's acceptance or rejection.

"I'll see you at the wedding," said Aunt Lucia at the station, "and don't worry, my dear." But worried, Amelia was. The possibility of change had shaken her stable way of life, working at Morgatti's pharmacy and living at home. But she would feel dreadful if she were not accepted at the university. However, she was so tired that she slept all the way to Milan. Carlo and Eva were waiting for her at the station.

"I have news Amelia. Roberto is coming to the wedding." Without any warning, Amelia broke into tears, out of joy and out of the released tension of the examinations.

"That's wonderful!" She managed to say between sobs.

"He won't be able to sing. Because of some health concern that he will explain when he sees us. But I have engaged a violinist and a cellist to play with the organist; so don't worry! Now, tell us, how did you feel after you completed the exams? I know you won't get the results for a while, but are you satisfied?"

"I am. I tried my best! Now we'll see." She suddenly felt light and full of life. She would be seeing Roberto again in a few days. "Oh Carlo, Eva, I feel so happy!"

The three days before the wedding seemed interminable to Amelia. She ran to the door every time the doorbell rang only to encounter one of the workshop clients or a delivery person. The house had been set up for a small reception. Amelia was to arrange and decorate the tables while Giannina and Renato cooked and Luisa went around checking to make sure everything was in place.

Amelia entered the room. Her mother stood there in silence. She embraced her as Luisa said: "Your father would have loved to be present at the wedding," Amelia understood.

CHAPTER TWENTY-EIGHT

The train entered Milan's Central Station. Roberto felt the same thrill he had experienced the first time he had arrived in Milan. He had marveled then and marveled now at the sense of belonging that enveloped him as he walked out of the building and along the streets towards the *Scuola di Musica*. His heartbeat quickened as he approached the building, anxious to see Maestro Stracciari again.

Like years before, he knocked and waited. The same butler opened the door. A look of surprise transformed his aging face as he recognized Roberto.

"Avanti! Come va?" The Maestro will be delighted to see you."

"Grazie Antonio! It's good to be back!" Said Roberto shaking the man's hand.

"Roberto, you're alive! I had given up hope." Stracciari had visibly aged but his smile and his tears showed Roberto how much he had missed him. Suddenly he felt alarmed about the news he was to give him about his voice. The butler interrupted. "Should I bring some coffee, Maestro?"

"Yes, please! That would do us good, Antonio, and some Sambuca too," then to Roberto "when did you get back?"

"An hour ago, Maestro, I came directly from the train station."

"It's so good to see you! Do you have a cold? Your voice sounds different."

"I have something to tell you, Maestro," started Roberto as Antonio entered the room with the coffee and the liqueur. He set them down and left the room.

"Salute, Roberto!" said the Maestro raising the small goblet.

"Altre tanto, Maestro!"

"Now, what is it you were telling me?"

Roberto started his account. It was difficult for both men. Stracciari was deeply affected when he heard what had happened at the front. He was aware that nothing could be done.

"At least, you are here, Roberto, alive and able to do something with your life."

"I know that I'm lucky," said Roberto, "not only for being alive but also for having encountered people like you, the Corellis, and the Antonellis who have been there to help me. I wouldn't be here without all of you, Maestro!"

After a few minutes, the Maestro said: "Tell me, have you gone to any opera performances lately?"

"No, Maestro, not since I left for the front. It would be too hard to take, just yet."

"You're wrong, Roberto! You can still enjoy opera, even if you can't sing. You don't stop loving something just because you cannot have it. True?"

"I know, but it would be frustrating."

"Maybe at the beginning, but you shouldn't deprive yourself of the pleasure of music, the music that you love. Years ago when I realized that I was losing the endurance needed for opera performance, I turned to teaching. I still enjoy the music and find enormous satisfaction in witnessing the development of the students.

It's an unparalleled reward. I am proud of your achievements. That glorious time on the stage you will have forever. Teaching might not be possible, but don't cut opera out of your life. That would be a terrible loss."

The Maestro knew that it was going to be difficult for Roberto to see the Corelli family again. He had confided to the Maestro that he was afraid words would escape his mouth about Cesare's tragic death. He firmly believed that he was to tell them only about being present at his funeral.

"Stay here tonight, Roberto," said Stracciari. "The guest's room is empty. Antonio will prepare us some supper in a while. You can stay for as long as you are in Milan. You can play the piano if you want."

"I haven't touched a piano in three years, Maestro," replied Roberto "and I really don't want to impose."

"It's not an imposition, Roberto. I'm immensely happy to see you and this is the only thing that I can offer you now."

Roberto understood then that the loss of his voice was also a loss for the Maestro. He had now been robbed of something that he had helped to create and had hoped to see grow. It was sad for him too. Roberto accepted his hospitality.

Later in the evening, he sat at the piano and attempted to play. In the three years at the front his hands had become stiff and calloused but it felt good to touch the keys again. By the end of the evening his playing had improved and Maestro Stracciari sat down to one side of the piano and started to play the voice part of on a cello. Even if there were no words being sung, Roberto was amazed at how the cello could express the feeling of the *romanza* without lyrics.

They played for quite a while until they both were emotionally drained and Roberto's love of music was renewed.

The next morning the two men walked to the Church of Santa Maria de la Passione where Carlo's and Eva's wedding was to take place. They entered the church and sat down well behind the front pews that were being filled by relatives.

Soon they heard a motorcar stopping at the church's esplanade. Everyone stood and turned towards the entrance vying for a view of the bride and groom. The priest was already there and he greeted the wedding party as the organ started to play and the group advanced.

Roberto's heart was beating wildly. He saw his friend Carlo coming in with Signora Luisa beautifully dressed in a grey gown and a broad-brimmed hat. Behind them, like a vision, walked Amelia wearing a new style wine-colored hat, which framed her face and her hair, cut short

Roberto couldn't take his eyes off her. She was a lovely-looking woman, elegant and serious. She walked down the aisle nodding gently.

The moment she spotted Roberto, her expression changed, becoming radiant. Her eyes shone with love transforming her whole countenance, inundating the place with light. As she walked by his pew, the two young people locked in an intense glance full of longing. Roberto thought his heart would stop. If someone had asked him what color Amelia's dress was, he couldn't have said, so enthralled was he by her face. Maestro Stracciari nodded happily.

Behind, the proud father walked with the bride. Eva was resplendent in a straight-line white gown, with long sleeves and rounded neckline, especially designed and made by Luisa and Giannina. She also wore a delicate lattice-work-headdress decorated with embroidered pearls and a long soft-flowing veil.

While the marriage rite took place Roberto found himself yearning to be in Carlo's place with Amelia by his side. Now he knew he wanted to spend the rest of his life with her. But his father's teachings rang loud and clear: "You don't ask for a woman's love unless you are ready to marry her and are able to support her," he had said repeatedly to his brother and to him and the way things were now, he couldn't even support himself.

It was a lovely ceremony and Roberto's singing could have made it perfect. A violin and a cello filled the church with the sounds of Schubert's "Ave Maria" and Cesar Frank's "Panis Angelicus."

The moment of regret that Roberto felt was soon overridden by the joy of being with the Corelli family again. He greeted Carlo and his bride with delight. Both men felt again the strong friendship that had united they from the moment they had met.

Luisa was in tears when she embraced Roberto and Giannina kept repeating how unbelievable it was to see him there.

And then came Amelia. "Roberto!" She said in her warm voice. How much he had longed for that sound. There was no need for words as they embraced tenderly.

"Amelia, *Cara!*" he managed to say as he gave way to other guests who were trying to greet the wedding party. Everyone present wanted to celebrate the triumph of love over the horror of war.

After the greetings outside the church, the bride and groom climbed into the motorcar and everyone else walked to the Corelli residence where the *pranzo di nozze* was waiting to be served. The weather was perfect for a stroll. Amelia introduced Roberto and the Maestro to Aunt Lucia and the other friends and relatives.

The veranda at the back of the house had been transformed into a dining area for the day. A long table had been set up with white linen, white china and crystal. Amelia had placed cherry blossom arrangements along the table. Even if the food shortages made it impossible to have fine meat, the "house chefs" Giannina, Renato, Luisa and Amelia had managed to produce *risotto, vitello col rosemarino e patate e una torta di nozze* –a complete wedding meal. Giannina's magical *cenci* accompanied the coffee which was extended with roasted chicory.

Eva's father raised his glass and asked everyone to join him in wishing Carlo and Eva a wonderful life together. Luisa's eyes glowed with tears of happiness wishing her husband and her younger son were with them on this special day. Amelia, Renato and Giannina were busy serving and it took them a while to join the others.

Amelia had noticed the change in Roberto's voice but hadn't said anything for fear of making it evident to others. She was worried but wasn't willing to upset the beauty of the day by asking him about it.

As the evening fell and the temperature cooled down, the celebrants went in and Aunt Lucia announced that she had brought a phonograph player. She placed a record on it and they listened as the music played.

"Carlo and Eva, you must start," said Aunt Lucia cheerfully.

Carlo stood in front of Eva and extended his hand for her to take. They walked to the center of the room and danced to the slow waltz on the player, as the others clapped.

"This song is popular in America," said Aunt Lucia. "Apparently, everyone dances to its music. It is by a Mexican composer. You must have heard it, Roberto."

"Of course! My parents used to dance to it. It's by Juventino Rosas."

"Can you sing it," asked Aunt Lucia.

"I don't think Roberto should sing these days," Maestro Stracciari intervened.

"Very well, Maestro. Let's dance then," and Aunt Lucia swiftly led Stracciari to the dance floor following the rhythm of the music.

The moment had passed unobserved by most, but not by Amelia. She wondered if Roberto had been seriously ill at the front. He was much thinner but so was Carlo.

The phonograph was wound up again and soon Roberto and Amelia were dancing to the music of "La Spagnola." *...stretti, stretti nel estasi d'amor..."* Amelia hadn't danced since she was a little girl. It felt wonderful to be dancing with Roberto.

"Have you been sick, Roberto?" Amelia asked tentatively.

"A while back, but it's a long story. I would prefer to tell it to you at a quieter time. Can I come tomorrow morning? If you are free we can go for a walk. I don't have to leave until the evening. I guess Carlo told you that I live in Padua now," said Roberto.

"Yes, he did. Oh Roberto, I'm so happy to see you! It's been such a long time...!"

"I know. I'm sorry I didn't come before..."

"Shshhh," she touched his lips lightly with her fingers, "let's just dance and enjoy the music, Roberto. Tomorrow we'll have time to talk."

As they danced Roberto could not stop his thoughts. Was it the music, or her closeness, or the touch of her hand? He didn't know, but he had to be with this woman from now on. He wouldn't live without her. His whole being was alive and he knew that he was in love!

The phonograph music continued and everyone was twirling around, Signora Luisa and Maestro Stracciari, Giannina and Renato, Lucia and Domenico, one of Carlo's friends, Eva's parents and, of course, the bride and groom.

The *sposi* departed in the motorcar while everyone smiled and waved. They were going to Lake Garda and Venice, their first trip together. Good-nights were said and Amelia kissed Roberto on the cheek in the most natural way as she said: *Ci vediamo domani.*"

"Till tomorrow," he replied tenderly. He wanted to dance on the street but Maestro Stracciari was walking beside him.

Amelia went inside the house with a beaming smile. Roberto was alive.

Early the next morning, as they walked away from the house, Roberto began: "Amelia, please forgive me for not coming before, I just couldn't face you."

"Wait Roberto, please. I want us to be tranquil when we talk."

They reached the public gardens and sat on a bench. The trees were still in bloom and the coolness of the morning invited confidences. Roberto leaned forward, his elbows on his thighs and his hand interlaced. His eyes were fixed in the distance.

He talked in a low voice trying to control his emotions. He told her about that morning in the mountains when he had found Cesare –the sadness and the horror of what had happened. He told her about the damage to his throat, his lungs and his voice.

She listened in silence, taking in every word, letting her tears flow. She understood how difficult all this was for Roberto.

"I'm so sorry, Roberto! I could never come close to knowing how you feel."

"I hope you can forgive me for not coming sooner to see you. I didn't know how to tell you."

"There's nothing to forgive, Roberto. On the contrary, I feel a certain comfort knowing that you were with Cesare, present at his funeral. It meant so much to us all."

Roberto was silent as he remembered that he couldn't sing to say good-bye to his friend.

"After the funeral I felt so angry, so helpless. Then, when I found about my voice I became despondent. That has passed now but the sadness of war and the death and destruction it caused, has not."

They were silent for a while.

"It's difficult to learn how to live with the losses," said Roberto sadly.

"Yes, it's hard. But you're a wonderful person, Roberto, with or without a voice. The feelings that made you want to be a singer are still alive. You can apply them to anything you want to do in life. Your enthusiasm, your dedication will always be there," said Amelia fervently.

"I wish I could sing to you the final duet of *Andrea Chenier*, remember...? *"Vicino a te"* –close to you my restless soul finds peace. It is true, Amelia. You are the answer to my every desire, my every dream, my every poem..."

"Oh Roberto, I would have loved to hear you sing this to me, as you did in the theatre a few years back, but just to hear you say that, is a miracle. How many times have I envisioned you in the battleground helping the wounded, carrying the dead... amidst gunfire and explosions, and here you are, alive!"

Amelia turned towards him and smiled. Her tears were still glistening on her cheeks.

Roberto stretched out his arms and tenderly held her face between his hands; he wiped the tears with his thumbs very softly and looked deeply into her eyes. Then he understood how much love Amelia harbored for him. Very slowly he kissed her lips. His heart was racing.

"Oh Amelia, how blind I've been!" He said as they embraced. "I love you so much!"

"I have loved you from the first time I saw you, Roberto. Do you believe me?"

"I do, I do! But now I have nothing to offer you, not even a sporadic singing contract."

"The war has taught us many things. One of them is that we can live with a lot less. The other is that there's no secure future. We attempt to build it but anything can happen. We can only try our best."

"Thanks to Dr. Antonelli I may now have a future but it will be a long road. Five years before I can become a doctor and make a respectable salary or have an independent practice. I cannot ask you to wait for me, Amelia."

"Roberto, if I'm accepted, I will be studying for three years. And," she added smiling, "I was ready to wait for you forever. The time frame is much better now," she said with a glint of humor. She felt suddenly light and optimistic. "I'll be in Bologna, not too far from Padua."

"Oh Amelia, I love you! I admire you too! Can you imagine what our life together could be?"

"I have dreamed about it for a long time, Roberto!"

CHAPTER TWENTY-NINE

Amelia

The house was silent that Sunday afternoon.

Luisa and Giannina had gone up to their bedrooms, exhausted from the activity of the previous day. The wedding had gone as planned and now they were enjoying peace and quiet. Amelia accompanied Aunt Lucia to the train station, but the train was delayed and they had the opportunity to talk at length.

"You have got yourself a wonderful man in Roberto, Amelia," said Aunt Lucia. "He seems to be totally in love with you. Seeing you two together makes me feel young again, my dear."

"You're young Aunt Lucia! Victor Hugo said that fifty is young and you're not there yet."

"Maybe, but I don't think I could fall in love like you two."

"Of course you could!"

"No, I don't think so." Aunt Lucia said pensively. "I never told your mother this, but a few years after my husband died, I fell in love with an artist. His name was Alessandro. He had come to see if I could make some book covers in leather for him, which he was going to paint. I had never seen that done. He explained the process to me. We talked at length. He came back several times and with each visit we became closer. In a few weeks our friendship evolved into a passionate relationship."

Amelia didn't dare to interrupt or to breathe. Aunt Lucia continued: "We spent the most magnificent month together and then he fell sick. When he was younger he had worked on the railways and his lungs had been affected. He started having problems breathing. Apparently he had some form of tuberculosis caused by coal smoke. Two lung specialists saw him but it was too late. Nothing could be done. No amount of rest or dry weather would have made him well. When he died, I was devastated. The war had started and I thought of volunteering as a nurse, leaving it all, the factory, everything. But then I realized that my employees, the people you saw in the factory, depended entirely on this work. Some were older and if I left they would have nowhere to go and most of them could neither read nor write."

"Oh, Aunt Lucia, I had no idea!"

"Nobody did, except perhaps some of my helpers. What was the point of telling anybody about Alessandro's death?"

"We could have come to see you, be with you," said Amelia.

"With the war everything became difficult and anyway, nothing could be done.

Sometimes I wish I'd had a child. But it didn't happen, not with Giovanni, when I was young and not with Alessandro. I guess I wasn't meant to be a mother."

At this point Amelia could only put her arms around Aunt Lucia. She had long suspected that her Aunt's cheerful demeanor had been learned through constant practice, in an effort to hide her pain.

"Apart from the wonderful memories, one good thing came out of it," Aunt Lucia continued, "I asked a friend to help me teach all the workers how to read and write. They all do now."

"That's good, Aunt Lucia! You gave them the best possible tool."

It was easy to talk to her aunt. The conversation turned back to Roberto and Amelia was able to tell Aunt Lucia what Roberto had told her about his time at the front and about the loss of his voice. She confided how much she missed his singing.

"Roberto put so much feeling into his singing that I often thought he might have left some great love behind, in Mexico. Now I realize he could feel as his own every word of the arias or the songs he sang. Perhaps this was his way of expressing the love he was hoping to find. I'm terribly sad for him. It must be hard to know that he won't be able to sing again," said Amelia.

"But is it for sure that he will never sing again?" asked Aunt Lucia.

"The doctors have told him so."

"It's tragic, my dear, but at least he's alive and he's in love with you."

"Yes, Aunt Lucia, I'm happy for that and ... what can I say? I have loved him for a very long time."

"Now, let's hope that you gain admission to the university and come to stay with me in Bologna. It will be wonderful to have you around. I so enjoy your company."

The train came into the station and they stood up and embraced.

"I'll be waiting for your news. *Ciao Cara!*"

"*Ciao Aunt Lucia!* I'll let you know as soon as I hear from the university. *Buon viaggio!*"

Amelia kept waving as the train pulled out of the station. She walked home slowly taking in the scent of the spring evening. The lights were now shining inside the cafes and piano and violin music filtered out into the streets as people came and went.

The goodbyes were still sounding in Amelia's head, Aunt Lucia's and Roberto's.

Something wonderful had happened. Something that she had hoped for had come true. It was unbelievable! She let the feeling sink in.

Between dreaming about Roberto and waiting to hear from the university, Amelia's week at the pharmacy went by slowly. Signor Morgatti, who had been at the wedding, noticed the change in Amelia and was happy for her –he would always remember her as the little girl who every so often came into the pharmacy pulling at her father's hand.

Morgatti was as anxious as Amelia to know the results of her university application. He thought she was cut to be a chemist. She truly enjoyed the work, much like her father.

Morgatti's younger brother, badly impaired by the war, was now learning the work, assisting in the pharmacy a few hours every day. Amelia treated him with kindness and was genuinely helpful to him, undaunted by his evident disability. Signor Morgatti admired her patience and her compassion.

A few weeks after the wedding as the Corelli family was finishing a late *pranzo*, the doorbell rang.

Amelia opened the door and in front of her was a good looking blonde woman dressed in a fashionable beige suit. She smiled and said with a marked foreign accent: "Is this the Corelli residence?"

"Yes, it is," replied Amelia smiling too. "You must be Clara! Roberto's friend."

"Si, si, sono Clara Gillespie. Piacere!" She replied in a well-rehearsed greeting.

"I'm Amelia Corelli. Please come in! Roberto told us you might be coming to Milan. He has gone back to Padua."

Amelia was pleased to finally meet Clara, but couldn't help but feeling slight apprehension upon seeing how beautiful Roberto's friend was.

Clara, for her part, seemed completely at ease.

They went in and Clara was introduced to Signora Corelli, Giannina and Renato.

In a mixture of Italian, English and Spanish they made her feel welcome. Amelia prepared some coffee and the two of them sat in the veranda, eager to know more about each other and trying to decide in which language they could communicate with some ease.

Amelia hadn't spoken a word of English since she had left school, but helped by the little Spanish she had learned from Roberto, she was able to communicate with Clara in a *pasticcio,* of three languages.

"Roberto wasn't sure if you would receive his letter before starting your trip," said Amelia. "He told me how happy he was for you and for your career in photography. He thought it was amazing and, if I may say, I think so too."

"Well, thank you! I don't know how it happened but I became fascinated with photography during my third year at school. I hope to become really good at it." Very soon the two young women were talking as old friends. "Now, tell me, how is Roberto, really." He mentioned to me very briefly that he could not sing at your brother's wedding because of a throat problem. Is he well now?"

Amelia had a moment of doubt. Was it proper for her to say anything? In the end she decided to tell the whole story to Clara just as Roberto had told it to her.

It was as if every time someone asked about Roberto's singing and she had to respond, the condition became more permanent and hopeless, as if it was she who had to be convinced that he would not be able to sing again.

"Oh, my God! That's so cruel!" said Clara. "He had such a beautiful voice. We were so impressed when we heard him sing on the boat. It was memorable. My uncle thought that Roberto's future was mapped out for him, especially when he wrote to us about his opera performances. It's a tragedy!" Clara was greatly affected. "He must be so upset."

"He is. We all are, but everything around us seems to shout to be thankful that he's alive! My brother, Cesare, as you know, didn't make it."

"I know. I'm so sorry!"

"At least Roberto is in good health and will be able to do something else. He has chosen another path, just as long and difficult. He has been accepted at the University of Padua to study medicine. Imagine that, Clara! I'm so happy for him. I'm sure he'll do well."

"That's really wonderful! He's lucky to have someone like you who loves him so much," said Clara.

"Why do you say that?"

"Because it's obvious that you love him, Amelia. From what he told me, and what I can see in you, there's no doubt. And his letters have always been full of praise and love for you. The only one who couldn't see that he was in love was Roberto, himself. It's crazy how sometimes we can be so blind to our own feelings."

"Well, I think he's seen the light," said Amelia happily. "And you Clara, where are you going to go? He told me just a bit."

"First, I'm going to take photographs of the battlegrounds in France. The journal I'm working for is trying to compile an archive of photographs of the various places like Ypres, Verdun, Somme, Passchendaele and the Marne where battles took place. It's not an uplifting job but I feel I'm doing something so that the sacrifice of all those men will not be forgotten."

"That's commendable! But, won't it be dangerous? Apparently grenades and mines still blow up."

"They are sweeping the fields in order to start planting crops again," said Clara. "I know they won't allow me in all the places. There's still a lot of heavy armament lying in the fields and along the roads."

"I don't want to think what those places must look like," said Amelia. "I've seen pictures in the newspapers of towns that are completely demolished."

"I also have to take photographs of cemeteries where American soldiers are buried."

"That's incredible! Are you doing all this by yourself, Clara?"

"No, no. There are two other people travelling with me; two men, a journalist and a technician who helps me with the equipment," said Clara.

"How do you do it? It must be difficult to travel and work with men only," said Amelia, feeling out of her depth.

"I'm used to it by now. I have been doing this type of work in the States for almost a year and a half. A couple of times I travelled with women but I found that more difficult because the magazine or newspaper makes us share the room in hotels. Instead, if I travel with men, I have my own room and privacy. I have time to read and think. I prefer it this way."

"You are brave, Clara."

"Not really, it's a learned attitude, Amelia. If I want this job, I have to be independent and look confident about how I do the work, even if I'm alone. The people that employ me don't want to have to worry about me."

"You're amazing. I couldn't do what you're doing."

"You could if you needed to."

"It's all so very different here," said Amelia. "Up until last April, women in Italy were not allowed to participate in any of the professions or have government positions. Can you believe that? Only very special women could attend universities. It's changing now, but slowly. I'm waiting to hear if I have been accepted at the University of Bologna to study chemistry."

"That will be exciting. One of the things that I enjoyed the most was studying with other people. I liked to hear artists explain their ideas and then be able to talk about them with other students.

And I like the developing work or "dark room work" as we call it and see as the images emerge out of the emulsion. Chemistry is important. If it weren't for chemistry and physics, there wouldn't be photography."

"Right! I hope I make it in."

"You will, Amelia. Just be strong and stand your ground. When I was studying in New York there were some young men who believed that women were there because they had nothing else to do. It was infuriating, but slowly they realized that I was there because I wanted a future in painting and later in photography. When a professor gave some recognition to my work, they started respecting me professionally. It wasn't easy, but here I am."

"Well, I hope I can be as strong as you, Clara."

Apart from her good looks, Amelia had been impressed by the self-assurance that Clara displayed. She was only three or four years older than she was but what a difference! Amelia decided right then and there that she would try to be more assertive from now on.

Luisa and Giannina came into the living room and tried to participate in the conversation. There was much laughter as they tried to understand each other. Giannina asked where Clara lived.

"New York City," replied Clara.

"New York! My son is in New York! He has a restaurant in Greenwich Village," added Giannina proudly.

"Really? I live in Greenwich Village. On which street is the restaurant?" asked Clara.

"A minute please!" said Giannina and ran up to her room. She came back waving an envelope.

When Clara read the address, she said: "That's just around the corner from my house. I live on MacDougal. When I get back to New York, I will go to the restaurant and I'll take some photographs, if they allow me to do that."

"Oh, please! You say it's for me, for Giannina, for Vincenzo's mother."

Amelia explained what Clara was going to do in France. The two older women were impressed and a bit in awe. Battlegrounds spoke only of death to them.

Later in the evening Amelia accompanied Clara to her hotel. On the way, they talked a bit more.

"Well, here's Roberto's address," said Amelia handing Clara a piece of paper. "I'm sure he would love to see you, if you can."

She suddenly felt that her fears had to be faced right on. If Roberto were to find Clara irresistible, it was better to find out now. Then Clara said something unexpected.

"I have to tell you, Amelia. Nothing will stop me from following my dream. I want to photograph the world –Africa, Australia, Japan, China, Egypt, Mexico, South America- any place where I can find interest and beauty. It can be around the corner from my house or in faraway places. My Aunt Margaret couldn't understand my feelings. Up until the time she died she wanted me to marry one of her friend's sons and settle down. But marriage is not for me. I need the freedom to move on my own wherever and whenever I want. Fortunately, Uncle Spencer has grown used to the idea. He's a good man with progressive thinking regarding women."

"I hope to see you again during your trips, Clara," said Amelia embracing her new friend warmly. "I wish you the chance to see the whole world and I'll think of you when I'm in a chemistry lab, where I hope to be for at least three years," said Amelia.

"Good luck, Amelia! Write to me once in a while and tell me how you're doing."

"Likewise!"

They said goodbye and Amelia walked out of the hotel. She heard drums in the distance and, as she turned the corner, she noticed that the groups of men and women walking down the street that evening were not the usual strollers. Instead the groups were walking elbow to elbow but carrying banners that stretched across the street. Others carried posters or banged on drums or pans. It was some kind of peaceful demonstration.

Amelia walked against this human river and was able to read the banners.

"Better pay!" "Shorter working days!" "*Fuori I pesce-cani!*" "Sharks Out!" Some people were coming out on their balconies or looking out their windows to see what the commotion was about.

As she was crossing one smaller street, Amelia's arm was gripped firmly. She turned around, surprised and angry. She thought it was a member of the parade but, no, it was Fausto Tozzi, who pushed her into the back seat of his car and shouted to the driver: "Get out of here!"

The driver started the car but was not able to advance. More men and women were joining the parade and intercepting the few motorcars.

"Drive! Move!" shouted Tozzi.

"*E impossibile!*" replied the chauffeur raising his hands hopelessly.

"*Imbeccile!* Honk the horn!"

"What do you think you're doing?" exclaimed Amelia when she recovered from the shock.

"We have to get out of here. It's dangerous!" Replied Tozzi, exceedingly upset.

"Dangerous? For whom? For you? These people aren't doing anything. They are just walking towards the government palace. They have grievances and they're showing their discontent."

"They are going to be stopped and then there will be trouble. Believe me! I know," replied Tozzi.

"Well, I'm not going any place with you," said Amelia as she opened the door and stepped out of the car walking hurriedly in the opposite direction. The car, which by now was flanked by the crowd on both sides, was stuck in place and couldn't move an inch.

Amelia was amazed at her newly found boldness. Never before had she been able to face this man and dismiss him so bluntly. For the first time in her life, she had fought for her right to make a choice.

Nobody bothered her or made it difficult for her to walk home. What was Tozzi talking about? Her anxiety had subsided but not her anger.

As the weeks went by Amelia worried constantly about encountering Tozzi. He was proud and persistent and anything could be expected of him.

He had come one more time to the pharmacy insisting that the marches were no longer peaceful and that there would be pillage and damage to property. He seemed to think that he was the only person who could protect Amelia. But it was clear to everyone that the groups were not concerned with the public in general. They were going after the big factories and storehouses and Tozzi was the owner of several of those.

Amelia let her mother assume that her nervousness was due to the long wait to hear from the university. One evening as she was opening the door to enter her house, Signora Luisa greeted her waving an envelope. "Amelia, a letter from the university."

CHAPTER THIRTY

Dr. Antonelli was sitting in his living room when Roberto arrived from the train station. The doctor, who seemed to be writing, turned around to greet Roberto.

"How was the wedding?" Did you have a good time?" He asked.

"It was wonderful!... Perfect!" Said Roberto with a big smile.

"Oho, sounds like romance!" Dr. Antonelli tried to joke but was unable to hide his concern. His desk was covered with open medical books and his expression was worrisome.

"Is something wrong, Professor?" asked Roberto. "I see you are in the middle of something."

"Do you remember I told you about some problematic medical cases in Milan, a few weeks ago?"

"Yes, I do, but I thought it was a false alarm."

"Unfortunately, it wasn't. We have some new cases of whatever it is here in Padua and the surrounding towns. At first, we thought it was typhus. It's not. It's something else. It attacks the respiratory system and causes internal and external bleeding. We haven't seen that before," said Dr. Antonelli, "and we're terribly concerned."

"Is there any cure for it?" Asked Roberto.

"So far it hasn't responded to any medicine or therapy. It starts with a severe headache and fever, in some cases, and then proceeds to block the respiratory tract. It seems to be spreading rapidly among young people, both men and women, between the ages of twenty and forty. It could be some new type of influenza, but we don't know for sure. Dr. Gamaggio and I have decided that you shouldn't drive the ambulance at the moment, if for no other reason, to avoid contact with any person who may be suffering from this."

"I don't mind, Dr. Antonelli, I've been feeling quite strong lately," said Roberto.

"Well, you should mind, Roberto. Young, strong people are dying."

"It's that serious! My God!"

"No use hiding the situation," said the doctor. "On your part, remember that your respiratory system is weak and it doesn't need additional complications. The hospital would like you to help from now on in the amputee wing. There you will help the disabled – amputees and paraplegics and even some quadriplegics. The hospital staff needs strong helpers to move the patients or carry them around. It's a sad job because the patients are disheartened and have no wish to live or to communicate with others. Maybe you will be able to help them."

"I'll try my best, Doctor," replied Roberto.

"Also, I would advise you to wear a protective mask during your working hours, whether you're in the hospital or outdoors on construction sites. You may not want to, it's your choice, but I think it's important. All the hospital staff will do the same, at least inside the hospital and so will I."

All the rapture of being in love was suddenly dampened by the distressing news. Roberto was worried thinking that maybe Milan was the source of the disease. That would put his friends and his maestro in danger. He was not able to share his good news with Dr. Antonelli.

That night he wrote a short letter to Amelia declaring his love again and asking her to be careful and alert about sick people coming to the pharmacy. Perhaps Signor Morgatti was aware of the situation by now.

While Roberto waited for the university classes to start he continued to work at the construction office. The workers were restless as a wave of discontent swept the country. The price of food kept going up and the factory and agricultural workers had started to organize themselves inspired by the soviet revolution in Russia. The Italian Socialist Party had gained momentum and the number of members had increased.

Roberto saw with despair the similarity of the situation with that of the Mexican Revolution, which had started in 1910 and was still going on –nine years of bloodshed with no end in sight. This time, however, he kept his opinions to himself. He made the construction drawings and talked with the workers only about the projects. The other two days he worked in the hospital.

Although Roberto had been exposed to seriously wounded and dying soldiers, the sight of a large number of maimed and paralyzed soldiers, lying helpless in one enormous hospital room was shattering. The ward was quiet except for the subdued moaning coming from one or two patients and the tinkling sound of the utensils being used by the nurses to tend the patients.

He took in the sadness and desperation that emanated from the place and he silently made a promise to do his best to help this people. He talked with the head nurse who explained that the patients who were paralyzed from the head down had little chance of survival because of lung congestion and bladder infections.

"What can be done for them?" Asked Roberto.

"Changing positions a few times a day helps to avoid bed sores. There's not a lot more we can do except to keep them clean and talk with them if they want to."

"This is terribly sad. When I was moving wounded men from the battleground my only thought was to keep them alive. I wonder if some of them would have preferred to die," Roberto said.

"Let's not brood over that," said Nurse Cristina. "You never know. Scientists are always finding new healing possibilities. Come with me, I'll introduce you to the patients."

Roberto followed Nurse Cristina; she was a petite woman in her early fifties who moved with a purposeful step, rushing around the beds, checking charts and greeting the patients. Nothing seemed to escape her watchful eye.

She took Roberto around the ward so that the patients could understand why he was there. The ones who could move waved a hand. The others just looked at him as he walked by.

"Where do I start?" Asked Roberto.

"We'll move the quadriplegics first."

Nurse Cristina called another nurse and they started to work. Although most men were thin, it was difficult work. They would find the positions in which they could be more comfortable and relieve pressure on the skin. It was frustrating not to be able to do more for them. Roberto thought that music could give them some emotional outlet, but, since he could not sing now, he would have to find some other way.

Soon Roberto learned why family members who came to visit their loved ones sometimes burst out in tears and didn't come back for a while. Sadly, that attitude reinforced the hopelessness of the situation. It was depressing work.

However, working with the paraplegics and the men who had lost limbs was a more positive kind of work. There was hope.

Roberto kept thinking of ways in which they could be helped. All of the men had been soldiers of the various corps whose lives had been shattered by the war. There were also two American soldiers waiting to be transferred to Milan and from there back to the United States.

Most of the men in the ward were visibly depressed and hardly listened to him when he spoke. That reminded him of his emotional condition after he had learned about his voice. *Use imagination and find something that can restore their desire to live,* Roberto kept this in mind, worked and observed.

There was also a feeling of hopelessness on the part of the staff. Most believed that the patients with total paralysis would die in a few months or weeks.

"Dr. Antonelli," said Roberto one evening. "I've been thinking that the men who cannot move their legs could benefit from a plan of exercises to strengthen their arms, maybe weight bearing exercises, pulling and stretching. That could help them move in and out of their wheelchairs and their beds on their own. What do you think?"

"It has to be done slowly and with supervision. We don't want them to get worse or to cause more damage," replied Dr. Antonelli, "and remember that the hospital has no money for equipment or new installations, you know that, Roberto."

"Yes, I do. I thought of asking the construction company where I've been working. Perhaps they can donate some materials and I will ask the workers to help installing them. Do you agree?"

"Very well. But first you have to inform the medical staff in that ward and ask the patients if they want to do it. If they do, then you can try."

Two patients decided to participate.

The construction company gave some metal bars and a few other materials to build a small exercise area with parallel bars, a small bicycle wheel with pedals for the arms and big elastic bands for pulling.

When Roberto asked the workers if they would help with the installation, he was impressed by their response. They could be angry at their wages or at the government but they would donate their time to help the men that had defended their country. In a few days the area was ready and the experiment began.

Amelia sat back in her second-class train seat. She had been leaning out of the window for a long time talking to Signora Corelli, Giannina and Carlo and Eva. She was also listening to their last recommendations.

They had accompanied her to the train station, with her suitcase full of clothes and mementos. Her mind was oscillating between hope and dread. For months she had dreamed about studying at the University in Bologna and now that the dream had become a reality, Amelia was experiencing the pain of leaving her mother and the rest of her beloved family. As the train started to move, she suddenly saw her mother in another light. Although she was surrounded by the others Luisa Corelli looked quite alone, standing on the platform, waving goodbye. She had appeared cheerful up to the last moment. But probably her heart was tearing apart. It was the first time that mother and daughter would be separated for more than a day or two. Amelia found it hard to leave but she understood that it was doubly hard for her mother to see her go away to enter a new phase in her life.

She was glad to be alone in the compartment.

She had the last glimpse of Milan as its urban constructions disappeared behind a line of poplar trees that divided the fields of grain soon to be harvested.

She remembered when her brothers, Carlo and Cesare, would return from their bicycle travels around these areas and she would listen eagerly to their stories. Those were good times —when there was no shadow of death and hunger. The war had changed all that. Men were maimed or dead. People were restless and life was no longer a poem. Amelia felt the sadness of time passing and of leaving behind a happy childhood.

"Look forward to a different future," she had told Roberto. Now she had to do the same.

Keep the feeling alive! She said to herself, remembering the feeling of success that had come over her when she had opened the letter from the university announcing that she had been accepted into the Faculty of Chemistry. At that moment, everything had seemed perfect. She had not counted on the sadness of separation.

Roberto had written to Amelia telling her what he was doing in place of driving the ambulance. He waited anxiously for her news and when her letter finally arrived, he was thrilled. She would be studying in Bologna. What a joy! She would be much closer to him.

About his work, Amelia wrote: "*I know how seriously you take anything you do, how you put your whole heart on the task. I hope this exercise plan works well for the patients. Even if only one succeeds, it will be fantastic. I love you and hope to be with you soon, my love.*" She would let him know as soon as she arrived in Bologna and, hopefully, they would see each other before too long. Classes would be starting soon.

The Morgatti pharmacy door opened and Fausto Tozzi walked in. He looked around and not seeing Amelia at the desk he approached the man sitting on her place.

"Good day!" He said. "Is Signorina Amelia in?" The man shook his head.

"Where is she?" Tozzi asked again, becoming impatient. The man shook his head again.

"Can't you speak and say something?" Tozzi was exasperated and raised his voice.

Signor Morgatti appeared at the back of the pharmacy. "How can I help you, Signor Tozzi, what's the problem?"

"I'm looking for Signorina Amelia and this *scemo* cannot tell me anything."

"Signorina Amelia does not work here anymore and this "scemo" as you called him is my brother who fought for us at the front. Never, ever talk to him like that again! Do you understand, Mr. Tozzi?"

"Where is Amelia?" said Tozzi dismissing the warning.

"Signorina Amelia went away."

"Where to?" Tozzi persisted.

"America!" Said Morgatti, almost smiling at the thought.

"America? But, I wanted to give her everything, money, position, you know… what women want."

"Not ALL women, Signor Tozzi. Good day!" replied Morgatti opening the pharmacy door and straining hard not to push the scoundrel out.

CHAPTER THIRTY-ONE

Amelia arrived at the Bologna train station but Aunt Lucia was not there to greet her, as arranged. She waited for a while and then decided to take a horse-drawn carriage to the house. She assumed that her aunt's business had kept her from meeting her at the station but when she arrived at the house Aunt Lucia's housekeeper, Assunta, opened the door, visibly upset.

"La signora non sta bene." Amelia dropped her suitcase at the entrance and ran to the bedroom. Aunt Lucia was in bed. She barely apologized to Amelia and fell back on her pillows.

"Has the doctor seen her?" asked Amelia to the housekeeper.

"One of the factory workers went to fetch him, a few minutes ago."

"What seems to be wrong?"

"Yesterday, Signora Lucia said she was tired, nothing else. She didn't want to eat anything. She said she had a headache," said the housekeeper.

Amelia remembered what Roberto had told her in his letter about the flu and hoped that it was something else that was ailing her aunt. When the doctor examined Aunt Lucia, he made his diagnosis discreetly.

"The authorities don't want the public to panic and that's why there's little information in the newspapers, but the flu epidemic has continued to spread and unfortunately, it has reached your aunt."

Amelia couldn't hide her anxiety. "What can we do, doctor?"

"Keep her covered but not hot. Cold compresses to her forehead to lower the fever and lots of fluids. Whoever takes care of her should wear a protective face mask at all times and use gloves when helping her to wash or use the washroom. Wash your hands as often as possible and scrub thoroughly. Disinfect all utensils such as bowls, cups and silverware. Keep a separate set for her. At the moment, there's not much else to do. And something else," said the doctor. "You should take turns for her care so that you can rest. That's the one way of protecting yourselves."

Amelia was dismayed. Aunt Lucia had looked so well and healthy just a few weeks back, at the wedding. How had she gotten infected? She decided not to tell Roberto or her mother about this. They would only worry.

"Assunta, let's get to work," Amelia said. "First we'll wash the cutlery and all dishes very well. We will disinfect them by putting them in boiling water for three minutes. Then we'll mark the ones to be used for her. We'll make a pot of clear soup, to help her build up her strength and we'll encourage her to drink water or tea as often as possible. I will understand if you prefer to stay away."

"Ma no, signorina! Signora Lucia has always treated me as part of the family and I wouldn't leave her in this situation. I haven't forgotten how she helped us when our little son contracted diphtheria. If it were not for her, he wouldn't be alive. No, I'll be here. You can count on me."

The days went by and the two women were permanently occupied in making Aunt Lucia as comfortable as possible but there was no change for the better. She was delirious with fever and her lungs were congested. One night she started to cough blood and had a heavy nosebleed. Both women stayed by her side expecting the end, while they waited for the doctor to come. They had even sent for a priest to give the last rites.

The doctor took a long time to arrive and their fears were rising. When he finally got to the house and examined Aunt Lucia he declared that the crisis had passed and she was expected to live. It looked as if the hemorrhaging had helped to clear her respiratory system.

"Now, it is important to look after yourselves. Rest and eat fruit, if you can," said the doctor "and if any signs of the flu appear, like severe headache, call me immediately and stay in bed. The same applies to Signora Lucia. Do not allow her to get up too soon. One of the greatest mistakes patients make is that upon feeling better, they go back to their normal activities and then, suffer a fatal relapse."

Amelia and Assunta watched Lucia's recovery closely. A week later, as she was feeling better, Aunt Lucia started fretting about her workshop.

"Everything is going well, Aunt Lucia. I have checked every day and things are under control in the factory. You have responsible and dedicated people working there –people who like you and respect you," said Amelia. "Please stay in bed. The doctor said that at this point of the disease it's of utmost importance to rest, until the last symptoms disappear and you are stronger."

"I feel badly, Amelia, about not meeting you at the station. I couldn't go."

"Please, Aunt Lucia. I was fine. You can't imagine how happy I am to see that you're looking better now."

"Have you registered at the university?"

"Not yet, but there's time. There's nothing to worry about."

"How long have I been sick?" asked Aunt Lucia.

"About ten days."

"Ten days! My God! And Assunta, is she well, is she here?"

"She has been here all along, Aunt Lucia. You are surrounded by people who love you," said Amelia smiling.

It was a Sunday afternoon and Amelia was reading by the window, beside Aunt Lucia's bed, when the doorbell rang. She heard Assunta opening the door and then a man's voice, which made her heart skip a beat.

"Is this the house of Signora Lucia Russo?"

"Yes, it is."

"Is Signorina Corelli in?" The voice asked, but by that time Amelia was running down the stairs.

"Roberto! What are you doing here?"

They embraced and he looked at her fixedly.

"Are you okay, Amelia? You look tired."

"Yes, yes I am. How come you're here?"

"Your last letter was a bit evasive," he said, "I decided to come and see you."

"Oh my dear! I'm sorry!"

They went into the house and sat in the living room.

"Where is Aunt Lucia?" he asked.

"She's in bed. She's been sick. That's why I couldn't write too much."

"Is she better now?"

"I can tell you now, Roberto. The danger has passed but she nearly died."

"The flu?" His expression changed. "Are you well? Were you wearing a mask, disinfecting everything?"

"All the time! Don't worry! We have done all the things that the doctor told us to do and both Assunta and I are feeling well."

"To think that I wasn't allowed to enter the wing of the patients with the flu in the hospital, while you were here, right beside one."

"We were awfully worried. I kept thinking that had I been working in the laboratory, instead of the pharmacy, I could have helped find some answers. What about Dr. Antonelli and his group?"

"They keep working but up to now, there are no answers. This influenza is not caused by bacteria, it's something else, and nobody knows how to fight it."

"This is the kind of thing that really interests me, the exhaustive study of collected samples and the unexpected findings. I hope I can do this type of work in the future, when I complete my studies or before," Amelia concluded, feeling energized for the first time in days.

She had thought only of illness and death for too many days and she felt deceitful towards her mother. *What if Aunt Lucia hadn't made it through?*

Roberto said hello to Aunt Lucia from her bedroom door. She smiled, happy to see him. "You two go for a walk," she said. "Amelia needs a change of air and a good strong coffee. Go, go and don't come back for a while."

They left the house arm in arm, delighted to be in each other's company.

It was a hot day and the cobbled stone streets seemed to be exuding steam. People walked under the ancient arcades for miles, enjoying their protective shade.

Students, mostly men and some women, talked animatedly in the cafes, despite the oppressive heat. An atmosphere of excitement could be felt as students arrived in the city to attend university. Amelia and Roberto were soon captivated by the prospect of student life and by the reality of being in love. The hours passed as they talked, until it was time for Roberto to take the return train to Padua.

"Please, my dearest, take care of yourself. Don't keep me waiting for news and don't tell me half of the story. I worry. I love you!" he said as he kissed her one more time.

"I won't, I promise. *Ti amo!*" She said as Roberto jumped into the train that was starting to move.

When would they be together permanently? It could be years before that happened.

She wanted to study and do research but yearned for Roberto's company and for his love. She desired most ardently to experience their love completely.

Classes started at the universities in Italy. Roberto was totally involved with his studies and on the weekends he worked at the hospital with the amputees. The hospital directors had approved the exercise program that he had proposed. More paraplegic patients had joined it. The process was slow but, as one of them had said jokingly to Roberto: "I don't have anything pressing to do just now." The exercise gave them a reason to wake up every morning.

"Roberto," said Dr. Antonelli, some time later, "the staff has noticed a great change for the better in the morale of the patients who are exercising. I must congratulate you for your perseverance. In the future, some of these patients may be able to do work that will not require the use of their legs. You have given them hope. Like giving a compass to a ship that's gone adrift."

"You told me that, doctor, remember? It's about finding new roads."

"Do you ever try to sing?" asked Dr. Antonelli.

"No, *professore,* I have closed that chapter of my life."

"You may not be able to sing opera again, but perhaps you will be able to sing a soft love song to Amelia," said the professor patting Roberto's shoulder affectionately.

Roberto assented silently thinking how may times he had dreamed of doing just that and how, instead, most of the time he didn't even recognize his speaking voice. The thought of singing to Amelia brought upon him a deep sense of loss. For years he had expressed the love of others through singing, through opera and although he tried to avoid that connection by not going to opera or concerts, music pierced his mind …a constant intrusion of memories.

Would he ever be able to feel complete as before? Would he be like the amputees —trying to replace what had been robbed from them by the war?

CHAPTER THIRTY-TWO

Roberto was standing by a window in one of the long hospital corridors, outside the amputee ward, reading a chart. This patient was getting more and more depressed and did not want to be moved, fed or even washed. He was studying the chart trying to find just one thing that could help him reach the patient emotionally.

He lifted his eyes at the sound of steps approaching. One of the nursing assistants was accompanying a well-dressed woman, who walked with determination.

"La signorina cerca lei, signor Roberto." The lady was looking for him and Roberto assumed that the lady was a patient's relative.

"Buon giorno! He said, bending his head, as handshaking had been prohibited.

The woman's hair was covered with a summer hat but something in her eyes seemed familiar.

"Roberto, is that you?" He was so stunned that he dropped the chart and had to bend down to pick it up. That voice... the accent... He controlled his bewilderment.

"Clara? It's been such a long time… I didn't recognize you. You look different."

She smiled. "Oh Roberto, it's so good to see you," and Clara opened her arms in a gesture of friendship. "How many years, is it, eight?"

"A long, long time. My God! What are you doing here? You look fantastic! How did you find me?" He asked still surprised.

"I was in Milan a few weeks ago and went to see Amelia and her family."

"Did you meet Amelia?"

"Oh yes, and what a lovely person she is! All of them are fine people, Roberto. No wonder you enjoyed living there all those years. Your letters were so full of them that, when I met them, I felt that I knew them. Amelia gave me your address and this morning I went to Dr. Antonelli's house to look for you, Signora Antonelli told me where I could find you. So here I am!"

"It's a wonderful surprise Clara! It's great to see you. Are you going to be in the city for a while?"

"Only this afternoon and tomorrow morning. We'll be leaving tomorrow afternoon."

"Are you with your uncle?" Asked Roberto.

"No, I'm travelling with a journalist and an assistant. We have an assignment from an American magazine," and she explained what the work was about.

"And your Uncle Spencer?"

"Oh, he's travelling to different places in Europe. I don't know if we'll be able to even meet while I'm here."

"I'd love to talk with you, Clara. I finish in about three hours. Do you have time? Can we meet somewhere?"

"How about the hotel where we are staying? It's on the Via Roma."

"I know, The Universo. I can be there at 6:30 is that good?"

"Excellent! There's a small café at the front and I'll wait for you there."

"Wonderful! See you then."

Roberto went back to the ward. He was thinking about all that he would say to Clara. She looked so independent and in control, so different from the girl that he had met on the train to Veracruz. It felt like another lifetime.

They had written to each other regularly up to the time of his joining the Red Cross. Through the changing times they had maintained that fine tie that linked them, a childhood and youth lived in Mexico. That was their only connection to the country now ravaged by revolution.

That evening Clara explained that Amelia had told her about the loss of his voice.

"I'm so sad for you, Roberto. I remember what a delight it was to hear you sing. But I admire the work you did at the front. Not many people would do that for another country."

"It is my country now, Clara."

"Of course, I realize that. I guess now you will dedicate yourself to looking after the health of people and that is wonderful too."

"I like the work. I did, right from the beginning. The front was a realistic teacher. It showed me how vulnerable we are. Now, I would really like to help, to make a difference. I hope to become a good doctor."

"And I'm sure you will become one, Roberto."

"It will take such a long time..." He added wistfully. "But now, tell me about you, Clara. You must be a successful photographer if you were able to get this kind of work."

"Like you, I've been trying my best and I love this work. Thank God I didn't get married, as my Aunt Margaret wanted me to. It would have been a terrible mistake. I like my freedom and I don't want a family, at least, not yet. Does that sound terrible?"

"No, not to me. I believe we must follow our dream, if we can and while we can… And we have to adapt. But it's good to know what one wants from life."

"It took me a while, but I know now what I want to achieve. I guess I'm different from the person I was when I met you," Clara smiled.

"We all have changed, Clara. But you and I have something in common that cannot be destroyed. The years we lived in Mexico have shaped who we are and how we feel. Often I have thought that you are the one person who can understand the feelings of nostalgia that creep up on me, thinking about my childhood and early youth. I miss the country, the traditions and, of course, my family and friends. But I don't want to go back, and live there; that part of my life is over. Italy is my home now. I love this country but I also love the country where I was born."

"I know Roberto. I often feel that way too. I was happy in Mexico until my parents died. I also love the country but I have stopped talking about it with my few friends. They tell me things like: "What's so great about the place? It's in the middle of a revolution!" And I realize they cannot understand. You have to have lived there to understand. Those were wonderful years!"

"Yes, never to be forgotten," said Roberto.

They were quiet for a moment. Then Clara said cheerfully: "here's something quite amazing. While we were chatting away in Signora Corelli's living room, it came out that Giannina's son has a restaurant in Greenwich Village in New York, close to where I live. I've never gone there. But now I'm going to go for sure and take photographs, which I will send to Giannina. She's a character!"

"Lovable, witty and tremendous support to the family. I wish I could be there to enjoy her cooking," said Roberto smiling at the thought.

Clara told Roberto of her Aunt Margaret's death and how Uncle Spencer was coping by immersing himself in work for the American government.

"He's the last person alive in our family, as far as I know. I never met my father's family and he never mentioned anybody else except for his parents who are dead. Aunt Margaret was my mother's only sister. She and Uncle Spencer had a daughter who died when she was twelve; she would be about my age now. Isn't it strange how families just end... disappear?"

Roberto wanted to change the course of the conversation. He didn't like to talk about family, the subject made him feel disloyal. He didn't have news from his brother or sisters, but he felt he hadn't tried hard enough.

He encouraged Clara to tell him more about her work. Clara explained how a single visit to an art gallery called 291 in New York City had completely changed her perception of art in photography.

"The owner of the gallery is a well-known photographer called Alfred Stieglitz," she said. "His photographs opened a new world for me. Immediately after that I started taking photography lessons. I have not given up painting, but there's not enough time for both."

"Isn't it unbelievable how lives can change through some minor event? I wish I could prompt some of the men in the ward to read or to even accept someone to read to them or talk to them, to find inspiration, to find a reason to live. Some are quite despondent."

"Will they be able to move again, Roberto?"

"It's hard to say, the doctors think not. But I feel that as long as the mind is working there's a possibility. Also, research carries on. There are many things that a man can do without the use of his legs or hands. It cannot be easy but if he becomes stronger in body and mind, there are possibilities. It won't be a perfect future but there can be a significant improvement from what it is now. And there are people out there who are coming up with new ideas, inventions or discoveries. Better artificial limbs are being developed, so there's always hope."

"I admire what you are trying to do for them, Roberto. Amelia explained your plans to me. Are there any Americans in the ward?"

"Yes, a couple, but there's another fellow that just arrived. I have not been able to convince him to join the exercises. He is American. He may be transferred to another hospital later on, when the flu epidemic danger is over. But he will be here for now."

"Would you like me to talk to him? He may identify my accent and decide to talk."

"Really? Would you do that?"

"I'll come tomorrow morning, maybe with Tom Reynolds, the journalist. He may find a story. We'll see what we can do."

They continued talking for hours about their losses and their hopes for the future.

It was almost midnight when Roberto stood up to say good night. It had been a pleasure to see Clara –a meeting that mixed nostalgia and happiness. It was just like seeing family again.

"I may not be able to see you tomorrow, Clara. I'm in emergency. But I thank you for taking the time to come to Padua. It's been great to see you!"

"You know, Roberto, you are my dearest friend." Replied Clara as they said good-bye.

As he walked home, Roberto thought of the two different beauties –that of Clara, blonde and blue-eyed and that of Amelia, his beloved, with her expressive dark eyes and her dark mahogany hair. A sudden recollection flashed in his mind –the words and the music of "Recondita Armonia" the aria he had sung a few years back in the opera house.

To sing *Tosca* had been one of his dreams and the dream had come true but had disappeared swiftly, like stardust. The memory, however, had stayed.

His step quickened almost to a run, trying to stifle the moan that was ready to come out of his throat, the dreaded surge of deep sadness.

CHAPTER THIRTY-THREE

Out of the window Amelia could see the magnolia tree in bloom again. What a year it had been! First, Aunt Lucia's serious brush with death and the imminent danger of the flu epidemic and then the strong current of communist ideas taking hold of the workers and the student leaders.

The world *sciopero* "strike" was in people's mouths constantly but, so far, it had not affected the faculties or the services at the university.

Amelia's first year of chemistry studies had ended successfully. She was satisfied with her work.

Just as she was getting ready to leave the Faculty for the term, she was called to the Dean's office. She trembled as she entered. At the beginning of the year all female students had been called for a meeting regarding "rules of behavior" and visiting restrictions to male quarters. There were more women in the university now and they tried to blend in quietly, but they still stood out, among all the male students.

With the Dean was the Chemistry Laboratory professor.

"*Signorina Corelli*, your name has been proposed by your professor, to form part of a study group. The work will involve analysis of samples, observation, tests and careful notations. It will have to be done after classes, three evenings per week. If successfully finished it will count as one-half course and you will gain experience. Are you interested and willing?" Said the Dean.

"Oh yes! Absolutely! *Grazie Professore!*" Words almost failed here. "When do I have to start?"

"In September, when the term begins but we want to get things organized earlier.

We need you to be here the week before classes begin to prepare all the materials. Can you do that?" The professor asked, without lifting his eyes from the papers he had in front of him. Amelia knew that this professor was not fond of having women in the laboratory.

"Of course, I'll be here. Thank you for the opportunity, professor.

"Good day *Signorina!*

Professor Pisanti didn't seem happy to have a woman in the research group, but there were new rules and the few women who had done research work before had been thorough and dependable. The number of women attending the university was on the rise and the Dean felt that they had to be acknowledged.

Amelia had returned to Aunt Lucia's home in a daze. She would be going to Milan soon and she had something good to tell her mother. She was anxious to be with her, to laugh with Giannina and to see Sofia, Carlo and Eva's newborn baby girl. She was suddenly excited to see the Duomo and the Galleria and to hear the streetcars.

She entered the house, eager to share her news but Aunt Lucia was not back from the factory. Assunta came to the door.

"Signorina, I'm glad you're back. La Signora is in the factory. There are problems."

"What problems, Assunta?"

"I don't understand but the workers are talking about *sciopero*, strike..."

"Strike? But I thought they had reached an agreement with my aunt, weeks ago."

"They say they are happy, but they are being pressured by the workers' council," replied Assunta, crying. Her husband was now one of the trusted workers.

"I'm going to see if I can help," said Amelia walking out of the house.

When she opened the gate to the factory, expecting to hear loud voices, she was surprised by the quietude. Only the sound of her aunt writing on the blackboard could be heard. All the workers watched and listened as Aunt Lucia wrote numbers.

She was saying: "This represents the amount that we spend on the leather and the raw materials. This is the cost of the work you do (in other words, your salaries). This is the cost of maintenance of the sewing machines and other equipment," added Aunt Lucia, underlining some figures, "and this is what I take home to live on and pay the city services and taxes," she continued. "This amount represents the average sales per month. Now, we calculate the difference between this column, the monies that come in, and this other column, the expenses. Can you see why it's impossible to raise the pay? Every month the leather goes up in price and I know it's not the workers in the tannery who get the money. Probably it's the chemical company that increases the prices but to us, it makes no difference, because we have to buy the leather to carry on with our business."

The workers were divided in their expectations. Most of them had been working with Aunt Lucia for years and were not only grateful but also protective towards the factory and their work.

A few had joined the communist party and they thought that the factories were to be run by the workers.

"Signora Lucia, we don't want to strike," said Leonardo, one of the oldest worker, "but the council is demanding for every Italian worker to go on strike. We're afraid," he added. "The Union has called for the occupation of all factories, starting in Turin, then Milan and then the rest of Italy."

"I understand," said Aunt Lucia calmly. "There's nothing I can do now. It's your decision." And in so saying she walked out of the large room and went inside her small office followed by Amelia who closed the door behind her.

Suddenly all her composure was gone and Aunt Lucia slumped on her chair in front of her desk and rested her forehead on her hands. Amelia put her arm around her shoulders. She could feel how her aunt was trying to control her pain and anger by taking deep breaths, but she was not succeeding.

"I hope this whole thing doesn't turn into a revolution," she managed to say.

"Oh Aunt Lucia, please don't say that."

"When people are stirred up, anything is possible."

Amelia thought of all the meetings that were taking place at the university on a weekly basis. Many students and some teachers had become members of the Italian Socialist Party. The Party was being pressured by the International to follow in the steps of the Russian Revolution. Amelia hoped for the workers to gain better conditions, especially those who worked so many hours without rest, but she was not ready to participate in any marches or protests. And women could not make much difference in Italian politics since they didn't have the right to vote.

Later that evening, Aunt Lucia asked Amelia to help her take out all the business papers and put them in a room in the house. There were bills to pay and letters to write and she didn't know if she would be allowed to enter her office again.

Two days later the red and black flag was hung at the front door of Aunt Lucia's factory. The front gate was closed and two workers mounted guard to keep anyone from entering. They would decide whether they could run the small factory without her.

Amelia didn't want to leave Aunt Lucia alone in this situation. She was pondering what the next step would be when Roberto arrived from Padua, taking her by surprise.

"Amelia *Cara,*" he said embracing her. "Aunt Lucia, are you all right? I just saw the red and black flag across the factory entrance."

"Yes, that's right! They have taken it. I'm worried, but hopeful, Roberto," said Aunt Lucia.

"What will happen, Roberto?" asked Amelia. "Should we warn my mother? Do you think she'll be affected too?"

"I don't think so. She only has two people working there. How many people do you have working in your factory, Aunt Lucia?" He asked.

"Fourteen. Not too many but enough for the council to come around and pressure them. I know that in a few weeks their savings will be gone. I feel badly for them because they are good workers and they have my respect, but it's their decision."

Amelia wrote to her mother to tell her that she had to delay her departure because Aunt Lucia needed some help. She didn't specify doing what. She was hoping to be in Milan in a couple of weeks and she had urged her mother to write back and tell her how she was doing.

Those were two weeks filled with tension for Aunt Lucia.

Amelia helped her with the office work and Roberto made drawings for the possible separation of the buildings. It was possible for Aunt Lucia to build a separate apartment to rent. They talked and made projections but hoped. Roberto also spent time in the garden cleaning, digging and making a vegetable plot.

"Do you remember, Amelia, when we planted vegetables at your mother's house?"

"How can I forget? It was a magic moment!" she replied.

"It was for me too," he said controlling his desire to make love to her right there and then.

It was both wonderful and difficult to be so close together. Their relationship was blooming and desire was intensifying.

Amelia often dreamed of fleeing with him for a few days to a chalet in the mountains, but that was only a fantasy. They were both loyal to their parents' teachings and conscientious in their love and respect for the family. Furthermore, they both had to complete their studies.

Aunt Lucia felt differently about love. But then, she had been alone when she had met Alessandro and had no one who could be affected by her decision to be with him.

After ten days of complete stoppage at the factory, the workers came to talk with Aunt Lucia.

"Signora Lucia," Leonardo said, "all the workers, except for two, have decided to return to their jobs. We want to continue working and we want to look for areas in which we can reduce costs so those savings can be put towards gratuities to be paid at the end of the year. Are you in agreement?"

"Anything that improves productivity affects our profits and I promise I will apply those in your favor. You know how I feel about this. For me, the most important thing in any company is the satisfaction of the people who work there."

Two days later, the factory reopened and Amelia, accompanied by Roberto, left for Milan.

The train trip was fraught with halts and delays. It seemed that the railroad workers were also involved in a process to slow down the service.

At last they arrived in Milan, tired and hungry.

Outside the station there were groups of people waving red flags and shouting "Viva Lenin!"

The whole scene mirrored the one that Roberto had witnessed outside the train station in Mexico City, in 1910. This time the groups sang in unison to the notes of a rousing melody called "The International." At the end of it came rallying cries about the rights of the workers and the claim that the factories were for the people. The participants were peaceful but ready for action. They were called *I Rossi*, the Reds.

Roberto took Amelia by the arm keeping well away from the turmoil. There were no carriages in front of the station so they started to walk in order to take the streetcar, but there was none in sight. The streets were unusually calm. They kept walking towards home. Suddenly out of an alley came a group of about twenty youths wearing black shirts and brandishing heavy sticks. They were running almost in unison towards the train station.

"Who are they?" asked Amelia.

"I don't know, but I don't like their attitude," said Roberto turning the corner, away from them, sensing danger.

He only felt they were safe when the Corelli's house came into sight and the two of them rushed up to it.

"Mamma!" exclaimed Amelia when Luisa opened the door.

"It's late! I was worried! Roberto, *caro, entrate!* Come in, come in!" said Luisa closing the door in a hurry. "You can't be too careful these days."

"What's happening, Mamma?" Asked Amelia.

"These groups of youths, gangs, I should say… they call themselves *fasci*. They go around scaring people, especially workers in groups. Apparently they use their sticks to break up any meeting. Nobody knows who they are or who they work for."

Amelia and Roberto told Luisa what they had seen outside the station and later recounted what had happened to Aunt Lucia in Bologna.

There was an undercurrent of apprehension but Giannina, as always, prepared a good supper, which made them forget, temporarily, their worries. Amelia was thrilled to meet Sofia, her baby niece. She wanted to hold her all evening long.

"She's not going to want to sleep in her crib tonight," said Carlo.

"Oh, she's beautiful! I'll have to teach her songs and rhymes," said Amelia.

"It'll be a while before she can learn those," said Eva, looking at her daughter.

Amelia gave the baby to her mother and sat down at the piano. She hadn't played in almost a year. Roberto followed her movements with loving eyes. It was a joy to hear her play in the same room where he had first been surprised by the girl who had turned into this magnificent woman he was so in love with.

CHAPTER THIRTY-FOUR

While he was in Milan, Roberto went to see Maestro Stracciari who was delighted to see him. The strong Maestro who had always had an impressive bearing was now looking frail. He wanted to know everything about his former pupil's life now as a student of medicine.

Roberto talked about his studies and about life in Padua. He told him about Amelia and her family but avoided talking about music.

"I'm so happy to know that you have found love," said the Maestro. "That's what was missing. *Amatevi!* Love each other well!" He said with tears in his eyes. *A memory of someone deeply loved.* When he recovered, the Maestro said: "Have you gone to the opera at all?"

"No Maestro, Not yet. It's been a busy year," Roberto replied avoiding the maestro's look. Then he said, "Maestro, I find it hard to talk about opera or even listen to it. Last night Amelia sat at the piano and played some classical songs. I felt such a desperate need to sing… it was unbearable. It brought back so many memories. When I first arrived in Milan, she used to accompany me at the piano, her brother Cesare playing violin and, at times, Carlo, also singing. That was long before I fell in love with her. Then it was a pure musical experience, now it would have been a glorious experience. I would have loved to sing accompanied by her for the rest of my life. Now, all that is lost..."

"*Ma no* Roberto! I don't agree. You have to look for something different to fill the void that the loss of your voice has left, not only with medical work but also with music. You have an excellent ear and your talent should not be wasted."

"Oh Maestro, I don't know what I could do."

"I'm going to give you something to work on," said Stracciari as he stood up and opened a cabinet that contained musical instruments. He took out a viola and wiped it carefully with a soft cloth. "This viola belonged to my father. I would like you to have it and learn how to play it."

The Maestro put it under his chin, tightened the bow and started to play. He brought to life Tosti's "Ideale". "Do you remember when you sang this for me, years ago? This instrument gives out the closest sound to a human voice. Learn to make it sing," he said as he handed the viola to Roberto.

"Oh, no, Maestro, I cannot accept it. It has special meaning for you."

"Precisely! That's why I want you to have it. Who am I going to leave it to? Please accept it and promise that you will try to learn how to play it. Did you hear the tone? It's rich, just like a tenor's voice. You may still be able to "sing" with this viola."

Roberto was touched. He couldn't believe how much kindness he had received from his Maestro. He would try to learn how to play the viola if only to honor him.

"Come to see me whenever you are in town, Roberto. Don't forget your old Maestro," said Stracciari.

"Maestro, even without a voice, I will never forget all that you have done for me," said Roberto. "I may never feel again the exultation of singing opera but I will never forget that experience. It's part of my life and for that I really thank you," he said embracing his beloved teacher.

"You two should get married," said Carlo that evening as he climbed the stairs to his apartment and found Amelia and Roberto embracing on the landing. "What's the point in waiting?" he added.

Roberto blushed deep red and apologized.

"Please don't!" Said Carlo, "I know you love each other. Things won't change that much when you become a doctor. Half of Italy is out of work, anyway!"

"I hope I will have enough to support us both in the future, but I also feel it's important for Amelia to finish her studies before we get married," said Roberto. "She wants to become a professional chemist and I want for her to achieve her dream. If we get married before she completes her studies, other things will get in the way."

"I realize that," said Carlo. "It's just that I want you two to be as happy as Eva and I are." He said, giving them a hug.

Amelia said nothing but suddenly became shy. Roberto would be leaving the next day for Padua and she was already dreading his absence. She would stay two more weeks at her mother's and then go back to Bologna.

The weather had been unbearably hot and humid in Milan and they had not gone out for walks as often as they would have wanted, coupled with the fact that the disturbances on the streets were on the rise and they could happen at any time of the day or night.

That evening Carlo brought the news that the workers had occupied Fausto Tozzi's factories. He had left for America, either gone to Argentina or the United States. Nobody knew for sure. However, before leaving he had managed to take away most of the money from the company's bank accounts. "Dishonest and greedy to the end." said Carlo. I wonder if professor Gozzano and professor Segni would hear about this. They were right about him." Both professors had returned from the war in poor physical shape and were now living in a residence for war veterans in Lake Garda.

Although Amelia hadn't seen Tozzi again, she felt great relief not to have to worry about the man anymore. There were other things on her mind that preoccupied her. First of all, Roberto had spoken to Luisa Corelli asking for her approval of their engagement.

"Roberto, I'm very happy for the two of you," she said with real joy in her voice. "She loves you and I hope you will make each other very happy. I couldn't hope for a better person to be Amelia's life companion. You have a lot to share and you certainly have my blessing."

But Amelia knew that her mother was aware of the implications. Most probably they would have to live in another city once they were married and she knew that Luisa had been missing her terribly since she had left to study in Bologna.

Her other worry was her mother's couturier business. She talked to Loretta and Rosa, the two seamstresses, but they assured her that they had no intention of leaving their jobs or taking over the workshop. They didn't belong to any union or party and they didn't have revolutionary ideas. They instead had children to feed and clothe.

She talked to Giannina about the social situation. "Is it affecting the business?" she asked.

"*E strano*, it's strange, Amelia," said Giannina, "things are going quite well in the workshop. The ladies who come here don't seem to be bothered by the disorders on the streets and they always have money. I don't know how they manage, but it's good for us. The *fasci* youths seemed to be after the protesting workers only. They don't interfere with wealthy people. I guess they are not after money. I try to avoid both the youths and the protesting workers. These days Renato is the one who goes to the market. The vendors know him well by now."

"That's good to hear. My mother always says in her letters that everything is fine, but sometimes I wonder. Renato is such a good person and I'm glad that he's still with us, Giannina."

"Maybe not for long. He's thinking of going to *l'America*. Imagine!"

"America! Why?"

"Everyone is trying to go there, Amelia. There's money to be made! And Renato is young," continued Giannina, "he has become a very good cook and I suspect he hopes to find a job in a restaurant, like my son when he first arrived in New York. Who knows, maybe my son could hire him for his restaurant."

"I guess he could make a good life there," said Amelia.

"We are his only family, if you can call us that. He has big hopes and he realizes that nothing much is happening in Italy, except for work shortages and strikes. He hears a lot of success stories of people gone to the United States. I know he is saving money to go."

"I hope he makes it, although I know we will miss him," said Amelia, "especially you, Giannina."

"Amelia, dear, you still have that little girl's charm I've always loved," said Giannina. "It's true, Renato has been like a son to me. But he has to make his own life."

"Oh Giannina," said Amelia putting her arms around the petite woman that she had always adored, "these have been some wonderful weeks at home. I will miss you even more now. I worry a lot about you and my mother and I'm happy that Carlo and Eva are here with you two. Please let me know how things really are, Giannina, Please!"

"Ma si! I will write and tell you," said Giannina.

Amelia left Milan just as the industrial workers went on strike and the factories closed. The same thing was happening in Bologna and then in all of Italy.

The newspapers announced that the whole country was on strike.

CHAPTER THIRTY-FIVE

Roberto sat on the train still worried about the angry crowd that surrounded the station. They were protesting. The people who had jobs were upset because their wages were insufficient and the ones who didn't have a job felt that they had lost it to the soldiers who had returned from the war unharmed.

Roberto closed his eyes and tried to sleep. The train was hardly moving. He wanted to stop all thoughts of war and revolution. It seemed to him that he had lived too much in one way and not enough in another. He had enough of war, but not enough of loving. Maybe his choices had been wrong.

He had left his parents to pursue a dream that was now lost, forfeiting the opportunity to be with them in their last years.

He had lost contact with his brother and his two sisters.

He had lost two of his best friends.

He didn't want to see any more killings or injustices, but he kept encountering them. Years ago he had thought that he could control his fate, but life had proven him wrong.

The three weeks that he had spent with the Corelli family in Milan had given Roberto a renewed sense of belonging. He felt part of the family again. However, the long road in front of him was distressing as he wouldn't be able to live with Amelia for a long time still. He loved her, as he never thought he could love anyone, but he couldn't be with her.

From now on, his studies would require working with the doctors and professors in every area of the hospital. Together with the other students he would have to observe, visit patients, be present at different procedures in the university amphitheater and study and report constantly. He would have to live part of the time in the hospital. He would be assisting in the emergency area on a rotating basis and still working with the amputees. It was going to be nearly impossible to go to Bologna to visit Amelia.

As he entered Dr. Antonelli's house, in Padua, the doctor asked:

"How was your trip to Milan? Did you enjoy yourself? I see you're carrying a violin. Are you thinking of playing it, Roberto"

"It's a viola, doctor. Maestro Stracciari insisted on giving it to me. But I don't know…"

"What do you mean you don't know? This is an opportunity to do something with music that will give you some relief from fatigue and an outlet for emotion. This is going to be a difficult year for you but you can always find the time for a short practice session. Can you play a bit?"

"Not really. When I was a little boy I had four violin lessons, but then I stopped. Later on I preferred the piano to help me practice singing."

"Well, I have a friend in the Accademia di Musica, Maestro Lorenzetti. Go to see him. I'm sure he'll be glad to help you."

Roberto was unsure but Dr. Antonelli kept a close watch on him and eventually he went. Although it was the end of the summer, there were sounds of string and wind instruments being played.

They mingled into the usual clatter typical of music schools and the sound carried his mind to a distant past. The recollection was so vivid and painful that he almost lost his nerve.

Maestro Lorenzetti reminded Roberto of the portraits he had seen of Nicolo Paganini, the genial Genovese violinist and composer –tall, very thin and with a remarkable aquiline nose.

"Have you taken other lessons at the Academy?"

"No, Maestro, this is my first time here."

"Your face is familiar. What did you say your name was?"

"Roberto Madariaga, Maestro."

"Madariaga...mmm. I know! I heard that name before. Four or five years ago I heard a young tenor in Milan, singing *Andrea Chenier.* Do you know him, by chance?"

Roberto braced himself. "That was me, Maestro," he said almost shaking.

"But, don't you sing any more?"

"No, Maestro, I lost my voice to gas during the war," his voice breaking. *This was the kind of thing that he had feared all along.*

"O, santo cielo! Scusa! I'm so sorry! So, so sorry!" Said the Maestro. He was so upset that Roberto came to the rescue.

"But I'm okay, Maestro. I'm studying to become a doctor now. A new life... A different life..."

"Yes, I guess..." said the Maestro. "I see you have a viola with you. *Permette?* Would you allow me?" he added opening the case. He took out the instrument, plucked the strings and adjusted the tuning. He started to play Braga's "Angels' Serenade."

The sound filled the room and Roberto felt the back of his neck tingling.

"This is a superb instrument!" said Maestro Lorenzetti, "you will enjoy playing it!"

"It's a gift from Maestro Stracciari."

"The famous baritone?"

"Yes, Maestro, he was my singing teacher."

Roberto explained about his tight schedule at the hospital; he would not always be able to come to his lesson. "But I'll try my best, Maestro."

He left the academy with mixed feelings. It had been a shock but he had survived the burn to his pride. And the thought that one day he could play together with Amelia the way he had heard Maestro Lorenzetti play, filled him with hope and gave him strength to keep the promise he had made to Maestro Stracciari.

CHAPTER THIRTY-SIX

The newspaper headlines read: *Contadini controllano le tenute.*" The farm workers had taken over the agricultural lands and farms in many areas. In Turin the army had been mobilized to the factories to suppress restless workers. The *Corriere de la Sera* informed in large print: *Camicie nere battono gli operai.* –youths wearing black shirts beat up striking workers. Who were they?

The next months were full of shocking events. These small squads of youths called "fascists" or "black shirts" were growing in numbers and their actions were extending their reach, fighting anything or anyone that represented socialism, with blood-shedding consequences. No one was sure where the groups were coming from but most of the members were young and aggressive. The hospitals were busy tending to people who'd been hurt or wounded in these encounters.

The workers and the farm hands organized themselves in councils and tried to take over the land and the factories from the big owners and to run the enterprises on their own but they were not successful. The government intervened and enforced an agreement that didn't satisfy any group.

Meanwhile, a voice was constantly heard in the newspapers, that of Benito Mussolini, a former teacher turned journalist. His articles were conquering the minds of the Italian people with his relentless proposals to strengthen the country by imposing order and rebuilding the concepts of pride in hard work and love of country. Many intellectuals and most socialists were suspicious or definitely against his ideas on how to achieve that, but a large majority was hoping for a strong leader. It was the fall of 1922.

Padua had been the center of operations during the war but now, four years after the armistice, the city had returned to its more important activities, teaching and learning. These were pursuits that dated back to the thirteenth century. Roberto took delight in knowing that he was studying at the same university where luminaries of the past such as Copernicus, Torquato Tasso and Galileo had studied and taught. The city showed pride in that fact by honoring these wise men with their statues in the quiet gardens of the Prato della Valle.

Although Padua was a city of pilgrimage for devotees of Saint Anthony, it had kept a small town feeling that allowed people to walk everywhere.

The *Orto Botanico* one of the oldest botanical gardens in Europe, came alive in the month of May with the scent of the opening buds of the flowers and the leafing out of the trees. Another full term had passed and Roberto's attitude towards life had changed. He was calmer and less prone to respond to his anger when encountering injustice or abuse. He had developed deeper appreciation for all that surrounded him, from the sounds of the city, its buildings, its atmosphere to all living things. The *Orto* provided him with an ideal place to clear his mind and ponder over medical conditions.

He was committed to a future of restoring people to health and he loved the work and the study more and more.

He didn't have much time for music but, as promised to Stracciari, he had learned to play the viola. He practiced whenever he could as a way to release the tension from hospital work. His Maestro had been right all along. Roberto enjoyed playing the instrument and was looking forward to joining Amelia as soon as he felt ready.

Amelia was about to graduate from the Faculty of Sciences of the University of Bologna with a degree in chemistry and pharmacy and Roberto was proud and excited at the thought of her becoming a professional scientist.

These two years had been extremely hard to take. They hadn't been able to see each other much as both had an enormous amount of work, reports and papers to turn in. They always wrote to each other however briefly but that was not enough.

CHAPTER THIRTY-SEVEN

Roberto awoke in the small room surrounded by white washed walls. He didn't mind the narrow space that the hospital provided for the residents. It was private and it had a window. It reminded him of the sleepers in the Pullman cars of the trains. One couldn't study or write notes in them. One could only think or sleep.

He was now in his fourth year of medicine. He had been up all night in the Emergency Room and now, in his room, he dozed off.

A persistent knock startled him.

"Doctor! To the administration, immediately, please! It's an emergency!!"

Roberto jumped out of bed, pulled on his white pants and lab coat and grabbed his stethoscope. He ran along the corridors to the head office.

"It's Dr. Antonelli," said the nurse who had called him, as they rushed along.

"Oh, my God!"

The office staff had just arrived and was frantic. Dr. Antonelli could hardly talk.

"Please! My wife!" He managed to say in a hoarse whisper.

"Please get *Signora Antonelli*," Roberto said to one of the orderlies who had come in the room. "Stay calm and reassure her. Go, go!"

Then to Dr. Antonelli: "Professore, please open your mouth, is *trinitrin*. Under your tongue, please."

He asked the staff to get a pillow or cushion and then turned the doctor on the floor with his head raised and opened his shirt.

He listened to his heart, "Help me to lift his arms above his head, up, down, up, down. Breathe in Professore."

The doctor's pulse was faint. He was drifting away and Roberto massaged his heart.

Two senior doctors had entered, with an orderly behind them. Together they lifted Dr. Antonelli onto a gurney and tried artificial respiration and heart massage, but by the time his wife arrived, Dr. Antonelli had expired.

"It cannot be!" she exclaimed, when the senior doctor told her. "He was fine this morning."

"These things don't give any warning, they just happen, Signora Antonelli. His heart gave up. I'm terribly sorry," said Dr. Gamaggio, the Chief of Staff.

Still in disbelief, Signora Antonelli said: "I want to be alone with him, please."

"Of course, Signora."

Caterina Antonelli was in shock. "I'll be outside if you need me," Roberto said to her. She nodded.

When she finally came out, Roberto could not see any trace of tears just a shadow of total desolation covered her face.

"I'll accompany you home, Signora Antonelli."

They walked in silence to her house. When she opened the front door she looked around as if expecting to see her husband coming out of his studio.

"Please sit down, Roberto," she said as she curled herself up, sorrow-stricken on the sofa.

"I'll make some tea," he said, disappearing into the kitchen trying to think of something, to soften the woman's grief.

"Should I inform anyone?" asked Roberto as he walked back with a cup of tea.

Signora Antonelli lifted her head. "My sister, please. Her address is in the book on top of the desk. Her name is Nicoletti, Rosa."

"Can I help you with the burial arrangements?"

"Gaetano must have known that his heart was failing," she said. "A few weeks ago he told me that he had arranged all that. *Se per caso* he had said lightly, just in case. Oh God! He knew!"

Still she couldn't cry.

"Signora Antonelli, please drink the tea. Maybe you should lie down. I'll advise your sister and I'll go to the *agenzia funeraria*. You try to rest."

Roberto was dismayed when he realized that Signora Antonelli did not have any family in town and only a few friends, mainly related to the doctor's work at the hospital. During the three years that he had lived on and off with them he noticed that Signora Antonelli was a shy and private person.

Roberto went out of the house leaving Signora Antonelli still curled on the sofa. He sent a telegram to Signora Rosa Nicoletti and to Amelia, to inform them of the death of Dr. Antonelli.

A day later, Amelia arrived in Padua. "How is she?" she asked.

"Not well," said Roberto. "She's still in shock. Dr. Biaggi has seen her and has given her something to sleep but I fear it's making her worse."

Then he said, "Oh Amelia dear, I have to go back to the hospital. I'm on duty for the next two days and nights, but I'll try to come around even for just a few minutes. Thank you *Cara* for coming."

"Don't worry, Roberto, I'll look after her and stay here until her sister arrives. You go to the hospital."

As he walked back to the hospital Roberto thought about Amelia's kindness and compassion and about how fast a life can change.

Amelia embraced Signora Antonelli tenderly. She had only seen her twice before but she immediately noticed that the twinkle in her eyes had disappeared. There was no expression.

Dr. Antonelli had been a well-respected physician and professor and the hospital staff and many former patients and university students attended the funeral. The ceremony was extremely sad, as their son was also dead and the sight of Caterina Antonelli accompanied by her sister, Amelia and Roberto was heartbreaking. When Amelia left for Bologna, signora Antonelli remained with her sister. She would help her deal with the situation.

In a short time Rosa Nicoletti came to the conclusion that her sister couldn't live alone. The loss of her son and now of her husband had left her spiritless. She decided to take Signora Antonelli with her to Florence. They both could live in the old family home.

One afternoon when Roberto entered the house Signora Antonelli told him the news. *"Mi dispiace moltissimo, Roberto.* I'm terribly sorry, but I have put the house up for sale. Gaetano and I had planned on moving and going to live in Sicily, in the future, but as we know, death is not predictable. I am going back to Fiesole, in the outskirts of Florence, to live with Rosa in our family home. I guess it's for the best." Her discourse had been delivered almost without feeling.

"I fully understand, Signora Antonelli."

"I'm worried that you won't have a place to stay when you're not in the hospital. Gaetano and I have been so happy having you here, with us, but now...."

"Please don't worry about me, Signora Antonelli, I'll manage. You have done so much for me. You have been tremendously kind to me all along and I will be forever grateful. Now, for you, it's important to be with family."

"I cannot stay here, Roberto. Do you understand? There are too many painful memories, our son, and now Gaetano… and this city, it only reminds me of war and loss."

She was now shaking and tears were running down her cheeks. Roberto held her against him and let her unload her grief. She had been so kind to him from the first moment when he had arrived at the Antonelli's home, disheveled and beaten down. Her unobtrusive but warm care had helped him regain his strength and Dr. Antonelli's guidance and encouragement had helped him find a new road. He felt terribly sad not to be able to give her the comfort she needed now. His presence was not enough. He could never replace her son. He hoped that Signora Antonelli's sister would be the kind of person who would give her strength. He could see Signora Antonelli had lost much weight but, finally, she had cried.

The death of Dr. Antonelli affected Roberto enormously. He had been his professor and his mentor. He missed him deeply! Only Amelia's love kept him on track. She was now back in Milan doing her practice and it was impossible for him to travel so far. After Signora Antonelli sold the house, his life changed even more. The hospital allowed him to live full-time in the residential quarters, but his scholarship money was barely enough to eat. He had just informed the viola teacher that he couldn't continue with the classes and was on his way back to the hospital when it started to rain. He stopped in front of a restaurant, debating whether he should spend the money and go in and have a coffee while the rain abated. He could hear a piano being played and decided to enter. He sat at a table and placed the viola in its case on top of a chair.

"Coffee, please," said Roberto.

The waiter touched the case and said: "*Lei suona?* You play?"

"A little."

"*Venga, venga.*" The waiter gestured Roberto to move to another table close to the piano. There were few customers at that hour and the piano player, who looked bored, without preambles said: "Want to play?"

"I guess, maybe," he answered a bit surprised to be asked directly.

"How about Toselli's "Rimpianto"? Here!" the pianist added placing the sheet of music on the table. "Good to have a fellow musician."

"*Va bene,* I'll try," said Roberto taking out the viola and plucking the strings and tuning. The piano player started the introduction and Roberto played for the first time in front of the waiters and a small group at the back of the restaurant. He managed to deliver the song. People applauded at the end and Roberto bent his head and swept his hand towards the pianist and shook hands with him. They continued to play for a while and then Roberto sat down to have his coffee.

"Do you play somewhere else? Asked the pianist.

"Not really. I'm a medical student."

"Too bad! You should be a musician."

An older man in a dinner jacket approached the table. "That was very good! I'm Giuseppe Marino!"

"*Piacere, Signor Marino, sono* Roberto Madariaga," Roberto said shaking his hand.

"Enzo, *un buon café per I musicisti!* He said to the waiter.

"Imagine Giuseppe, he's a medical student," interjected the pianist.

"At the university here?"

"Yes, I'm at the university hospital most of the time now."

"Do you ever do work with the amputees?" Asked the owner.

"Yes, I do," answered Roberto.

"You must know my son, Vittorio."

"Vittorio is your son? Of course I do! He's a courageous young man," said Roberto. "He's working hard to regain some mobility,"

"So you are Roberto? Of course! Vittorio talks a lot about you; about the exercises you give him, about how you encourage him. You have restored his will to live. I'm forever grateful to you! You play well too! You can come here whenever you want to eat or play or both, if you wish. *Questa e la vostra casa,* this is your house!" The owner said putting his hand warmly on Roberto's shoulder.

"Thank you, Signor!"

"Another thing, are you available to play on Saturday or Sunday afternoons? For a fee, of course!"

"I'd love to! But I'm not sure of my duty hours until the week before. I can come and let you know a week in advance. I'd certainly like to play here. It's a lovely place! Thank you, Signor Marino. It's been a pleasure meeting you," said Roberto glancing at his watch. "Now, unfortunately, I have to run but I'll come back. *Grazie di tutto!*" He shook hands with Mr. Marino and with the pianist and rushed out of the restaurant.

It had rained heavily while Roberto was in the restaurant and the cobblestones glittered under the evening lights. He walked briskly enthused by the prospect of playing his viola in the restaurant and earning some money. The atmosphere was heavy and humid but a wave of optimism enveloped him. That had been a good coincidence.

CHAPTER THIRTY-EIGHT

Amelia had completed her required practice at a pharmaceutical company and submitted her thesis to the university. Then she waited for the date of her professional dissertation. The entire family, including Luisa, Carlo, Eva, Giannina and Renato travelled from Milan to Bologna. Signor Morgatti and his wife drove their motorcar with Signora Luisa and Giannina as passengers. The others took the train. Roberto travelled from Padua. Everyone was excited but also nervous. When Amelia came out of the dissertation room with a big smile on her face, they rushed to congratulate her. The professors had given her their unanimous vote of approval. She was jubilant and ready for a new life.

Aunt Lucia celebrated Amelia's accomplishment with a reception with champagne and canapés. This type of festivity had not been seen in her household for a long time.

After the celebration the Corelli family returned to Milan and Amelia started to work in the pharmaceutical laboratory where she had completed her research, in Milan.

Roberto returned to Padua, to his medical studies and, when possible, he played the viola at "Marino's", Vittorio's father restaurant.

Signora Luisa considered it improper for Amelia to go by herself to see Roberto in Padua since the Antonellis were no longer there. Amelia waited impatiently for the days when Roberto was able to travel to Milan. Their reunions were few and far between.

"Roberto," she said one day. "If you haven't changed your mind about getting married?"

"Of course I haven't!" He interrupted.

"Then, let's get married after Christmas, when you have a few days off. We can welcome the New Year in a chalet in the Alps or the Dolomites," said Amelia.

"In three months! But we can't Amelia! Since Dr. Antonelli's death, my situation has changed so radically that I can barely make it through each month," said Roberto imagining Amelia living the way he was living now.

"I have enough money for us to rent a small apartment in Padua for at least two years. And I may find work in a pharmaceutical company or a laboratory right there. At least we can be together. Separation is becoming unbearable to me."

"It's unbearable for me too, Amelia. But I can't do that. It's against everything I've been taught all my life. I have to be able to support you, Amelia."

"Roberto, we are living in a new time. Just think of your friend Clara. Look around you. Do you consider me your equal?"

"Of course I do!"

"Well, right now our life requires something that I can provide. Let me be a real partner and share in every part of our life together," said Amelia. "I know that further ahead things may change."

"But, this is crazy! I can't accept that."

"You mean to tell me Roberto, that all your thoughts about equality of women, their important contribution to science, government, planning and so on, are so shallow as not to be able to apply them to your own life? It's all right for other people but not for you? Imagine," she added, "women have now the possibility of holding some public offices and maybe one day they will be paid the same salaries as men are paid. Everything is changing!"

Roberto was beside himself. He could hardly talk.

"Amelia, I love you with all my heart and respect you. That's all I know."

"Then, if you really love me, you will not want to prolong this situation. We both know what we want from life. We can do it together. Please, my love!" she said taking Roberto's hand in hers. "Forget pride and think of the dreams that were truncated by the war. Think of the people who died, of the terrible things that happened. Our lives changed, but we are here, you survived and… my love for you survived all that," said Amelia.

"Oh Amelia," said Roberto embracing her. "Let's walk and clear our minds," he said tenderly. He would have liked to talk this over with Dr. Antonelli. He had been a wise man, a mentor.

"I'll take care of everything –the licenses and the arrangements. You come after Christmas and we'll get married on the 27th of December. What do you think, Roberto?"

Roberto didn't know what to say. "You are amazing, Amelia! And I adore you," he said kissing her.

They walked until they came to a church. Amelia stopped.

"Ti piace la chiesa? Do you like this church?" She said as they stood in front of the Church of Saint Barnaba.

Roberto assented. How he loved this woman. He wanted what she wanted.

"I like it, Amelia. I'll be here."

He returned that evening to Padua and when he entered the hospital in the middle of the night, he could not stop smiling.

In seeing him the nurses joked: *"Il signor medico e innamorato!"* Yes, he was very much in love, and wanted to spend the rest of his life with Amelia, without doubt. But, what would his parents say? Everything was different now. Walking along the hospital corridors he felt qualms about what his father would have thought of his getting married without having a secure income. However, when he entered the amputee ward, he knew that what he was doing was right –to live before life was mutilated or cut short.

He played his viola at the restaurant, whenever possible, to be able to bring some money to their future household. Every time he thought about this Roberto trembled from desire but also from misgivings. *It's not easy to forget childhood teachings.*

In Milan, Signora Luisa and Giannina were tremendously excited at the prospect of Amelia's marriage.

"I'm so happy for you, my child!" said Luisa. "I know how long you have waited for this. I still remember your expression when you first set eyes on Roberto. You were so young. I thought that the feeling would pass but I guess it only grew."

"Yes Mamma, it grew through war and loss. Do you remember how I used to read D'Annunzio's poetry? Then, maybe I was in love with love, but now I'm in love with Roberto. It was a miracle that he came to our house to live. I will always be grateful to Maestro Stracciari for sending him to us."

That night Amelia sat at the piano and played her favorite Schubert's Impromptu and Saint-Saens's "Mon Coeur Souvre a ta Voix," as the magic of love enveloped her.

For the next weeks the Corelli family was in a whirlwind. Signora Luisa and Giannina worked on the wedding dress while Eva and Amelia planned for the ceremony, the music and the flowers.

Soon it was time to prepare the meal. Everyone worked fever-ishly making ravioli. Renato went in and out of the house on con-tinuous errands. Even the Morgatti's had brought small baskets of homemade confections for the wedding.

Eva planned for a lovely bride's bouquet with small white roses and also a tiny one for her little daughter Sofia, who would be the flower girl. And Aunt Lucia came from Bologna to decorate the church with vases of white canna lilies and white gladioli. The music was to be played by an organ accompanied by a cello and a violin.

Carlo was looking forward to walking his sister down the aisle. He believed that his dear friend, Roberto, would make Amelia very happy. His father would have approved.

They were so busy that there was no time to think of the effect that Amelia's marriage was going to have on her mother. She had been back for some time and Luisa had again grown accustomed to having her around. Her absence would leave an emptiness that couldn't be filled even by her chatty granddaughter. Sofia, the lit-tle girl, had discovered the wonder of words and wanted to know everything from her *Nonna* –her grandmother.

Roberto boarded the train for Milan the day after Christmas hav-ing spent two busy days and nights in the emergency ward at the hospital. He didn't feel tired, the excitement of his marriage kept him awake. He visualized his future with Amelia as he looked out of the window into the falling darkness and thought of his mother and how much she would have liked his future wife. The train fi-nally arrived in Milan two hours late. He jumped out and rushed to the flower shop where he bought one red rose, which the atten-dant wrapped carefully in cellophane.

"*Per la sua bella? Auguri!*" She said smiling.

"Yes! It's for my beloved, my beautiful Amelia!" Replied Roberto almost flying away.

The streets were peaceful and the sounds of the *zampognari* could be heard, probably playing their pipes close to some piazza.

He rushed to the Corelli's house and was greeted at the door by Amelia. He handed her the rose saying: *"Per la mia bella, in-namorata! Tesor mio!"* wishing he could sing the words of Luigi Gastaldon's song.

Amelia and Roberto were married at St. Barnaba's, the lovely church they had seen a few months back. Amelia had wanted it to be a simple affair. Although the war had ended nearly five years before, the economic situation in the country was still difficult and there were many people still suffering and without work. She had chosen a private and tasteful ceremony.

Roberto waited at the foot of the altar for his bride.

Amelia entered the church accompanied by Carlo and pre-ceded by Signora Luisa and her granddaughter, Sofia and walked down the aisle with the background music of the "Intermezzo" of *Cavalleria Rusticana.* Roberto trembled.

She was exquisitely dressed in an elegant cream-colored two-piece suit, trimmed with suede and a small matching hat that framed her beautiful face. Her ankle-length skirt had no train and she wore no veil. She looked stunning in her simplicity. Roberto felt the rest of the world disappear; there was only Roberto and Amelia.

Then at last, they swore their love to each other with the prom-ise: *to have and to hold – till death do us part.*

Amelia wished so much for her father and Cesare to be present and Roberto wished for his father and mother and his brother and sisters to be there too.

As they walked with beaming smiles on their faces towards the church exit, accompanied by the notes of Händel's *Ombra Mai Fu,* Roberto noticed that Maestro Stracciari wasn't there. Only his faithful butler, Antonio, was present.

"The Maestro is not well. He's sorry he could not come," the valet said when he approached to offer his congratulations a few minutes later.

"Can we come and visit him for a moment?" Asked Roberto.

"I'm sure he would love that."

After they were greeted and embraced by all their family and friends, Roberto asked Amelia, if she would go with him to see Stracciari.

"Of course, my love! Let's go right away. People will take a while to arrive at the house."

After they told Signora Luisa and Giannina they were driven to the Maestro's house, accompanied by Antonio.

Maestro Stracciari looked weak but made an effort to be cheerful. "What a joy to see you, Roberto! I'm sorry I missed the ceremony but, believe me, my heart was there with you." He took Roberto's hands in his own. "The doctor said I suffered a cardiac arrest. It's just an old heart that doesn't want to work anymore. The doctor says I'll be well soon if I rest," he added smiling sadly, "but I feel the end is near, Roberto."

"Don't say that Maestro," replied Roberto. "Amelia and I came to see you and to share our joy with you."

"Where is she? That beautiful girl!"

"Just outside, Maestro."

"Please tell her to come in, if you don't mind. I'd love to wish her happiness with you, my son. Am I presentable?"

"You're fine, Maestro!" Roberto said as he walked to the door to show Amelia in.

She greeted the Maestro warmly.

Animated by their radiant appearance, the Maestro said: "*Un bicchierino?* The doctor has ordered no wine or spirits, so it will have to be mineral water for me and a little *Cinzano* for you two," he said lifting his glass as Antonio filled the small goblets: "*Roberto e Amelia, Vi auguro una vita piena di musica e d'amore!"* I wish you a lifetime full of music and love. The three of them stood up for a moment, with Antonio standing by watchfully.

"Andate! Siate felice!" Time to go, be happy!" said the Maestro feeling that he was about to cry.

They embraced warmly, Roberto felt a knot in his throat thinking that perhaps this would be the last time he would see his dear Maestro. Just before going out the door he said quietly, to Stracciari:"I have learned to play the viola, Maestro. What a wonderful idea it was! *Grazie!"*

The Maestro smiled knowingly.

Amelia couldn't stop thinking how wonderful it had been for Roberto to find Maestro Stracciari. He was like a father to him and their mutual affection was evident. Yet, although Roberto didn't say anything, she too realized that the Maestro's life was coming to an end.

They set aside the apprehension and joined in the merriment of the family that was waiting anxiously for them.

"To the bride and groom!" *"Salute a gli sposi!"* "To Love! To Life!" Everybody was making toasts.

Roberto stood up and said: "To my beloved Amelia, who waited for my hard-headed love to wake up."

"Ti amo," she answered.

It was a delightful meal and everyone praised the efforts of the cooks. The Morgattis thought that the ravioli were the best they had ever tasted and the *vitello al rosemarino* was outstanding. At the end of the meal everyone enjoyed the *confitti* prepared by Signora Morgatti.

Aunt Lucia and her gramophone was the perfect touch to complement the occasion and Luisa Corelli smiled happily seeing her daughter dance with Roberto looking completely in love.

"Amelia," had said Aunt Lucia the day before as she handed her an envelope, "my gift to you and Roberto is one-night at a hotel in town before you travel to the mountains and to Padua."

"Oh, Aunt Lucia! This is the most expensive hotel in the city," said Amelia when she opened the envelope. "I don't feel right about you spending that kind of money. The train can be romantic too."

"Romantic? Of course! But not very comfortable! Leave that for later, my dear. Please accept this. I do it with all my heart."

And Lucia didn't want them to travel the same evening after the wedding. She had gone to the hotel and reserved a beautiful room, on the top floor and had decorated it with flowers, a bowl of fruit and a small bottle of champagne. She did things with style.

The party ended with all the guests saying goodbye to the *sposi*. A motorcar would take them a few streets down to the hotel.

"Mia cara piccola figlia!' said Signora Luisa making a big effort to hide her tears. She kissed and blessed Amelia, her little girl, her *piccina*. An avalanche of mixed feelings invaded Amelia. She was touching perfection being with Roberto but her heart was also breaking by leaving her mother.

Roberto and Amelia entered the hotel feeling self-conscious. Everyone seemed to be giving them a knowing smile.

Once in their room, they relaxed.

Amelia got closer to the balcony and admired the view of the park below. It was beginning to snow and the street lamps shone their light on the falling snowflakes. Roberto stood behind her and slowly turned her around to face him. He kissed her softly. Her response was full of desire. She took his face in her hands and looked at him deeply and lovingly. He could hardly control himself.

She took off her jacket and he did too. She started unbuttoning his shirt but could not take off the stiff collar he was wearing. They laughed, partly out of nervousness.

He was gentle and purposefully slow, sensitive to the fact that this moment would mark the rest of their lives. The night covered them with its mantle of yearnings and desires as bit by bit they discovered one another.

With the morning light, Amelia awoke. She marveled at the perfection of human nature and at her new knowledge. She looked at
Roberto, still asleep by her side and gave silent thanks to the life
that had given her this wonderful man. He opened his eyes slowly
exultant at the sight of her beside him.

"You're beautiful!" he said.

"You're beautiful too!"

The small train threaded slowly through the Ampezzo Valley in
the Dolomites. Amelia and Roberto were awestruck by the view
of the colossal peaks now almost covered in snow. Inwardly, they
couldn't help but remembering that a few years before alpine soldiers had been fighting on those same peaks, but they made no
mention of it.

The town had healed from the effects of the war and Roberto
and Amelia walked around breathing the crisp air and admiring
the wooden chalets decorated with shrubs and potted flowers that
soon would be wilted by the frost. A light cover of snow had fallen
during the night but disappeared by noontime and the town came
alive with the smell of baked bread and the delivery of cheese and
cream to the various *pensione.* The church *campanile* rang twelve
times and people stopped to pray. It was another world, a world
that, although damaged by the war, had not been touched by cars
and modernity. For the next few days Amelia and Roberto walked
around the town and the valley, climbing the paths of the shep-
herds breathing the mountain air and getting to know each other
leisurely in the warmth of their small chalet, the flames of the
fireplace witnessing their love.

CHAPTER THIRTY-NINE

The day before New Year's Eve the weather turned foggy and rainy in the mountains. Amelia and Roberto decided to return to Padua and start their new life a day earlier than planned.

As the train made its way south, the weather cleared up and through the window they could see some signs of prosperity in the countryside; newly built barns adorned the landscape, although every few miles they still saw traces of bombed out buildings. They were quiet but at ease with each other.

Unable to hold his secret any longer, Roberto suddenly said to Amelia: "I have a surprise! We already have a small apartment close to the university hospital."

"Really?" she turned towards him with a big smile. "This is wonderful news! But how?"

"A colleague at the hospital returned to Perugia, his home town, and I took over his rental contract. I hope you like it. It's small but airy, with lots of light and it's heated with hot water radiators. Can you believe that? I jumped at the opportunity. He left just before Christmas, when I was at the hospital, so I didn't have time to arrange it for your arrival, Amelia."

"Don't worry, Roberto. We'll do that together. That's incredible!"

"Yes, it is! I had had no time to look for an apartment and this came unexpectedly. It's almost impossible to find an apartment close to the university, especially at this time of year. I'll be able to walk home in ten minutes."

Amelia's lips were smiling as they dozed off with the lull of the train.

In Belluno a group of *alpini* soldiers got on the train. They were on leave, going home for the New Year and were in high spirits. They passed around some wine and bread to start celebrating the end of the year. It was impossible to sleep as they started to sing their alpine songs.

Amelia held Roberto's hand tight as the group sang "Monte Canino" *Non ti ricordi quel mese d'aprile* –Do you remember that month of April?"

How could he forget? The memory of that morning when he had climbed the mountain and found Cesare and the rest of the company... came sharply into mind. He shivered and Amelia tightened her hold and touched his cheek. Roberto knew that he couldn't stop the memories from returning but he could look ahead and help build a better world. As the wine began to take effect, the soldiers moved on to happier songs.

The train finally pulled into the station in Padua.

It was extremely cold and Roberto decided they should take a taxi to their new home. Amelia was thrilled when they stopped in front of a three-storied classical building with an impressive entrance. He explained that every floor was divided into small apartments.

They climbed the marble staircase to the first floor. It had an elaborate wrought iron handrail that became simpler in design as they went up to the second floor and walked along the spacious corridor to their apartment.

"Voila!" said Roberto as he opened the door.

He immediately walked towards the two tall windows and drew back the curtains. The winter light inundated the room and unlike outside, the place was warm.

"It's beautiful!" exclaimed Amelia.

"Wait! I'm supposed to carry you in," said Roberto. He picked her up and carried her across the threshold. Both were laughing. She looked around happily. The apartment was only partially furnished and that would make it easy to decorate. She sat down on the small chesterfield with a big smile on her face and extended her arms to him. "This is absolutely lovely, Roberto. We'll be very happy here."

"It's a bit the worse for wear," he said as he sank down beside Amelia.

"Let's see the kitchen," said Amelia standing and walking towards the next room, "Oh, look at that stove! And this!" she exclaimed. Roberto's colleague had left some ground coffee, a small bottle of wine and dried fruit and nuts with a card that read: *Buona fortuna! Auguri!*

"What a thoughtful gesture!" Said Amelia. "Should we stay in and celebrate the New Year quietly? We still have a large piece of that delicious cheese and the bread that we bought this morning in Ampezzo."

"Splendid idea!"

So they greeted the year 1923 in the secluded warmth of their small apartment.

Signor Marino had invited Roberto and Amelia to his restaurant for the fifth of January to celebrate *La Befana*, the eve of the feast of Epiphany, when children in all of Italy receive small presents of candy, dried fruit and honey.

Da Marino's restaurant lights shone brightly that night. The tables were beautifully set up with white tablecloths, crystal, silver and flowers.

Roberto was beaming when he introduced Amelia to Signor Marino.

They soon realized that this was a celebration in their honor. To his enormous surprise, among the guests and sitting on a wheelchair was Vittorio, the owner's son.

He was smiling as he stood up slowly on his artificial legs and embraced Roberto. "What do you think, *Dottore?*"

Roberto looked at him in disbelief, "Vittorio! Fantastic! This is Fantastic!" He introduced him to Amelia who held his hands in hers as he expressed his good wishes. Everyone was clapping for the newlyweds and for the amputee who had finally come out of the hospital to join the world again.

Glasses of *Lambrusco* went around and toasts were made. Vittorio's mother approached Roberto and kissed him: "*Grazie!*" she said and controlling her tears went to embrace Amelia.

"A song! A song!" clamored the group.

So Roberto approached the piano and took out his viola, which he had left there before going to Milan. He tuned it up and looking at Amelia, said:

"For you!"

"Malia, Maestro?" He said to the pianist and started to play Tosti's song. He had not told Amelia that he was playing the instrument. He had wanted to surprise her.

Amelia couldn't take her eyes off Roberto's face. She was transported to higher ground. "Malia" was the first aria Roberto had sung at her mother's house, when she had asked him to sing. The sound filled the restaurant and the guests were mesmerized and so was she. Roberto's playing was a gift just as his singing had been. She envisaged the two of them playing piano and viola duets in the evenings in their home. Tears were flowing down her cheeks. Roberto had rediscovered music.

Winter turned to spring and there were changes in the hospital. Roberto had become increasingly interested in the rehabilitation of spinal injury and loss of limbs but the new hospital director had decided to move those patients to another facility.

"They will be in a chronic care unit," he explained. "There they will receive regular care."

"But then, doctor, they we will not be doing the rehabilitation work and they won't be part of the research work that we have been carrying out here," said Roberto.

"That's right, Dr. Madariaga. Here we'll be concerned with acute care and emergencies. Rehabilitation and research will be carried out in another facility."

Roberto was upset. He would not be working any more with the amputees or the paraplegics. He considered them his cases and was disheartened by the fact that the new director was not interested in that field. He had not told him or Nurse Cristina about the changes. Roberto felt some of the patients were close to succeeding in their efforts to walk or move their limbs and the change would affect them but soon realized that there was nothing he could do. The decision had been taken.

He talked to Amelia about this: "It seems to me that we're abandoning them," he said. "Some of them are progressing, but without constant support and encouragement they may fall back or worse, the progress may stop altogether."

"You have to have faith in them, Roberto," she replied. "You have given them hope and now they have to find the courage within themselves to keep going. That's the only way that they will be able to survive physically and emotionally, accepting their own disabilities and coping with them on their own. You won't be able to be with them always."

"I know, but at least until they have reached a level of movement and confidence," he replied sadly.

"That's not possible now, my love. I know how much you care and I love you all the more for that," she said tenderly, "but you have to accept their decision."

"That's what bothers me too. I don't know if I would like to work with the new director."

"Right now, it is this way; only eight months to go, my love. Be patient. Just do your best."

They were settling down in their life together and getting used to the hospital shifts. Sometimes Roberto could not get away for two full days. Amelia thought it was time for her to look for a job. She went to the Faculty of Science of the University to see if she could work in the laboratories.

"I'm afraid we don't have any positions at present," said the administrator. "However, I saw in your documentation that you speak French. We may need some translation work done. Are you fluent in that language?"

"Yes, sir, I am."

"We receive monthly research papers from Grenoble University and we would like the advanced students to be able to read them. You have the science background. Do you think you could translate them for us?"

"I think I could," said Amelia, already interested in the project.

"We will pay you by the page and you can do it at home. Do you have a typewriter? If not, there's a place on the Via Savonarola that sells used ones. So, Signora, can you do it?" *It felt strange to be called Signora.*

"Can I take a look at one of the papers just to be sure?"

So she sat down and read one of the papers and then reached an agreement with the administrator of the faculty. She walked home in high spirits. This would be an excellent way to keep informed about new research work and she would earn a bit of money too.

When Roberto came home after two days of emergency duty, Amelia had already laid out her small workspace, close to one of the windows, with a table, a chair, a typewriter and a stack of paper.

"What do you think?" she asked as she explained to him what she would be doing.

"I think it's great! *Cara.*" He was happy for her, as she would be working on something she loved. He took her in his arms and carried her to bed unable to think of anything else at that moment. And as with each and every time they made love, Amelia wondered whether other people in the world were enjoying similar glorious moments.

Just as things were settling down in the Faculty of Medicine and the hospital and Amelia was totally adapted to the irregular hours of work and to Roberto's time off, the news of Maestro Stracciari's death arrived. They had been worried about him ever since their wedding day, when they had last seen him, but they were unprepared for the effect his death had on them. When Roberto read the telegram he was devastated. Maestro Stracciari had been more than a father to him. For nearly six years he had been his teacher, his mentor, a true friend.

His studio had been a haven for Roberto. Even after the war, the Maestro had given him guidance and strength. His death was a terrible loss and both Amelia and Roberto were extremely sad on the train ride to Milan.

The School of Music organized a solemn ceremony in honor of Maestro Federico Stracciari. His world-famous former student, Gianni Seneschi, sang Faure's "Crucifix" together with another singer. All this brought back sad memories for Roberto, for this was the piece that the maestro had helped him rehearse for his mother's memorial mass. This new loss was terrible for him.

The choir of the Faculty of Music sang Mozart's "Ave Verum" at the end of the ceremony and the mourners walked slowly to the *"Cimetero Monumentale"* to the sound of two clarinets playing Chopin's funeral march.

Roberto and Amelia walked with Antonio, the valet, followed by Signora Corelli, Giannina, Carlo, Eva and Renato, followed by the teachers and the students of the Faculty of Music. It was a long, sad funeral procession.

At the end, Signor Seneschi walked over to greet them.

He took Roberto away for a moment and said: "Roberto, it's been a long time. Our dear Maestro told me about what happened at the front and I'm terribly sorry!"

"Well, that's war, Signor Seneschi," replied Roberto. "But, I'm alive, I have married a wonderful woman and I'm about to finish my medical studies. It hurts enormously not to be able to sing, I miss it, but... what else can I say?"

"Coraggio, Roberto!" Seneschi embraced Roberto, saluted the others and walked away.

On the train ride back to Padua, they were very quiet. Roberto couldn't bring himself to talk and Amelia shared his silence. No words could comfort him. With Stracciari's death and Seneschi's encounter, the thread to singing had snapped. The faint hope that Roberto had harbored to be able to sing once more, even quite softly, was over. He would not try to train with anybody else. No singing teacher would sustain even a few notes without recoiling from the harsh sound that came out of his throat. People who knew him were used to his speaking voice while others sometimes winced.

He told himself that he was about to become a doctor and he should be happy. He had by his side the most magnificent woman that he could have ever dreamt of finding. She loved him and he loved her with all his heart.

Singing was part of his past history. That chapter of his life was closed. He breathed deeply and turned to look at his wife.

CHAPTER FORTY

It was now time to find a medical position in another hospital since Roberto did not want to stay in Padua. There were openings in Mantua and Como. He submitted his applications and when his acceptance papers arrived from the *Ospedale Valduce* in Como, Roberto was pleased. The hospital, founded in 1853 by the Nursing Sisters of Mary of Sorrows, was known for the excellent care it gave to its patients.

Amelia was delighted too because Como was only an hour away from Milan and it would be easier to visit her family. Her translation work would have to stop but she was really hoping to find work in a laboratory.

"With this position, I may be able to have a private practice some afternoons," said Roberto. "Maybe we'll even find a house with an adjoining office."

"Nothing would please me more," replied Amelia.

A few months later they were installed in Como and Roberto started his work at the hospital.

On the second Sunday in July, Amelia's family visited.

She had prepared a special meal that everyone praised, particularly Giannina.

"Giannina, how are you?" asked Amelia. She knew that Giannina was sad because Renato had gone to live in the United States.

"I'm happy," replied Giannina, "Renato is working at my son's restaurant. Isn't that incredible! Look at the photographs that Signorina Clara sent," she added.

As promised, Clara had gone to the restaurant and taken several photographs and Giannina had brought them for everyone to see. They all smiled at the sight of Renato wearing a chef's hat, standing beside Vincenzo, Giannina's son and owner of the place.

"Life doesn't stop," she said.

Amelia always admired Giannina's practical mind and the ease with which she adapted to situations. She was a source of strength for her mother. It was good that she had never wanted to go to America to live with her son. She would never leave Italy. She loved Italy. It was her homeland.

Sofia, Carlo's and Eva's little girl kept everyone on their toes with her questions and funny remarks. Roberto entertained her by modeling animals out of the thin metal wrappers of the Gianduia chocolates that they had brought.

"Una giraffa!" She exclaimed, quickly. *"Un gabbiano!* A seagull!" Little Sofia seemed to be tireless, until she finally fell asleep on an armchair.

"She's a vivacious little girl," said Roberto.

"Always on the go. It's time for a brother or a sister," said Carlo, "or ... a cousin."

Signora Luisa turned around hoping for a sign, but Amelia only smiled.

She sat at the old piano that her mother had sent from Milan and started to play. Soon Roberto joined her with his viola and everyone listened as the summer afternoon spread its tranquility.

It had been a wonderful family reunion –a mirror of that outing they had enjoyed so many years ago. Since that time so many things had happened.

Everyone was gone now.

Roberto and Amelia sat in their balcony surrounded by the blooming wisteria. He turned to look at her and she extended her hand to touch his face.

In the distance small row boats drifted on Lake Como and a lone sailboat spread sail on the rippling waters.

In the silence of that afternoon, everything was alive.

COVER DESIGN BY PETER GRIMALDI

www.ingramcontent.com/pod-product-compliance
Lightning Source LLC
Chambersburg PA
CBHW032207190626
46810CB00019B/2139